Dor Slinkard is an unstoppable storyteller. Be it through writing or voice, her stories will enthral. Inspired by life, especially as a jillaroo in outback Australia and later as a race horse trainer, her imagination thrives. In her lasting marriage to Wade, a jackaroo now horse trainer, they have produced two children and they, in turn, five grandchildren.

For the Love of Justice is the third book in the trilogy.

Dedication

To the Aboriginal Stolen Generation.

*

The pain may lessen.

But the memory never fades.

God forgive us all.

Doreen Slinkard 2019

Acknowledgements

Once again I give immense gratitude to my proof-readers,
Sandy Gray, Julie Sanderson, Amanda Norton-Knight,Betty Holman,
and my dear husband Wade.

To my wonderful, effervescent, editing team, Denise Dorisarmy
and Margaret Mooney. A sincere thank you.

I do hope this book brings the reader alert images of how it was
for the stolen generation. And an insight into the exciting life of
being a Horse Trainer. My other profession.

Special thanks to our talented photographer, Danny Mayson-Kinder.
And to my beautiful young friends, Bianca Tolhurst, Thomas Norton-Knight
and to our darling racehorse, Stradazzle, for your time and patience in
producing the perfect cover. Thank you.

A very special thankyou to my Computer Wizards, Deb and Mick Jones
from Computus Australis. Without them, my stories would not survive
this technical world, nor would I. Bless you.

For the Love of Trilogy

Book 1 – For the Love of Patrick
Book 2 – For the Love of Freedom
Book 3 – For the Love of Justice

Dor Slinkard

FOR THE LOVE OF JUSTICE

Chapter 1

Northern Territory, Australia: 1957

A whirlwind of hot air swept the red earth and swirled its heavy mix towards the battered ute. Tarni's strength had almost left by the time PJ pulled up outside the homestead. The closeness of PJ, when he gathered her close in his arms, allowed her to float in a euphoric state before she passed out. Limp in his hold, PJ carried Tarni to the sick room and yelled out for Gwen, the nurse-cum-nanny.

"Jeez that's nasty," Gwen said screwing her face at the sight of Tarni's wound. "just as well you radioed me P.J, I got straight onto the Flying Doc. Now tell me what happened?"

"It's a long story Gwen. Let's just say she's lucky to be alive. I need to tell Ian what happened first. Any idea when the Flying Doc' will be here?

"Yes, Tarni's in luck again. They were in the area: shouldn't be too long."

PJ smoothed a strand of sun-bleached hair off Tarni's forehead, smiled at Gwen, and left to find his boss.

As usual and especially in the heat of the day, Ian sat at his desk attempting to catch up on his book work.

"Come in," Ian said when he heard the knock. His head remained buried in accounts.

"Ian, I've just witnessed an attempted murder." PJ said with conviction.

"Bloody hell, what do you mean attempted murder? Who was it? What happened?" He spun his swivel chair around so fast it nearly fell off its spigot.

PJ took his hat off and asked. "May I sit?"

This amused Ian. He'd never had such a well-mannered, highly educated Jackaroo work on his property. Sometimes he felt inferior to this young man, Patrick Darcy Jnr (PJ), who despite being a lawyer and the grandson of the famous Adelaide Magistrate Jonathon Darcy QC, he was humble and so bloody well mannered. Ian had to lift his own game many times to meet with PJ's standards.

Ian indicated with his hand for Patrick to be seated.

"So, tell me PJ, what happened? You're not kidding me, are you? It wasn't just Bluey and Drongo at it again?"

"I wish it were, but the trouble lies with Tarni and Robbo. Their dislike for each other was apparent the first day I arrived and today it almost turned to murder."

PJ took note of Ian adjusting himself more comfortably in his seat, before he brushed away a pesky fly.

"Well go on, fill me in."

"I arrived at the river just in time. I saw Robbo pointing a gun at Tarni. He ordered her to tame the croc, which was about to attack her. Obviously, if she had made a run for it, Robbo would have shot her."

Ian sat forward in his seat. "But why?"

"I don't know why. All I can tell you is that the morning after I arrived, I was trying to catch a young horse, supposedly broken in by Robbo. I couldn't get near it. Tarni was nearby and stopped to watch. Before I knew it, she was standing alongside me. 'Shoosh, stay still,' she'd said. I watched as she took over. She ran the horse around in circles throwing her arms out to shun it away. Before too long it started running along with its head close to the ground and ears twitching. That's when Tarni turned her back on him. The horse stopped and then walked right up to her. She stroked his head and walked away with him following her. I'd never seen anything like it before. Robbo wasn't too pleased when I sang her praises later in the day. He called her a smart-arse bitch and said he'd teach her a thing or two when the time was right."

Ian nodded his head, relaxed, and let a wry smile creep onto his face.

"Yeah, I know about him and her. He's been in trouble with Tarni before. She reckons he tried to rape her. It's a bit hard for the men out here, especially when they get a skin full. They're used to having their own way with the black girls. But not Tarni. She's a real beauty and thinks she's a cut above the rest, so I reckon she brings a lot of it on herself. I've had to talk Tarni out of reporting him on a few occasions."

PJ's pained expression revealed he could not believe what he'd just heard.

"I think you should consider what you're saying Ian, even if you're unable to change your views. The words, 'bringing it on herself would not go down too well in a rape case, especially in cross examination. But now it's gone a lot further than rape. Robbo was about to murder Tarni and make it look like an accident."

Ian was still thinking about the accusation of rape when he answered.

"All depends on what you're referring to, regards raping a black girl. Up here in the Northern Territory we have our own rules for black and white. But murder; well that's a different thing. Maybe the jury wouldn't look the other way for murdering a black girl. Rape yes, but not murder."

"This is 1957 Ian, not 1857. I'm sure things would have changed a lot by now in this part of the land."

PJ felt uncomfortable. He hadn't been aware of Ian's prejudice before this day. However, he'd not been surprised by the hired station hands sexual use of the Aboriginal girls. These young women seemed to enjoy the attention and favours they received for their services. However, he was shocked by Ian's casual attitude towards Tarni, who'd remained aloof from the rest. PJ had rarely noticed her talking to the other girls or going anywhere near the men.

"Well anyway, I've seen for myself the way Robbo treats her, Ian. I stood witness today. I saw him aim his gun at her, forcing her to walk into the jaws of a croc. That's a murderous attempt, one way or the other."

"Shit, I can't believe Robbo would go that far. Fuckin' hell. What's wrong with that silly bastard?"

"I don't know the full of it, but you have to report him to the police. Nobody should get away with attempted murder."

Ian scratched his head then shook it, trying to be rid of the picture PJ had painted in his mind.

"Maybe he was just tryin' to scare her. You know, get his own way without having to slap her around."

PJ's anger at his boss's continuous degradation of Tarni began to rise, but being trained to nail it down, he said firmly:

"It would have been cold-blooded murder if I hadn't arrived in time. I insist you report this to the police Ian, or I will. Tarni's lying in the sick room with a gushing wound to her lower leg. Gwen radioed the Flying Doctor Service, and they'll be here soon. This was no idle threat by Robbo. He would have shot her if the croc didn't get her first."

An arrogant tone surfaced in Ian's reply.

"Well then, tell me, PJ. How come you were there to witness it? You were supposed to be on the dry run, checking on a herd of steers."

"I was, until I saw Robbo driving his ute at a hundred miles an hour towards the river. He was supposed to be heading my way with a packed lunch and then, we were going to do some fencing together. I don't know what it was, but something told me there was trouble. So, I followed him. I pulled up a good distance behind his ute, which was nearer the riverbank. I could hear him yelling at someone, so I crept up with my gun. I didn't know what to expect until I saw him aiming his gun at Tarni. He yelled at her, 'So ya think ya can tame any bloody thing? Well, tame that fuckin 'croc ya black bitch!' That's when I noticed the croc – I managed to shoot it twice, before I told Robbo to drop his gun, which he did, but then he ran and took off in his ute, like the coward he is."

Ian sat with a quizzical look on his face.

"I still can't fathom what would drive Robbo to do that, PJ. I know he's a hot-headed bugger and sometimes he gets a bit violent, but Jesus, that's a terrible thing to do to a poor little girl."

Ian then picked up the phone and asked the operator to connect him to the police. PJ stood, placed his hand on Ian's shoulder confirming approval, before he walked out of the office and left Ian to his phone call.

It seemed to Patrick, whether he liked it or not, that he would soon be in court, but this time as a witness, not a prosecutor.

He sat vigil over Tarni while waiting for the flying doctor and wondered what he would do with the rest of his life. That was the reason he'd come here, to try and work his future out. His love of horses far outweighed his interest in the law, but he knew it would be a tough road. Being a horse trainer meant a great deal of luck was involved. On the other hand, as a lawyer, he'd be readily furnished with clients introduced by his grandfather Jonathon Darcy QC. Plus, his older cousin, James Darcy, also a lawyer, had offered him a partnership. If he accepted, PJ would be assured of a lucrative business and a grand lifestyle.

Horse training meant working seven days a week, with long hours and early morning starts, no matter what the weather. Heart breaks and disappointments were guaranteed, yet the sensation of a win, especially a city win, would perpetually push those deficits into oblivion.

PJ was a gentleman, not a fighter. His father had been a hero in World War One and PJ could think of nothing worse, than going into battle to fight for your life and country against some presumed enemy. But of course, he would feel duty bound to do it. He would never turn from a fight for justice and this, apparently in a small way, had intervened in his life.

He gazed at the beautiful Aboriginal girl lying before him. He thought back to that first day and how she'd handled the wild horse. Suddenly he realised that she'd shown him how to look into a horse's soul; how to understand the animal and respect it. He'd been around good horsemen all his life, including his father, but this young woman owned a spirit that truly connected to the horse. Something surreal shone from within her. She was a lone soul, belonging only to her own spirit guide. Maybe she's be my guide to show me the way.

Chapter 2

A week later, on 22nd of November, just before the wet season arrived and made it impossible for PJ to leave, he packed his bags and said farewell. Gwen drove him to the 'Merriola' air strip, which in reality was a half-mile-long graded strip of red earth. He searched the flat horizon, shimmering with the certainty of change, like his heart; a wry smile crept on his face at the memory of why he'd come in the first place, it struck a vibrant and constant pledge. Follow your heart.

"Are you going to visit Tarni, before you go home to Adelaide, PJ.?" Gwen asked, head tilted.

"Yes of course, Gwen. I have to stop in Darwin anyway to give my statement about what happened." Gwen donned a sorrowful expression.

"Poor little thing. She's a loner that one. I could never work out what she was thinking, not ever. So unlike the other Aboriginal girls, but I suppose she doesn't look like them. That beautiful honey coloured skin." Gwen shook her head consoling the fact that Tarni walked the line in-between black and white. "I just hope they catch that bloody Robbo. He's always looking for trouble. I wouldn't trust him as far as I could throw him."

"Yes, its times like these that I feel the need to don the wig again. I have no faith in the law around here. Still, I'll have time to think about it when I'm in Darwin and after I've spoken with Tarni. I'm sure I'll be able to get a lot more out of her than the police have. From what I've heard, it's nothing."

The four-seater plane sat with its engine running. PJ threw his bag on board, while Gwen took the opportunity to thank the pilot for the medical supplies and mail. Their kiss caused PJ to raise an eyebrow.

The noise of the engine, when in flight, gave little chance for conversation so PJ reflected on the months he'd spent on the station. Mostly it had been what he'd expected. Six months straight of cattle mustering amongst continuous dust and heat. Camping out under the brilliant stars, so bright, and seemingly so close he could reach up and hold them. Bush stories and laughter shared in between a song or two while sitting around the campfire. The station hands and jackaroo's, apart from Robbo, were a happy lot. They were friendly and helpful, playing the odd practical joke now and then, which PJ was used to as his father was renowned for the same.

Still, had he advanced towards his final decision? He would let it rest until he met with the Darwin police. Maybe the attempted murder of Tarni was a sign for him to continue his life as a lawyer? He almost shuddered at the thought.

*

PJ breathed a sigh of relief when signing into his hotel and feeling the coolness of the air-conditioning. Not too many places held such luxury. It was moments like these, when his other self-reminded him of the swish lifestyle he'd be assured of if he travelled the road of the law, that indecision plagued him. Then he relaxed and smiled at the thought of another pleasure that awaited him – a long warm shower.

Clean, fresh water flowed over his muscled body and he delighted in the fact there was no rotten egg smell like in the bore water used on the property. PJ, when done, dressed in tailored grey trousers, the only pair he'd packed when leaving Adelaide and checked his white shirt. It looked not-so-white after a few washes in the property water, so he chose a pale blue one. He polished his riding boots, straightened his plaited leather belt, looked in the mirror and said with humour:

"Even my clothes are town and country. How am I ever going to make up my bloody mind?" Then laughed.

*

Tarni sat in an armchair facing the window, with her bandaged leg elevated on a stool. The moment Patrick entered the room, she smiled and turned to face him.

The nurse, who'd followed PJ, said from behind:

"That's the first time I've seen her smile since she's been here. She's hardly spoken a word. I've even tried to bribe her with sweets, but she won't accept them. I'd say that's why she has such perfect teeth – no sugar!"

The nurse laughed a little before PJ turned around. His captivating eyes took her breath away as she stammered out the words:

"I … I … I'm sorry, Mr ..?"

"Patrick Darcy Junior, everyone calls me PJ."

"I'm pleased to meet you, PJ. My name is Helena Stravinsky. I'm here to take her observations, I won't be long."

"That's fine, Helena, take your time. I'll be here for a while."

Helena batted her eyelashes at Patrick; it seemed she couldn't help herself.

"I'm so pleased, PJ. What I mean to say is, it's good for the young lass to have a visitor. She's had no one here except the police."

"The young lass's name is Tarni, Nurse Helena," PJ said with an edge.

She nodded before doing her duties, and then walked out of the room sideways, beaming her admiration at PJ.

Tarni's smile accompanied a giggle:

"I think she likes you, PJ."

"Maybe she does, but I'm here to see you, Tarni. How are you? You're looking much better. What do they say about your leg? Will there be any more surgery?"

"I feel good, thank you, and no, they said they've stitched me up good enough. Well, that's what the doctor said. I should be fine to leave on Monday. The doctor said there should be no chance of infection now." Her large brown eyes lowered as she continued softly, "thank you for saving my life PJ."

He gently patted her arm.

"I'm only pleased I followed my instincts Tarni. You know this isn't the end of it though, we have to bring Robbo to justice." Tarni hung her head even lower, so PJ gently lifted her chin to meet her eyes. "I'm sorry Tarni. It must be very hard for you to think about it. But I'm your friend, I'll listen and understand. You know I'm a lawyer, I'll help you."

Tarni suddenly lifted her head high, her eyes flashing in anger.

"I don't want to tell anyone. That mongrel will be punished."

"What do you mean Tarni?" P.J thought of the indigenous people and their renowned payback method. She remained silent. "If you're referring to your people, they can't take the law into their own hands."

Tarni turned to face the window. A tear trickled down her cheek. PJ held her hand, and with this she began to sob. Moments passed before she regained her composure.

"I'm sorry PJ I try hard not to cry."

"It's only natural Tarni. You've been through a dreadful experience."

Suddenly, her cynical laugh and firm retort surprised him.

"My whole life has been a dreadful experience. Well almost. Sometimes I wish I'd never been born. But a voice inside keeps telling me I'm meant to live and there's something important I should do. All I know is, the only time I'm happy is when I'm around horses. But I'm a girl and especially black girls are not supposed to know how to train horses. Everywhere I go, I'm stopped from doing what I want."

She took a sip of water and noticed his interest. Tarni gave a relaxed sigh, as if she was finally going to reveal the truth.

"I was taken away from my mother and fostered out to a white family-the Browns. Their son and daughter had a pony each. The girl was scared and the pony knew it, so he'd buck her off all the time. After she broke her arm in a fall, the father decided he'd have the poor pony put down. I was really upset and begged him to let me ride and show him how it should be done. Later when I'd got the pony going really well, he asked me to ride him in front of a man who wanted to buy it. He was happy with how he went and paid a lot of money for the pony, but Mr Brown never thanked me or even said, well done Tarni."

This was a turning moment for Patrick. He sat silently, feeling her frustration. He looked almost lovingly at this young woman.

I wonder if given the chance to prove her talent with horses, she would be happy? She seems to know her worth. The day at the river showed she'd been prepared to die with courage and dignity – no grovelling for mercy.

It was often said by Patrick's family, he was the one most like his grandmother Sally, especially when he'd bring home stray dogs, or feed a hungry child. And every now and then, PJ would ask his grandfather if he would help out a mate with a legal problem; free of charge off course. Whereas PJ's older sister, also named Sally, was likened to her grandfather Jum Watt. She was a warrior, who'd fought with the French resistance in the Second World War.

"You know Tarni, I've been tossing up options about what I should do with my life, whether to be a racehorse trainer or remain in Law. I think you may have unintentionally helped me make up my mind. What say, when you're free from hospital, and we sort out this attempted murder case, we go home to Adelaide and start training racehorses together?"

"Your home is there? That's funny. Adelaide is near Victor Harbor and that's near the home of my tribe. It's where my mother was born. My Aboriginal name means the sound of waves. My mother always loved the sound of waves. I lived there too, until the white men took me away!"

This memory suddenly triggered a verbal outburst from Tarni.

PJ was taken aback.

"I won't talk to the Police PJ; I won't go to court. I hate the white man's law! So, if this changes your mind about me, then leave me alone. Forget about me." Patrick groaned in dis-belief.

"You can't let Robbo get away with it Tarni. We have to at least go to the Police Station and write a statement. We'll do it together."

Patrick saw the determination in her eyes. "What you do is your business Tarni, but I want you to think about it. If he's allowed to go free, he may murder some poor little girl next time. That would stay on your conscience forever."

A cunning smile curled her lip to one side.

"It won't happen again. He'll never be able to murder anyone."

Her statement, or was it a cloaked threat, shocked PJ. He would have liked to ask why? But he chose to let it go, for fear she would close up entirely, so he softened and changed the subject.

"You haven't answered my question Tarni. Would you like to live in Adelaide and help me train racehorses?"

Tarni gazed out the window and her face brightened when a seagull, so rare in the outback, suddenly arrived as if by messenger. It remained fluttering outside the window, taking Tarni away to another place where she had been happy. She turned and smiled into PJ's amazing eyes. She could lose herself there.

"Yes, I'd love that PJ. I'll work very hard – all day every day. I'll even sleep with the horses; I'd never leave them."

PJ was humoured by the thought.

"You don't have to go that far Tarni." He laughed a little. "I'll find you board and lodgings nearby and I'll pay you well. And I insist that you have off one day a week." Patrick shook his head still amused. "Just as well you won't be working for my old boss at Morphettville. He'd have you working twenty-four hours, seven days a week and pay you nothing!"

PJ left after patting Tarni on the head, some may say in a patronizing fashion, but Tarni saw it as affection. PJ felt happy about his decision when he stood at attention in front of the nurses desk.

"Nurse Helena I will be collecting Tarni on Monday and taking her home to Adelaide, if her release is approved by the doctor of course."

"Really Mr Darcy, is that so?" She looked up with a mixture of amusement and a tinge of jealousy.

"Yes, nurse Helena, I will be taking care of Tarni from now on."

Helena then raised her finely plucked eyebrow, tilting her head to one side she said:

"Platonically of course Mr Darcy?"

"Of course, Helena, she's only a girl."

"That's where you're wrong. Tarni turned nineteen yesterday."

Patrick chose not to show his surprise or take the conversation any further. He simply smiled and left.

*

The Darwin Police station was within walking distance from the hospital. This gave PJ time to consider the crush he felt Tarni had on him. If she were only fifteen, it would be classed as a schoolgirl crush, nothing to worry about. But the fact she was nineteen, an age when most girls were either married or engaged to be married, concerned him. He would have to stay at arm's length from her in future. However, it hadn't changed his mind about employing Tarni as a rider, and what he felt was his duty to help her.

*

PJ's meeting with the police went as he'd assumed it would. Little interest was shown in the case by the sergeant in charge. When questioned by PJ, the sergeant assured him that they were, and would remain, searching for Robbo.

"So far this Robbo bloke seems to have disappeared into thin air," the sergeant said light heartedly. "We have all the information we need from you at this stage Mr Darcy. We'll be in touch when we find the accused, although it would help a great deal if the young Aboriginal girl would talk. If she won't talk, then the case might just have to be dismissed."

"I'm working on helping Tarni reveal the facts, Sergeant."

Then there was a brief pause before PJ added:

"I will be totally responsible for Tarni's care, and I'll accompany her back to Darwin when and if we're needed. Is there a problem with me taking Tarni back to Adelaide and giving her a job?"

"No, not at all," the sergeant eagerly replied.

Considering all matters that stood for Indigenous people in the Northern Territory, PJ felt they may be fighting a losing battle. Before he left, PJ simply wished the sergeant good luck.

The thought of Tarni's age then struck PJ. The police, it seemed, had also assumed her to be a younger. And another point: while everyone else kept calling her Aborigine, her skin was no darker than his mother's, who was from Hawaiian heritage. Tarni's features were definitely European and yet they still referred to her as being black. He thought she could be any suntanned girl swimming at Glenelg beach, especially with her mid brown hair streaked with gold.

Chapter 3

Through his friends in Adelaide, PJ had found Tarni board and lodgings with an elderly woman, Mrs Stenning. She lived not too far from Morphettville racecourse, walking distance in fact.

After helping Tarni settle in, PJ drove to his family property, Bulkawa. It sat forty miles north west of Adelaide. Almost all of PJ's family had gathered to welcome him home. A feast was duly presented with the very best Barossa Valley wines, which made it a true celebration. During their leisurely three-hour lunch, PJ told tales about his six months spent on the cattle station. Afterwards, he found an opportunity to sit alone with his parents and explain in detail about Tarni's life to date, including her attempted murder. He waited until their shocked expressions disappeared.

"I brought Tarni home with me, because I've made my decision. I'm going to be a horse trainer and Tarni has a real talent with horses; she'll be a great help.

PJ's mother, Addy, saw the admiration in PJ's eyes.

"Have you feelings for Tarni PJ?"

"No mother. I see her only as a friend and as somebody who needs my help, and I need hers."

Patrick Senior laughed out loud.

"I can hear my mother again! I tell you son; you're so much like her. Anyone who was in need was her friend." He stood and shook PJ's hand.

"Congratulations PJ, I'm pleased you've sorted it out. As your mother always said and so do I, you must follow your heart, or you'll never be truly happy, so good luck with your horse training venture." He sat down again and looked under his eyebrows in all seriousness. "Now I'll tell you something that I've kept from you. Your uncle Angus is going to give you two yearlings to train. They've been broken, had a spell, and they're ready to go into their first racing prep. Their breeding goes back to Freelance, your grandfather Jum's stallion, so they should be able to run." Patrick Snr looked lovingly at Addy. "Your mother and I are going to accompany you to the tried horse sales at the end of January, the twenty-ninth to be exact. You choose a few horses you like; we'll pay for them and you train them. I've been talking to a few mates who'll take shares with us."

Patrick Snr smiled and placed his hand steadfast on PJ's shoulder.

PJ was overwhelmed. "I never realised you'd help me out that much, Dad. I don't know what to say, except thank you, thank you both for supporting me. I know it may seem a step down from being a lawyer, but I think I have the horse disease and I just can't shake it. I need to have a go, or I'll regret it. And I can always go back to law."

"That's right son. We decided not to let you know about the horses any sooner. We thought you needed to make your own decision, because it's tough to get started, and you had to be sure. We didn't want to sway your decision in any way. So let's drink a toast to your future in the racing business." Patrick Senior raised his glass and winked at Addy.

And so with that announcement put to rest, the day turned into evening; spent reminiscing over the family's lifelong passion for horses.

*

As a young boy, PJ loved to wake up to the summer mornings on 'Bulkawa', with the silver mist covering the treetops and the sun filtering through leaves, warming his face. The scene would transport him into his own wonderland. This morning was no exception. Birds sang the new day in, as the horses neighed, calling for the hay PJ was about to feed them. He stood outside the barn breathing it all in, feeling great relief and enthusiasm at beginning his new career. His instincts were correct again, he'd made the right choice.

First, he'd have to submit his trainer's application to the South Australian Jockey Club (SAJC). This, he assumed wouldn't be a problem. He'd worked for many years as a part-time, rider-come-strapper for a leading trainer, and he'd come from a long line of thoroughbred breeders and racehorse owners. His uncle Angus had on two occasions received an award for being the most successful breeder and owner of racehorses in South Australia. His mother and father had dabbled, along with Angus, in taking up small shares in various horses, which had all won a race or two. Sadly, and so far, a champion racehorse had eluded the family. Maybe he would be the one to choose and train a champion for them. PJ drew fresh air into his lungs and declared to himself.

"I'm going to be the leading trainer in South Australia within five years. This I promise." Then laughed at his audacity.

*

A hearty brunch was later taken with the family, who'd stayed over the previous night. Sally, PJ's sister, along with her husband-Frenchy, as they called

Alain and their two children, Peter and Suzan now teenagers were there. Also present was Uncle Angus and Aunty Clare and their son James, a 39-year-old bachelor. James was also a lawyer and hoped that one day PJ would take up a junior partnership in his practice. Grandad Jonathon was now the grand age of eighty-six and as he'd said, was 'a little under the weather,' he'd decided not to take the long drive to Bulkawa.

Granddad Jonathon's wife Margie had telephoned to explain about Jonathon not being up to the journey. She did ask, however, if PJ could visit them the day after next for lunch. Granddad Jonathon was literally bursting to hear all the details about PJ's time out west. He agreed to this request with pleasure.

Older cousin James was not sure if PJ would last long at being a horse trainer.

"I'll give you twelve months PJ. I'm quite sure you'll have had enough of the early mornings and late nights, tending to highly strung thoroughbreds. You'll be knocking on my door to take up my offer!"

"You're on, James! I'll even bet on it."

"Definitely PJ, what about if we purchase a yearling together and if you give up training in twelve months' time, then your share will become mine. What about that cousin?"

"As long as you pay your share of the training fees James!"

Patrick Sr didn't have to think too long before he'd seen a hole in the deal.

"What if the horse becomes a champion and PJ needs for some reason to give up training? I think you should make another bet gentlemen or this one may just cause a family rift."

"Yes, you have a point, Uncle, maybe we should just lay a monetary bet. Say a hundred quid!"

"You're on, James!" PJ repeated, more than pleased with a chance at stealing a hundred quid off his older cousin.

They shook hands, while James remarked, "I still think we should buy a yearling together PJ. I'd really like that, how about you?"

"Yes, although we'll have to put a lid on the price. The old piggy bank has to be emptied out to fund my new business. Saddles, horse rugs and feed don't grow on trees you know. What say we make the purchase price a one-hundred-pound limit?"

The deal was just about sealed when Alain, PJ's brother in-law, asked if he could be in it too.

"Why not!" said James, "You're a lucky bugger Frenchy, just look at your lobster business. It's thriving!"

"No, no. It is not lucks—it is just bloody 'ard work mate." Alain thought himself to be a fair dinkum Aussie, now he'd become an Australian citizen, so he used every colloquialism in the book.

PJ later found the opportunity to talk privately to James about the business with Tarni.

"Any man, who would do such a thing, PJ, would definitely kill again. You shouldn't let this lie, even if Tarni wishes to. I feel the buck stops with you. It's obvious the girl is scared out of her mind, and from what I've heard about the difference in law between the blacks and whites in that part of the land, she'd be put through hell in court. In the end, it would look like it was all her fault."

"Strange you should say that, James. My boss Ian said much the same thing. He said she may have provoked Robbo into it because she wouldn't give Robbo what he wanted. He said Tarni brought a lot of it on herself. It sickened me. I just can't tolerate their way of thinking. The cattle work and the time spent alone did me good, but their bloody single-minded attitudes got the better of me. I just couldn't stay the full twelve months after what happened to Tarni."

"Well, don't give up, PJ. Keep trying to reach her."

"I have. And all she said is that Robbo won't ever be able to murder anyone. I tell you James, the look in Tarni's eye and the way she said it, gave me shivers down my spine. I even suspected she may have had one of her people point the bone at him." PJ stopped to think seriously about his last sentence. "You don't really think that works do you, James?"

"Bloody oath it works! The Kundela they call it. I've heard stories from people I know who don't lie. It doesn't take long apparently, only days after the Kurdaitcha man hunts the victim down and puts his curse on him while he points the bone. There's been many victims taken to hospital, and even the medical profession can't explain why they die. They just become listless, they won't eat and then they die – in agony."

Patrick ran his fingers through his hair, a habit he had when he had a problem to solve, or something worried him.

"Poetic justice I suppose you'd call it. That's if Robbo's fallen victim to their voodoo. Anyway, it's no good surmising. Surely the police will track him down sooner or later."

*

The next morning PJ set off for Adelaide, his first call was to the SAJC to collect his application form. He arrived and asked the secretary Jane, whom

20

he knew quite well, to make an appointment with the committee at a later date. Happy with the fact he'd started the ball rolling, PJ then decided to visit Tarni.

Mrs Stenning's home was a modest California red-brick bungalow, surrounded by gardens manicured to the extreme. Mrs Stenning a widow for ten years, was in her late seventies. She was still physically active with her charity work and being the president of the church committee. At first, PJ wondered how Tarni would get along with the orderly Mrs Stenning. However, before ringing the doorbell he could hear Tarni say.

"I'll put the kettle on Mrs Stenning."

"Thank you my dear," was her reply. This put a smile on PJ's face.

The door opened to a beaming Tarni.

"Hello, I was just about to put the kettle on. Would you like a cup of tea?"

"Yes, thank you, Tarni."

He entered the lounge room where all ornaments and family pictures sat upon lace doyleys and rose wood furniture. Neatly folded patch-work quilts hung over each armchair and the house smelt like furniture polish mixed with bleach. Patrick's attention was drawn to a photograph of the late Mr Stenning, standing with his arm around an Aboriginal boy in a pristine school uniform holding an award. PJ picked up the photo, just as June Stenning walked into the room.

"Hello Mr Darcy, I was hoping you'd drop by today. We have such a lot to talk about." She smiled at the photo he held.

"That picture is of my late husband, Jack. And the boy is our adopted son Aboni, or Adam, is his European name. He's now teaching on an Aboriginal mission in the Northern Territory. Tarni knows him. It's a small world, isn't it Mr Darcy?" She laughed, the memory bringing a sparkle to her tired eyes.

"It certainly is Mrs Stenning." Patrick said returning the smile.

"Please call me June, Mr Darcy, and I'll call you Patrick if I may? I'm so pleased you heard about me having a room to let. It's such a pleasure to have Tarni living with me and especially after hearing how she knows Adam. We haven't stopped talking since Tarni arrived. Please sit down and I'll get us some tea and biscuits."

Tarni placed her hand on June's shoulder. "No, please Mrs Stenning, I'll get it."

"No, you won't my dear. You need to rest your leg. It's still not properly healed."

Tarni nodded, took a deep breath and let it out slowly before sitting down opposite PJ.

"I try and help, but she won't let me. She spoils me."

Tarni's look of gratitude was unmistakable.

"I can't thank you enough for what you've done for me PJ. Mrs Stenning is the nicest white lady I've ever met. She doesn't seem to notice that I'm black. She just treats me like a normal person. And her son Aboni is a very nice young man. He was the teacher on the mission where I lived, before I began working at Merriola. The children on the mission love him." Tarni hung her head, feeling self-conscious at how PJ seemed to be studying her face as she spoke.

"I'll never know why you keep calling yourself black, or Aboriginal, Tarni. Your skin is no darker than my sister or my mother. I wish you'd stop labelling yourself. You're a beautiful young woman and you have more European blood in you than Aboriginal. Not that that's anything to be proud of - just the opposite. But I don't go around calling myself a white man." PJ lifted Tarni's chin high with his finger, smiling into her alluring brown eyes. "I'm sure you know your value Tarni. Hold onto that and be happy." Impulsively he kissed her on the forehead. "Now I have some wonderful news. We'll soon have some horses to train. My family have been very supportive. I've just been to the Race Club and filled in my application. I'm sure there won't be any problem getting a licence. So, the wheels are in motion and your leg should be healed and ready to start riding when the first horse arrives. Which reminds me, I'm going to have a look at some stables to rent at Morphettville. Would you like to come?"

"Yes, I'd love to." Tarni said still in a romantic trance. PJ touching her face and looking deep into eyes was almost too much to bear.

June Stenning entered, carrying a china plate laden with cakes and biscuits. She placed it on the coffee table and ordered:

"Eat up. There's plenty more and the tea won't be long."

PJ waited until she'd left before he spoke:

"You'd better watch your weight while you're here, Tarni. I think Mrs Stenning would like to fatten you up and then you'd be too heavy to ride."

"I'd starve myself for the chance to ride, PJ. I'd like to be the first girl to ride in races."

He laughed.

"Well, anything's possible." His expression then changed to serious.

"I'm pleased you didn't say the first Aboriginal girl to ride. I'll make a deal with you. If you don't ever refer to yourself as black in the next six months and if you ride well enough, I'll ask the SAJC Committee if it would be possible to indenture you as my apprentice jockey. I must admit though; I don't like your chances. But that's my deal, okay?" PJ put his hand forward, Tarni took it.

"Okay. It's a deal!"

*

Joe Stallero lived in the house in front of his stables, which PJ had now leased. Joe, a retired fisherman, told PJ that the previous trainer went bust, due to being a huge and un-lucky punter. Joe had bought the property, including the stables, with the thought of renting them out for extra income, and so far, it had prospered.

"Punting is the one thing I'll stay clear of, don't worry, Mr Stallero," PJ said. "I'm sure if my uncle Angus hadn't gambled away a fortune, he'd have money for better stallions for his mares. Then he may have bred that elusive champion. Me, I'll only ever have a small wager to cover the jockey sling, that's all."

Tarni nodded, understanding PJ's reasoning, although she felt they could make their own luck. Like the trainers she'd heard of, where they purchased an un-fashionably bred youngster, then trained them to win good races. Some trainers concentrated only on tried horses that possibly weren't trained well in the first place and after they'd sorted the horse's problem, they became top racehorses. She hoped PJ would remain instinctive and not put too much emphasis on breeding and conformation. Tarni knew she had the gift to look beyond the obvious, to sense the spirit within the horse. To her this was more important than breeding or even conformation.

The realisation of what was about to happen, truly hit PJ when he signed the lease on the ten stables at Morphettville. His excitement was unleashed when he shook hands with Joe. Joe, then put a blanket on his verve by asking for one month's rent in advance. As PJ made out the cheque, Joe's smile revealed a gold-capped tooth, it caught the sun and sparkled, PJ couldn't help but laugh. A bloody old pirate this bloke is!

"Good luck, PJ. I think you've got what it takes to make a real good trainer." Joe winked at Tarni. "And you look like you might be a good rider, Miss Tarni."

"And I think you might be right, Mr Stallero," Tarni replied with confidence.

Now that she had the chance, PJ felt that Tarni was about to reveal all her horse skills. Suddenly, he checked the time on his watch.

"I have to go. I'm sorry Tarni, but Granddads a bit under the weather. I'll drop you off home before I go see him. I'll take you to meet him another time, I'm sure he'd love to come here one morning and watch you ride."

A south-westerly breeze, cooled by the ocean, streamed through PJ's car. Tarni's hair became a tangled mess about her face and she laughed while trying to brush it aside.

"Why so happy, Tarni?"

"I'm happy because I'm doing what I've always wanted to do?"

"Not yet you aren't, but it won't be long."

PJ gazed sideways at Tarni. He delighted in seeing her happy.

*

After dropping her off, he drove the ten miles north east, to his granddad Jonathon's palatial home, 'Wildflowers'. PJ had always loved this home. It was where his dad and uncle had grown up. It had given shelter to all the Darcy family at some stage; plus, close friends who'd stayed in contact and those who'd attended the many celebrations held there. The first thing PJ noticed was the driveway had recently been tarred. He remembered when he was a small boy it was covered with gravel. He'd constantly had busters off his bike and couldn't wait to go to school and show off his scars. The two-storey mansion he admired so much had been built in the late 19th century. Another wing had been added for PJ's mother and father when they'd returned from army service in the Middle East after World War One. Addy was a doctor, and Patrick Snr was an officer in the Light Horse. Six months after PJ was born, the family finally moved to 'Bulkawa' to live. The vast and what appeared magical property had been bequeathed to PJ's mother Addy, by her birth father, Jum Watt.

'Wildflowers' named because of PJ's birth grandmother, Sally's love for the Australian wildflowers, had originally sat on twenty acres, until Jonathon purchased the adjoining one hundred acres of bushland. He was now in the throes of having the extra acres sub divided due to the threat of bush fires. He'd never had it cleared. Jonathon had held it as an expansive cross-country course, where Patrick Snr and Angus his half-brother, had enjoyed riding when young.

A beaming Margie opened the massive front door.

"My darling, PJ. It's so wonderful to see you. You look well. And so tanned." The smile left her face and she spoke like a school mam. "Are you aware that too much sun is harmful to your skin? I hope you wore a hat out in the Wild West?"

"Yes, Nan, I did, but I think the sun burnt through it."

Her smile returned, and she clutched him to her.

"Your granddad is looking forward to seeing you and hearing your stories. He would have loved to have spent some time on an outback cattle

24

station. When he was younger, of course."

Margie furrowed her brow and peered from over the top of her glasses.

"I've heard about the trouble you had concerning a young Aboriginal girl. You saved her life your mother tells me." She waited for him to answer but he just nodded. "I must say, PJ, saving lives seems to be a family habit."

He laughed, "I hadn't thought of it like that before, Nan, but you're right. Perhaps we should write a book about how to save lives. I suppose I shouldn't make light of it though, as the culprit hasn't been caught yet."

After leaving Margie's embrace, PJ walked towards the den. He knew, even if Jonathon wasn't in the best of health, he'd find him relentlessly compiling legal information in his office. Margie followed, almost skipping with joy.

"You know your granddad very well, PJ. Of course, he's in his office, he always is, and always will be. I think we'll have to bury him there!" she said with a chuckle.

Chapter 4

PJ opened the door to see Jonathon sleeping, his head back on a head rest attached to his chair. Margie had had it especially designed for Jonathon's 'thinking naps,' as she called them. She was concerned he would literally snap his neck off if she didn't do something.

Jonathon's hair had finally turned silver, but his face was barely lined. When PJ placed a kiss on his cheek, Jonathon stirred and opened his eyes to see his favourite grandson, not that he would divulge this fact to anyone. Jonathon, like Patrick Snr, thought PJ to be the most like his grandmother Sally. Not in looks, but in nature he was her to a tee.

"PJ, my son, you have returned." Jonathon struggled to stand. "Help me out of this wretched chair and let us go to the lounge room." He looked towards Margi with a smile, "Would you mind bringing us a pot of tea, my dearest?"

"Not at all Jon. Has your headache gone, or do you need some more aspirin?"

"I'm fine Margie, please don't fuss. Just a cup of tea would be very nice. Come on PJ, I want to hear all about your adventure!"

PJ assisted Jonathon to his old tapestry chair, the one Grandma Sally had had crafted for him many years ago. It had been re-stuffed several times, but the paisley pattern was still evident. PJ, then sank into the feather cushions of the enormous couch. It too held memories; as a small boy, he would be left there all night after falling asleep during family celebrations.

Jonathon's face gleamed with enthusiasm.

"You may begin your stories, PJ. I'm all ears. Please, transport me to the Australian outback. I'll close my eyes and pretend I'm young again, riding my horse behind cattle, amongst the mulga bush and the red earth, and camping beneath the Southern Cross."

"I suppose it was a bit like that Granddad. I loved it. It was everything I imagined it would be, only a hell of a lot tougher. The enormous land mass of Merriola made Bulkawa look like a suburban back yard. The property was huge. It covered over 980,000 acres.

"As you know, I arrived in late March, just after the wet season. We spent the first two weeks at the homestead, organising the horses and gear, plus maps had to be drawn up. I spent those first weeks getting acquainted with the boss and the other men before we headed out. We then set off like a caravan of gypsies. The horses travelled in an open cattle truck and another cattle truck was used for the jackaroos and station hands. Thank God it was covered in, although it only protected us a little from the dust. We travelled along some of the worst bone-shaking roadways. I tell you Granddad, I felt like every part of my body had been turned inside out. Last in line came the cook, he followed in a smaller truck with all his gear." Jonathon sat on the edge of his chair listening intently, as PJ leaned back placing his arms behind his head.

"We started by mustering the paddock furthest away. Each paddock was approximately thirty-four thousand acres, and in the middle of each sat a huge yarding pen, which held over a thousand head of cattle. It took us well over a week just to muster each paddock – four in total. There were five of us jackaroos, ten Aboriginal stockman and four ringers, or station hands, if you don't know what a ringer means." Johnathon nodded, yes.

"It was bloody hard work. Not the riding, that was great. I didn't even mind the rough ones, the broncos. That was a bit of fun. We'd lay bets on who'd stay on board the longest. But that only lasted for the first couple of days, then the horses became like us; too buggered to buck. I'm sure you could imagine, Granddad, that after castrating eighty or so young bulls in a day, branding them, giving vaccinations and then de-horning them, there wasn't much time spent singing around the campfire. And the perpetual cloud of dust produced by a thousand head of cattle entered every orifice; ears, nose, eyes and especially our throats. We were eating the stuff all day long."

"Did you lasso the cattle and then throw them to the ground to brand them?" Johnathon asked enthused with the story but starting to feel weary.

"Yes, we roped them one at a time and then we'd attach the rope to one of our Clydesdale's, who'd drag the steer up to the branding fence. I tell you, Granddad, after the first thousand head I was ready to bolt for home. I was totally knackered by the end of each day. So, I can assure you, I wasn't lying on my back admiring the stars for long. And the food the cook dished up was nothing to write home about. Beef every night – mainly stew. He'd cook it for hours to tenderise a tough, old cow and then the next night, he'd throw a handful of curry and some sultanas in to spice it up a bit."

Patrick paused a moment, noticing Jonathon had closed his eyes, and wondered if he was sleeping or daydreaming.

"You would have loved the barramundi fishing Granddad!" PJ yelled this and Jonathon jumped a little.

"Barramundi – now there's a real fish PJ." Jonathon opened his eyes wide. "I caught a huge barramundi in my younger days. A client of mine owned a small property, not far from where you were. That place also bordered on the Victoria River. He called it a get-away farm. It held no stock, simply a reserve for wildlife. He owned his own aeroplane and flew me up there for a fishing weekend. So yes, I've experienced the thrill of catching barramundi, and then I can't tell you how much I enjoyed cooking and eating the delicacy." Jonathon was now wide awake.

"Yes, I remember when I was a boy and you telling me about that weekend, Granddad. I think my dreams began to take hold after you told me that story. I knew one day I'd experience the outback. And as you've always said, 'God does have a plan for each of us'. I know that even more now, because if I hadn't been there, Tarni would have been murdered." Jonathon inclined his head.

"You know PJ, I too saved a life – your grandmother's. Well, at least I played a major part in it." He then laughed before asking. "I say, you haven't fallen in love with this young lady, just like I did with your grandmother all those years ago. Have you?"

"No, Granddad, although she is beautiful; no, I just wanted to give her an opportunity to prove herself. She's a talented horse woman and I think she has a lot to offer in my horse training business and the community."

"It sounds like she's running for council, PJ. You must bring her here, so I can meet her."

"Yes, I'll ask her to join us for Christmas at Bulkawa. I can't believe it's just three weeks away."

"Tarni will be most welcome but you obviously don't know; we're having Christmas lunch here at Wildflowers. I enjoy being home for Christmas. Maybe I'm just too lazy to travel these days."

Margie entered the room in time to hear Jonathon's remark.

"You're not lazy, Jonathon, and after all, this is your family's home. It's a safe haven for all who have needed it, so I must tell you, PJ, your young friend, Tarni, is most welcome."

"Thank you, Nan."

"I'm hoping all the family will be able to stay overnight. We've had the pool re-tiled this past winter, so we can have some fun again. And now gentlemen, lunch is served in the dining room." Margie said as she bowed to the waist.

They took their place at the formal dining table, which seated up to twenty people.

Jonathon chuckled, "You're very sweet, Margie, trying to make PJ feel special by sitting us at the dining table. Though I'm sure he'd have felt a little more comfortable in the kitchen. Isn't that right, PJ?"

"This is fine, Granddad. I need to be reminded of the finer things in life. I may be in for a long hard slog with horse training, minus the refinements, unless I can produce winners. It could be a sobering business."

"I suppose you're right. Now I'll remind you of something that you may have forgotten. My mother, Kate, married a horse trainer, my father of course, many, many years ago. She was from British aristocracy. Sadly, her family shunned her for marrying a man who was deemed well beneath her station. However, my father was in fact a gentleman, in the truest sense of the word." Jonathon sighed deeply. "It was such a shame my mother and I lost him when he was so young. I was only a boy, seven years old in fact, and then more tragedy came when my mother died three years later." Jonathon paused, sad in his reflection.

PJ had not forgotten the story. He'd heard it many times and although Jonathon held no blood ties to PJ, he would insist that PJ's passion to train racehorses was due to Jonathon's father being a racehorse trainer.

"Well Granddad it's obvious where I get my passion."

PJ would never embarrass this amazing old man, who'd taken Patrick Snr from the orphanage and into his home and heart, by denouncing this lack of blood tie.

Their lunch of cold chicken, with salad and fresh bread, was taken in-between laughter and more tales about PJ's time spent in the outback.

"PJ, are you going to pursue the matter of your friend Tarni's attempted murder? I do have considerable contacts in the Northern Territory you know."

"I'm leaving it up to Tarni, Granddad. I don't want to push her into it. She hasn't had the best life so far. She was taken from her mother at age six and fostered into a white family. They treated her as a slave. Only one good thing came of it, a good education. She did well too. She's very intelligent, but they gave her no opportunity to pursue a career, instead they turned her into a housemaid and cook for the family. The only thing she enjoyed when living with them was riding the children's ponies. Tarni was only allowed to ride because the kids had trouble handling them.

They lived near a racetrack, and when Tarni turned thirteen, she'd sneak out early in the morning to ride a couple of racehorses for a local trainer. This was until a year later when he became amorous towards her, so she ran away from the family. But the authorities found her. This didn't deter Tarni; her running away continued and when brought home, the father would belt her with a strap and then he'd fondle her while saying he was sorry. After she told the counsellor about this, they sent her back to a mission near 'Merriola Station'.

She was sixteen when the boss gave her a job as a housemaid-cum-gardener. It was on the second day after I arrived, when I was attempting to catch a horse in the yard next to the veggie patch, that I saw her. Tarni had watched me for a while before she came to show me her way of 'tuning in', as she called it. She amazed me with how she caught and handled that horse. It was one of the wildest horses I think I've ever come across. At sunrise the next morning, I saw Tarni riding him around the yard. I watched enthralled; she had him as quiet as a lamb."

Jonathon listened and in his usual manner of weighing things up, offered his advice.

"I think this young woman, after what she's been through, may need some counselling. I can put you in touch with an excellent female therapist who is renowned for helping young Aboriginal women, or half-castes if you like, to overcome their insecurities."

"That would be great, Granddad. But I think Tarni may refuse the offer. She has her mind set on forgetting all about the past and the attempted murder. She just wants to concentrate on her future with racehorses."

"And you, PJ, are you included in her plans? Just be careful, son, you may break her heart, that's if you don't have feelings for her. You know what I mean. And this is the reason I strongly urge you to seek out the therapist, Sarah Brown. She's an amazing young woman. Sarah not only deals clinically with her patients, but spiritually, which I'm sure helps in the long run." Jonathon shook his head and smiled the way one does when a fond memory comes creeping back. "Sarah is also the funniest young woman, or person, I've ever met. I'm sure her sense of humour is why she's had great success with her patients."

PJ gave only a shy smile.

"It would do you no harm to laugh a little more, PJ. I think the worry of what you wanted to do with your life, has bogged you down, plus of course the disturbing attempt on Tarni's life. You seem to be taking it all very seriously, especially the task of setting Tarni on the right road. I remember you used to be so funny. You were the best practical joker in the family. I trust you will soon find that same happiness."

"You're right as usual, Granddad. I have become a little morose. I suppose it is all due to weighing up my future and now wanting justice for Tarni. But what good is pursuing justice if she won't cooperate with me, or anyone else for that matter?"

"Have you heard any more from the Northern Territory police?"

"No, I haven't. I thought I'd give them a ring later today."

"Why not now? I'm interested to hear what they have to say. I may be able to get things moving a bit quicker. That's if I'm not satisfied with how they're running the case."

"Of course, Granddad. Just let me digest my delicious lunch and then I'll phone them."

PJ rose to kiss Margie on the cheek.

"Thank you, Nan, it was just what I needed. You must have known I was totally sick of beef. The chicken was superb. I think I'll take a walk outside and have a look at the re-tiled pool; I'll be back in five."

PJ stood transfixed on the edge of the pool, recollecting the hours he'd spent with his cousins and friends, dive- bombing, playing water polo and running around the edge playing tag, while Margie yelled, 'NO RUNNING BOYS!'

Mesmerised gazing into the stillness of the pool, PJ thought of how he'd miss his granddad terribly when he passed away. This thought came upon him like an unexpected wave. Jonathon had been PJ's rock throughout the endless hours of studying law. Jonathon was his mentor and his confidant. Even as a young man, when PJ came to him with women troubles, he'd laugh and tell him, not to worry. His father's charm with women had simply been inherited. Although PJ had never taken up as many offers as did his father, Patrick Snr, PJ enjoyed the company of females. He'd had the privilege of making love to some of the most beautiful young women in Adelaide. But none had touched him deeply. Tarni then came to mind. She had touched him. He shook the un-wanted feeling and returned to the house where Jonathon was talking on the phone. He beckoned with his hand for PJ to come closer.

"He's just walked in, Sarah. I'll put PJ on the phone. You can work out the appointment time with him. Thank you and I hope your parents are well. Please give them my regards. Goodbye."

Jonathon handed the phone to PJ who exchanged pleasantries before making an appointment for the following morning.

"Well that was easy, PJ, although it may not have been if I were not acquainted with Sarah's parents. I do apologise though; I've taken a liberty that perhaps was not mine to take. But I think it's imperative that Tarni receives counselling. You wouldn't want her to break down mentally from un-resolved problems. I've seen this happen many times to seemingly stronger people, and I can tell you, it is not pretty. Sometimes these people need to spend time in a mental institution. Let us give Tarni every opportunity to make her way through the rest of her life on a happy and stable note. She's had a lot to deal with in her short life. Do you know if her mother is still alive?"

"No, she's not. She died when Tarni was eight years old. Tarni said her mother died of a broken heart after the authorities took Tarni away. I can understand why she is so bitter against the white man. I think I may be the only white person she's ever trusted, and that's why I haven't pushed her into talking to the police. To be quite honest, Granddad, I'm on both sides of the fence. I can see her point of view and of course what should be done legally. But you were right to contact Sarah Brown. It will be good for us both to talk to a professional. I need to know how far I can push Tarni."

Jonathon nodded before he called the Darwin police. The sergeant in charge of Tarni's case, Sergeant Ralph, said the news was still negative. They were unable to find any trace of Robbo. Ralph then asked to speak with PJ. He inquired into Tarni's health and asked if PJ was any further informed on why Robbo would attempt such a drastic thing.

"No, I'm not Sergeant. Tarni still won't talk about it. I'm sure the station manager, Ian Davies, has supplied you with the story of Robbo attempting to rape Tarni, several times I believe. She'd fought him off each time, so there's Robbo's motive." There was no reply from the sergeant, so PJ added. "Tarni's made a speedy recovery, injury wise, and tomorrow I'm to meet with a counsellor who will hopefully help Tarni through this mess, plus her initial traumas in life."

"What do you mean initial traumas Mr Darcy?"

"It's a long story but it's more or less about her being taken away from her mother and then the treatment she received by the so-called do-gooders. I'll explain in detail if I need to return. When you find Robbo, Robert Timer, that is."

"Well, all I can say, Mr Darcy, is that Tarni's a lucky girl to have you and your family as friends. Just keep a close eye on her though, she's known to go walk about and quite often. We'll need her here to lay a charge when we find this Robbo bloke."

Jonathon asked if he may speak with Sergeant Ralph again.

"Hello, Sergeant, Jonathon Darcy again. I'd like to ask you one more question. Are you using Aboriginal trackers to try and find Robert Timer?"

"Yes Sir, of course, but they all seem to come up with dead ends."

This was all Jonathon needed to know.

"Thank you, Sergeant, I'm sure you are doing your best to find him."

He turned to PJ and asked if he wished to speak further with Sergeant Ralph. PJ shook his head, so Jonathon bid the sergeant, goodbye and good luck.

PJ gathered Jonathon to his chest and kissed his head.

"I have to go now Granddad. I have a lot to organise."

Chapter 5

At ten o'clock the next morning, PJ walked into Sarah Brown's stylish office and immediately guessed what she would be like. He then remembered his mother saying, 'Never judge a book by its cover, PJ. Always give people the opportunity to show who they really are before you make an opinion'. He smiled at the thought.

Sarah Browns secretary was an Aboriginal girl, who spoke eloquently.

"Good morning Mr Darcy, Miss Brown will be with you shortly. She has a client with her at the moment. Please take a seat."

Patrick did what he was told but couldn't help compare this young full-blood Aboriginal woman with Tarni. If they stood side by side, he was sure most people would never guess Tarni had even an ounce of Aboriginal blood in her. He began to think, if he were Tarni, he would've made a new life for himself and never let on about his heritage. Then he changed his mind. That would be wrong, but then, where did Tarni fit in with a white majority. This Aboriginal secretary would no doubt have a family who was proud of her for making her way in the white man's world. PJ was sure this young woman was at ease with her colour and race. It showed in her confidence.

The office door opened to reveal what PJ thought to be a woman dressed in men's clothes. Her black hair was slicked back, most probably with Brilcream. Her masculine, grey suit looked as if it had been tailor made. The only feminine touch was her pink shirt under the blazer. The woman held the door open for a tall slender woman dressed in a figure-hugging, beige, crepe dress and long strawberry-blonde hair draped around her shoulders accentuating hazel eyes. Patrick was expecting to keep on admiring this beautiful woman, as she left. He thought for a moment about finding out from the secretary who she was, when the opposite happened. The manly dressed woman left after kissing the strawberry blonde on the cheek. The real Sarah Brown then stood above him with her slender hand extended. Patrick felt his mouth drop.

She laughed. "Ah got you. You thought she was me!"

PJ stood up and held Sarah's hand. She turned and almost dragged him into her office then closed the door with a bang. And went straight to the point.

"It's so nice to finally meet you, Patrick." She turned to face him, eyes dancing with eroticism, her voice stimulating. "I've read many articles and admired photos of you in the social columns and always accompanied by beautiful women, of course." She laughed. "It sounds like I'm envious. Mmm, I'll have to look into that. Envy is not healthy."

Sarah then sat gracefully in her red leather chair, behind her black desk and rested her chin on her hand.

"Now let us begin, Patrick. You have a problem with a part white Aboriginal girl your grandfather tells me?"

PJ sat a little gob smacked. He assumed a woman so glamorous and obviously intelligent would be a little more demure. He found Sarah almost confronting and he wasn't sure if his granddad had been correct in sending him to her.

"Yes that's right, Miss Brown, Tarni is a quarter caste Aboriginal. And I prefer to be called PJ. It saves any confusion with my father."

He then filled Sarah in on what he knew about Tarni. This took about thirty minutes. There were no interruptions and no questioning. Sarah sat statuesque and listened intently to every word PJ had to say. He finished, relieved that his observations had changed towards Sarah Brown. She seemed sincere and to be transforming his information into fathoming out how she would approach Tarni. She then looked at her watch.

"I'll need to meet Tarni as soon as possible. Our time is up for today, PJ. Please make another appointment with Miss Brown at the front desk."

PJ raised an eyebrow, "Miss Brown?"

"Yes, I adopted Ella. Her parents were killed when she was a baby. She was brought to me as a troubled and abused child. She's lovely, isn't she? I'm so proud of her. And the years of elocution helped tremendously don't you think?"

Once again, Sarah didn't wait for his answer. She seemed to glide to the door before PJ had time to rise from his chair. They stood face to face in the open doorway.

"Thank you, Sarah. May I call you by your first name?"

"Yes of course, PJ and you may call me anytime for a dinner date."

She didn't seem to mind that two of her clients had witnessed her brazen statement.

"I'll take you up on the offer with pleasure. Thank you, Sarah. Until we meet again."

PJ made an appointment for five days hence with Miss Ella Brown.

The day before Tarni was due to visit Sarah, PJ received a letter from the SAJC. He ripped it open with the same excitement as a child opening his first Christmas present – he wasn't disappointed. The letter said he had permission to train racehorses. He was sure that the fact had at least five horses to begin with, had gone in his favour. He also had a number of outstanding references, one of which was written by the leading SA trainer at the time. It explained Patrick's fine horsemanship, which he'd shown when he'd worked in the trainers' stables on school holidays and most weekends. All Patrick needed to do now was to attend a meeting with the committee to seal his future.

The first person he shared his good news with, was his father. It was an extremely hot day for late November. Usually this intense heat would not hit Adelaide until January - February, but today the temperature had reached nearly one hundred degrees by 10 am, so PJ knew where his father would be. Patrick Snr was sitting reading the morning paper on the west side veranda of their rambling country homestead. Come afternoon, it would be the last place he'd sit, due to the afternoon sun.

"Dad," PJ said, waving the letter about, "I've been given permission to train."

Patrick looked up from under his glasses and said dryly. "Is it too early for a celebration drink, son? I know it's bloody hot enough."

"No, it's not too early, Dad, and I hope this will be the first of many when my horses win!"

Patrick Snr poured the Shivers Regal neat. "'To be enjoyed how it should be'. That's what Jum Watt, your paternal grandfather would say if he were alive."

They drank a toast to Jum's memory. Jum would've been so proud of his grandson, becoming a horse trainer. Jum owned 'Freelance', the horse favoured to win the Melbourne Cup back in 1895. Sadly, Jum was shot dead the night before the Melbourne Cup. And so PJ poured another whisky and made Jum a promise.

"I will make amends, Grandfather. I will train the winner of a Melbourne Cup one day and I'll accept the trophy in Jum's honour."

Addy had just returned from an early morning ride and heard the men talking on the back veranda. Her slim figure, still the same as when she was twenty, was extraordinary. She'd knock back compliments, saying, 'oh for heaven's sake, it's only the riding that keeps me trim.' She was now sixty but looked forty. Her olive skin remained un-wrinkled and her long black hair contained only the odd grey. Every time she appeared before Patrick Snr, his eyes beamed. Their love for each other seemed as binding as the day they first met.

"Good morning, gentlemen," Addy said with slight surprise at seeing the whisky bottle half empty on the cane table. "And what may I ask is the reason for the bar being opened so early?"

"PJ's received good news, Addy. His trainer's licence has been approved. So, my love, we've decided to celebrate."

Addy hugged PJ while Patrick poured her a whisky.

"Thank you, Patrick my love. Here's to you my darling son. May you become the leading trainer in Adelaide, in… "

"I've given myself five years to accomplish that feat Mum."

"Well then, in five years it is!"

After taking time to discuss where he should live, now that he needed to be closer to his stables, Addy suggested that PJ move into a unit they owned in Adelaide that would soon be vacated by the tenant. She seemed just as excited about doing up the apartment, as she did with PJ's good news.

"I'll get on to it straight away and have the apartment painted and re-decorated in no time. It's about time we used it for the family. It'll come in handy when we're in town to see a live show. That's if you don't mind, PJ. We usually stay at a hotel, but it would be fun to stay with you. And please tell us if it's not convenient, you know, if you have a young lady friend staying." She paused to take a sip on her whisky. "I haven't heard of any budding romances since you returned from the outback, PJ. Have I missed something?"

Patrick Snr shook his head. It seemed to him that Addy was always in a hurry to see PJ married with children.

"Addy let him be. Stop badgering PJ about finding a wife. It'll happen if and when it's supposed to happen." He placed his whisky down and stood to slap PJ on the back.

"Let's get started, son. I'll give you a hand to set yourself up and we'd better go look at uncle Angus's horses, or he'll think we're not interested."

Addy called after them. "So, PJ, would you like me to take over organising the interiors of your new abode?"

"Yes, thank you, Mother. I won't have the time; besides, I trust your good taste!"

Patrick Snr laughed. "That'll keep her busy and out of your love life for a while."

With all the work needed to set up the stables and to bring in the very best horse feed that PJ could find, the week soon passed. Then the day arrived for PJ and Tarni's meeting with Sarah Brown. PJ felt a little uncomfortable that he hadn't yet made a dinner date with Sarah as he'd been far too busy.

On their way, PJ spoke to Tarni about Sarah's daughter, Ella, being Aboriginal and how efficient she was as her secretary.

"I can't wait for you to meet her Tarni. She's a lovely young lady, and a credit to Miss Brown."

Tarni threw a sarcastic look at PJ. "Perhaps she's a credit to herself." He didn't like her tone.

"If you have that attitude Tarni then you won't make any headway with Miss Brown."

"I don't want to make headway with Miss Brown. I'm only going there because you insist PJ. I'm happy as long as I don't look back at my life."

"But that's exactly what you need to do. Look back, so you can come to terms with what's happened. Only then will you be able to move on and handle the bad memories that are sure to come back occasionally. Sarah will teach you how to deal with them."

Tarni turned her head and imagined the houses flashing by were her memories – all gone in an instant- obliterated. They drove the rest of the way in silence.

PJ approached the front desk and introduced Tarni to Ella. There seemed to be an instant dislike between the two. Their eyes met for a second, before they drew apart. In unison, they said, 'Pleased to meet you'. The exchange was cold and abrupt. PJ chose to ignore the tension between the two women, although it had him wondering if Sarah had given Ella information about Tarni being a quarter-caste. Tarni and PJ took a seat.

When Sara's office door finally swung open, PJ was once again bedazzled by her beauty. Today her hair was swished up in a French roll and she wore a navy blue fitted dress with a split long enough to expose her perfect thigh. PJ stood up with Tarni, but Sarah asked him to sit and wait. She needed to talk to Tarni alone. Sarah smiled at PJ like a seductress, before slowly closing the door. He heard the door being locked and wondered why. PJ turned to Ella who'd obviously found Sarah's animation quite amusing. She giggled while looking into her appointment book.

After thirty minutes, PJ was fully expecting the door to open, hopefully with a smiling Tarni. When the door remained closed he asked Ella:

"I think Tarni's time is up. Should I be concerned?"

Ella replied sweetly. "I'm sorry Mr Darcy, I should have explained. Miss Brown has allowed another thirty minutes for Tarni, although she may ask you to join them soon. Would you like a cup of tea?"

"No, I'm fine thank you, Ella. I'm busy reading the rules of racing. I've only just been given permission to train horses and I wouldn't want to do anything wrong unintentionally."

"Of course not, Mr Darcy. At least your time is not wasted then."

After another thirty minutes, the office door opened at the same time as the waiting room door. Sarah recognised and acknowledged her next client with a nod and then focused on PJ.

"I am sorry PJ. I intended to spend a further ten minutes with you alone, but time is up. Call me later and we'll work out another time to talk." She lowered her voice, "perhaps over dinner?"

Sarah had remained standing in the doorway and beckoned the client to come into her office. Before closing the door, she smiled sweetly at Tarni and then shot a seductive look at PJ. He was now feeling obliged to at least ask her out to dinner. I really don't want any romantic complications at the moment. I need to focus on my horses, and Tarni, of course..

Driving back to the stables, PJ asked Tarni:

"Do you think Sarah will be able to help you Tarni. I mean, do you feel comfortable with her?"

Tarni smiled, then giggled.

"She's very funny, PJ. The first thing she told me was, we should never label anyone, except nymphomaniacs who are also kleptomaniacs." Tarni, then laughed out loud. PJ had never heard her belly laugh before.

"Well, let me in on the joke."

"I'm sorry, it's private. I think it's too rude to tell you."

"If you don't tell me, Tarni, it'll bug me for the rest of the day. Please tell me."

"I'm sure you're clever enough to work it out all by yourself, PJ." Tarni said still giggling.

Chapter 6

Christmas day, 1957, was planned by the Darcy family to be held at "Wildflowers'. Tarni had refused the offer to join them, due to Mrs Stenning's son Adam returning home. He'd been a good friend to Tarni, and he'd be staying only two days before he had to return to the mission.

Tarni and Adam were lucky; the overcast sky had protected Mrs Stenning's home from the searing sun. However, the promise of storms brought a humidity that reminded Tarni of the build up to the wet season in the NT.

Each Christmas, no matter how hot it was, Mrs Stenning would cook the traditional hot roast lunch and set her finery on the dining table, which sat unused for eleven months of the year. They pulled their cracker bonbons apart, donned their silly paper hats and read aloud the jokes written on the paper inside. Tarni would have liked to tell them the joke Sarah Brown had told her but thought it inappropriate. She smiled to herself.

It was a happy day for Tarni. She felt right at home and not once did Adam raise the Robbo story. He'd refrained from telling Tarni that everyone in the Northern Territory was still talking about it. Although the talk of the attempted murder had gone quiet, concern was now about the young man Robbo who had simply disappeared. Many assumptions had been made, which had swung the pendulum in favour of Robbo, he remained innocent until proven guilty and now the general consensus was, particularly under the influence of alcohol; 'it was those black bastards that did away with him'. The Police had finally found Robbo's burnt out ute but there was no sign of a body. It had become one of the biggest mysteries in the NT in the last decade.

*

Tarni had offered to feed the racehorses on Christmas night, plus take them for their usual afternoon pick. PJ was most grateful. If Tarni were lucky, Adam would help her, and he did. After they'd finished their Christmas lunch and had a rest, they tended to their duties.

Later, the intense humidity caused Tarni and Adam to take in a refreshing dip in the ocean at Glenelg. Intermittently, lightening lit up the steely sky and claps of thunder created ripples on the water. So loud was one clap that Tarni

jumped into Adams arms. In that moment, she felt something; a kindred spirit –
an attraction-maybe. But then it was gone and once again Tarni became aloof.
She wriggled away from Adam. She felt neither black nor white – a nobody.

"It's all right, Tarni. I won't bite you. You know if you're ever scared,
I'll always be your friend." He smiled broadly and then asked in a caring way.
"Are you as happy as you say you are? Because if you're not, you could come
back and help me at the mission?"

"I'm very happy thanks, Adam. You know how much I love horses and
I've found another good friend in , PJ. He saved my life. I owe him."

"You can't spend the rest of your life paying back what you think you
owe somebody, Tarni. But I'm happy you've finally been given an opportunity
to be with horses. I remember at the mission, when you rode that poor old sway
back around all day. You cried for over a week when he died. You thought you
killed him because you rode him so much." Adam laughed and Tarni punched
him playfully on the chest.

"That wasn't funny Adam. I still believe I killed him. I only thought
of myself and how I wanted to ride. I never thought of him, the poor old boy. I
hated myself for that!"

She turned and swam away. Adam remained where he was, chest deep
in water, watching and thinking how Tarni would always run away from the
things she didn't want, or care to remember.

Before Adam left Adelaide, the day after Boxing Day, he made Tarni
promise that if she ever became unhappy, she was to let him know. He would
come running. Her warm embrace gave Adam hope that she felt something for
him. He certainly did for her.

*

When the Christmas festivities and New Year's Eve parties were well
over, PJ set to work on preparing his first runner. He and Tarni had joined his
parents at a tried horse sale in January. A certain horse had caught PJ's eye, so
he approached the trainer.

"He runs like the bloody clappers, but he's a bastard," the trainer said.
"He won't go anywhere near the barrier stall. I don't know why the missus
named him Volunteer; he won't volunteer for any bloody thing."

They were able to buy the renowned barrier rogue for a song, Five
Pounds to be exact. But he'd be worth only dog meat if PJ and Tarni weren't able
to get him over his barrier fears.

PJ approached the racecourse curator at Morphettville and asked for
special permission to use the barrier stalls throughout the day, explaining they

needed to try different methods on their hopeful first runner. After consent was given, PJ tried nearly every trick in the book, until the blind fold was used as a last resort. Thankfully it worked, at least in getting Volunteer into the stalls. But before this, Tarni had done her 'tuning in' with the horse and a strong bond had formed between the two. Every day she'd taken Volunteer to the beach, just to play. No galloping, only moderate exercise. PJ agreed, as in his opinion, Volunteer had been over trained. This was probably done to work the energy out of him, in the hope that he wouldn't have any when they tried to load him into the barriers.

Over a month later, on 28th of February, their patience with Volunteer was rewarded. The group of new owners, including PJ's parents, had come to see Volunteer's barrier trial. He walked straight up and into the barriers going on to win the trial by six lengths. This exhibition set tongues wagging.

Two weeks later, a very nervous PJ saddled up Volunteer for a maiden race at Murray Bridge. The horse had opened at odds of twenty to one, but by the time PJ arrived in the betting ring, smart money had been laid and the bookies had Volunteer at three to one favourite.

PJ's stomach churned as he paced up and down the fence, knowing a hell of a lot of money would be lost if Volunteer refused to load and PJ would be the brunt of the punters anger.

Tarni sat alone and sent mental telepathy messages to Volunteer; 'Calm, stay calm, calm there's a good boy. Stay calm'. She'd even had the courage to confront the race starter.

"Please don't use the whip. If he refuses to load, just scratch him from the race please."

The chief barrier attendant smiled arrogantly.

"I'll use whatever method I have to, Miss," and walked away.

Tarni's prayers were answered when Volunteer, although a little hesitant, walked up and into the barriers and stood quietly. When the gates flung open, Tarni repeated her silent mantras for Volunteer to stay calm. He did. He dropped back to last.

PJ almost passed out when he saw this. He was feeling the punters scorn already. PJ's old boss had never failed in giving instructions to his jockey's. 'Follow the fence and ride for luck, even if you're last into the straight,' he'd say. PJ hadn't given his jockey, Billy Paton, any instructions but he wished he had.

PJ now thought Volunteer couldn't possibly win, because he was tailed off in this 1200 metre race. Coming into the home turn, Volunteer lost at least four lengths by rounding the field. This took him ten wide; he was almost trimming the Photinia hedge down the outside fence. The cheering didn't begin until the final 80 metres when the leader got the staggers and Volunteer after making steady ground, flashed home to beat him by a head.

PJ felt sick but elated at the same time. When Volunteer returned to the mounting enclosure, he questioned Billy about his riding tactics. Billy replied:

"I know this horse Mr Darcy, and I know how much ability he has. I reckoned the only way he was going to get beat, was if he wouldn't load in the gates, or he got blocked for a run. Now I'll give you a tip Mr. Darcy. What you lose on the home turn by going wide, you gain in the straight with a clear run. That's if you've got the horse that can do it. You'll win plenty more with this fella. Thanks for the ride Mr Darcy. You can see me later in the jockeys' room."

He gave PJ a wink before walking away, assuming he would receive a tidy sling. And then Billy remembered something and turned around.

"This was your first starter. Am I right Mr Darcy?" PJ nodded. "Well you've done a great job. I'd like to hear how you got him to overcome his fear of the barrier. You can tell me over breakfast one day. I'll come and ride a bit of track work for you if you like."

That day began a great partnership between Billy Paton and PJ; it was also the beginning of PJ's romance with Sarah Brown. Unbeknown to him, Sarah was a silent partner in the ownership of Volunteer. This was after Tarni had given her the tip on how much talent the horse had.

"Of course it's a big gamble, Sarah. We have to get him to load in the barriers first, but I have such an incredible feel for this horse. I reckon if they still had the rope start, we wouldn't have bought him under a thousand pounds!" Tarni had said.

Sarah, in turn, spoke with PJ's granddad Jonathon about wishing to take a share in the horse and him being the front man for her. She didn't want PJ to think she was stalking him. Jonathon thought it a great idea.

"It will be our secret Sarah." He promptly signed his name on the papers and Sarah went as his representative on race day.

PJ smelt a rat when Sarah turned up at Murray Bridge that day; especially when she became overwhelmed by Volunteers win. She showered PJ with kisses and congratulated him on training her first and his very first winner. When PJ was free of Sarah's embrace, he asked in an almost confronting manner.

"I thought Grandfather said you were only representing him here today, Sarah. And didn't I hear you say, your first winner, as in, you own a share?" Sarah's excitement waned, and she appeared humble.

"I'm sorry, PJ, I didn't want you to think me a stalker. The truth is, Tarni put such a good spiel on the horse, I thought I'd like to own a share. If you don't want me to be part of it, then I'll sell."

PJ saw Sarah's vulnerability, her somewhat cocky over confidant approach was not present today. On first meeting Sarah, PJ thought she was a man-eater. Someone who assumed her beauty and wit would allow her to have any man she wished, and PJ didn't like that type of woman. Maybe I should give Sarah a chance to prove my judgment wrong. He quickly softened and offered her an olive branch.

"There's no point in selling your share, Sarah. You're more than welcome to join the fun and tonight I think we will be having just that. I'm sorry it won't be the intimate dinner I've promised you, but we can still enjoy the evening together." He then said jokingly, "And I think you should change the ownership back into your name. I wouldn't trust that old codger, he might run away with the prize money!"

Sarah belly laughed before taking on mock seriousness.

"I think your right, PJ. You can never trust magistrates who've been dubbed with the Order of the British Empire and the honour of being, 'Australian of the Year.' You're right. I'll go and see that rascal Jonathon Darcy tomorrow and get him to sign his share over to its rightful owner." She and PJ then joined the other horse owners in bar.

Being the strapper, Tarni had no other purpose than seeing Volunteer cared for. This came before anything else.

After PJ had finished at the bar with Sarah and the others, he joined Tarni at the tie-up stalls.

"Come to the party tonight to celebrate, Tarni. It'll be fun!"

"No thank you, PJ. I'll stay with Volunteer. Besides, I'm tired and I have to be up at four in the morning. You go. I'm happy to stay home with the horses."

PJ handed Tarni a wad of ten-pound notes, but she pushed it away and he pushed it back.

"Please take it, Tarni. All the owners had a big win and they want you to have it as a gift. They know if it weren't for you, Volunteer would never have won. So keep it, and tomorrow, we'll go to the bank and start an account in your name."

"I might lose it, PJ. I don't think this money will fit in my Milo tin. I've never had this much money before."

PJ kissed her on the forehead, "You will from now on."

His kiss lingered a little longer than usual and she wished he would stay with her and not go off celebrating with his friends, especially Sarah. She kicked herself for mentioning the horse to Sarah.

*

The night air sat heavy with the promise of rain. The humidity gathered around the party goers who were celebrating their win at a seaside restaurant at Glenelg. Sarah began waving her menu to create a cool breeze and this act amused her. It reminded her of the movie 'Gone with the Wind', in which Scarlet O'Hara waved her fan and batted her eye lashes at Ashly. However, Sarah was unable to accomplish this because PJ was the centre of everyone's attention and he'd hardly looked her way all evening. Thankfully and eventually, Sarah breathed a sigh of relief when the last happy owner said his farewell. It left her alone with PJ. He smiled into her hazel eyes, and for one moment she saw what she'd hoped for, an attraction. He spoke softly.

"I'm sorry we didn't have much time to talk, Sarah. Did you come by cab or did you drive?"

"I caught a cab."

"Well, would you like me to drive you home?"

Sarah's pulse raced, and she could hardly speak.

"I…I'd appreciate it, thank you, PJ."

After driving for only one minute, PJ pulled the MG sportscar up outside her seaside home and laughed.

"You could have walked home, Sarah." He lowered his head and looked at her as a schoolteacher would if you were in trouble. "Did you really have to catch a cab to the restaurant, Miss Brown?"

"Yes, I did. My feet were killing me from walking around the races all day, Mr Darcy!"

He smiled. "Would you like me to massage them for you?"

"Of course I would, but not tonight, it's late and you have to be up in four hours. Can we make a date? One you will keep, Mr Darcy?"

"You're right, Sarah. I'd better get some sleep. Thanks for reminding me." PJ jumped from his British Green MG and quickly ran around to open the door.

"You didn't answer me, PJ. Can we make a dinner date? I don't mind cooking. In fact, I love it, what do you like to eat?"

"I eat just about anything except beef curry. The cook on the cattle camp cured me of that."

"Okay, what about Saturday night at my place for a sea food

extravaganza?”

“I accept with pleasure, Miss Brown. What time?”

“Say 7 o’clock?”

*

Friday morning brought a downpour of rain so intense that Tarni was unable to ride the horses. So PJ excused himself.

“Are you able to manage here Tarni, I’m a bit knackered, I didn’t get to bed until one this morning, so I need to take a kip.” He yawned as he sat watching Tarni go about her duties.

“I’m fine, PJ. I don’t need you. Get some sleep and then we’ll go to the bank this afternoon if you like.”

“Oh, the bank, I almost forgot. Of course, I’ll take you to my bank. I’ll pick you up from Mrs Stenning’s at one.”

PJ left, and the rain continued heavy and loud, like small sacks of flour being thrown on the tin roof. It blocked out the sound of the young man entering the stables. Tarni turned around to make up the horse feeds when she faced a smiling Blue Boy. His skin was black as black, and those haunting eyes hadn’t changed. What they held, nobody could guess. He’d been a real troublemaker at the same mission where Tarni had lived for two years. He stole, he lied and basically annoyed the shit out of everyone there.

“Oh hell! You gave me a fright, Blue Boy. What are you doing here? How did you know where to find me?” Her heart rate quickened, she felt ill.

“Mr Adam tells me you here, Tarni. I need money. You got money, Tarni? You got pay job now.”

“Yes, I have some money Blue Boy and I’ll give you just enough to buy a bus ticket home. You don’t belong here.”

Tarni went to her secret hiding place and grabbed the money she had hidden in a Milo tin.

Blue Boy followed and looked over her shoulder.

“You want to know how we fix Robbo, Tarni. We fix him real good for you.”

“I don’t want to hear anything about Robbo. Here take this money and go home. It’s a lot more than your bus fare. You can buy something to eat and some new clothes. Now go home to the mission. Leave me alone!”

Blue Boy smiled at the wad of pound notes Tarni held in her hand.

“It take me four week to come here, Tarni. I not go back now. I think I stay in Adelaide. I like city places. Lots to see.” He snatched the money and turned to walk away, then stopped for a moment, not looking back. “I come see you tonight Tarni, down the beach, near the pier. If you not there, I come back when money runs out." His evil laugh made Tarni's blood boil. She'd given him a month's wages.

PJ arrived at Mrs Stenning's home at precisely one pm, freshened up and ready to take Tarni out. He knocked on the door and Mrs Stenning answered, looking a little glum.

"I'm sorry, PJ, but Tarni said to tell you, she's unable to go with you today as she feels ill. But she says she should be fine in the morning. She'll see you then."

"Oh, that's a shame. I was going to take her out for lunch to celebrate our win."

"Yes, how exciting. I must congratulate you. Fancy training your first horse to win his first race, I must say it was quite an achievement. Tarni tells me you both worked very hard to get him to accept the barriers. Well done. Now I must go and see if Tarni is alright. Goodbye," and she turned and shut the door.

PJ left a little miffed.

At four o'clock the following morning, PJ arrived at the stables and, as usual, he found Tarni there.

"How are you feeling today, Tarni?"

"I'm fine thanks. It was just women's problems."

Her answer took him back a little, as he still found it hard to believe Tarni was a woman. She looked so young.

"How's Volunteer? Did he eat up?"

"Yes, he licked his feed bin clean. He knows he's won a race and he wants a reward. I'll take him for a play on the beach and then I'll give him a pick of grass. But of course, I'll ride the others first."

PJ was happy for Tarni to organise the morning work. It meant he could get on with the business of meeting interested, would-be racehorse owners. He'd figured to make a decent living from racehorse training, he'd have to have twenty-five horses in work if he were to have a chance at winning the trainer's premiership. At the moment, he only had five, however, after his win he'd been approached by several people to train their horses. He knew for a fact, that changing Volunteer's barrier manners and then having him win his first race, had a lot to do with these offers.

The newspaper scribes had also taken an interest in 'the new kid on the block.' One sporting headline read: 'Rooky trainer wins with confident plunge!' The article explained how Patrick Darcy Jnr, aka, PJ, had bought 'Volunteer', the barrier rogue, at a tried horse sale. It was an excellent story and sure to bring

PJ more business, although a worrying thought came to him. He may only be offered barrier rogues. He smiled at this but knew he shouldn't.

Tarni worked the four horses, then rode Volunteer to the beach. PJ always followed to make sure it was safe to cross the road and he'd hold the traffic up if need be. At six thirty am, as they approached the beach, they saw an invasion of police vehicles and an ambulance. An officer smartly walked over to Tarni.

"Go home please, Miss. There will be no riding along the beach this morning. A man has been found drowned."

Tarni, unemotional with the news, turned Volunteer around and spent the next thirty minutes giving him a pick around the racetrack. PJ stood alongside contemplating.

"We don't hear of many drownings at Glenelg, Tarni. I wonder who it was. Maybe it was a suicide."

Tarni remained unfazed and gave no comment. But she did offer PJ her opinion on Volunteer, if only to change the subject.

"This horse is as tough as nails, PJ. I think if we just keep him ticking over, we should be able to race him again pretty soon."

It became obvious to PJ that Tarni had her own way of dealing with other people's tragedy. It was the same as she did her own; she simply blocked it out.

"Yes, I reckon you're right, Tarni. There's a race here at Morphettville next Saturday and it's over seven furlongs. They don't usually have improver races here on a Saturday, so I'll nominate him. I think we should take the opportunity while we can. But we'll see how he does between now and acceptance time."

The morning progressed as usual at the stables, until PJ received a telephone call from a prospective client, a Mr Harold Jones. He wished to meet PJ that afternoon and inspect his stables. He said he had four well bred horses to be trained.

PJ got to work immediately, cleaning the tack room and feed bins and the horse's coats were brushed free of dust until they shone. At this stage of his enterprise, PJ had leased ten stables, so the hunt would be on for bigger ones if Mr Jones sent his horses across. However, this would mean splitting his team and having to hire responsible staff, staff that could be trusted to do what he said without constant supervision.

Mr Jones arrived on time, driving up slowly in his Mercedes Benz. He rolled his enormous frame out of the car and offered PJ a robust handshake.

When he then noted Tarni's beauty, an admiring smile crossed his face.

"Well, you are a pretty little thing. I like girls looking after my horses. And your name is?"

"Tarni, Sir, and I will look after your horses very well and I'll ride them track work."

"Really? You don't look strong enough to ride a racehorse."

"It's not all about strength, Sir, it's about feel and respect." He raised his bushy eyebrows.

"I see, well maybe you can show me one morning when you ride my horses, especially one of them. He's a hard puller and there are not too many male jockeys who can hold him. But you're welcome to try, Tarni." He then laughed, imagining the improbability of such a frail-looking girl being able to accomplish the feat.

The meeting was successful and ended in a handshake to seal the deal. Mr Jones's four horses would be arriving the following Monday, and if successful, more would follow.

PJ hadn't thought it necessary to tell Tarni about his dinner date with Sarah that evening. But he decided to mention it as they were locking up the stables.

Tarni didn't comment but she turned quickly and walked away, saying:

"Don't worry about being here early tomorrow morning, PJ. I'll be here to feed up."

"I'll drive you home Tarni, wait a minute."

"No, I'd rather walk thanks."

PJ left her and went home. He showered and shaved while listening to the radio announcement.

"The Aboriginal male, who was found drowned at Glenelg beach, remains unidentified. We are therefore asking, for anyone who may have seen, or knew of this Indigenous man, to please inform the Adelaide police?

While driving to Sarah's home the story haunted PJ. He parked the car, turned the ignition off and shook the thought away, saying aloud: "It's just the lawyer in me. Let it go, PJ."

Sarah answered the door, wearing a white sleeveless cotton shirt and pink pedal pushers, with her hair tied in a ponytail. She studied PJ's somewhat formal attire.

"I'm sorry, PJ. It appears I'm not dressed for the occasion."

"No, I'm the one who should be sorry, Sarah. I should have asked, whether it was formal, or informal."

"Well, I hope to make you feel extremely comfortable and very informal. I get sick of dressing up for work, and I like to relax on the weekends, unless I'm going out." Sarah threw him a sultry look, then moved across the room in cat-like-steps and deepened her voice. "So, loosen your tie, or take it off if you like." She then lightened her tone, "What would you like to drink PJ?"

He smiled at her play acting. Maybe she chose the wrong vocation? She even looks like a movie star.

"A beer would be fine, thank you."

The apartment, spacious and modern, held furniture pieces designed in the latest fashion. They paraded along the walls, ultra-sleek and impressive though perhaps a little uncomfortable, similar to the furniture in her office. Sarah was obviously taken in by looks, not comfort. PJ considered himself the opposite.

While Sarah was attending to the drinks, he looked at the photographs that sat on every available surface. One, in particular, took his eye. It was of a tall young girl with long frizzy red hair, smiling shyly, obviously trying not to expose braces. She wore bifocals and a frumpy outfit. He couldn't imagine her being any relation to Sarah.

"Who's the young girl, Sarah?" PJ asked when she appeared with the drink tray in hand.

"Don't you recognize me, PJ?"

He nearly dropped the photo. "No, I'd never have guessed this was you."

"Well, you know a little more about me now. I had a massive complex when I was growing up." Sarah paused to look at his shocked expression. "Wouldn't you, if you looked like that?" There was no answer, so she continued.

"My parents were old fashioned and not much help with, 'the modern look.' They thought I was beautiful, just the way I was. They never understood why I was unhappy with the way I looked. I suppose my sense of humour kicked in by the time I was a teenager and I learned to laugh at myself. It was either live with self-loathing until I went mad or accept what I looked like and laugh about it. So, when I was in college I became the class clown. Then one day a miracle happened. The girls in our sewing class were asked to put on a fashion parade in front of the entire school, including members of the staff. We had to model the garments we'd designed and made. Of course, being thin, tall and a clown, I willingly offered to do more than my share of the modelling. We were lucky enough to have an Audrey Hepburn look alike for our design teacher. Thankfully, she saw beneath the frizzy hair and bifocals and transformed me into a beautiful princess. I never thought it possible. I can tell you, PJ, when I strutted my stuff down the catwalk that day, I became the envy of all. It changed my life forever."

Sarah focused on pouring PJ's beer and then looked up to see him smiling, his white teeth perfect against his tanned unblemished skin. His eyes, softened with the glow of moonlight, gave him a look she'd never seen before. *Oh, how I'd like to make love to you right now, PJ – this very minute.* Sarah forced herself back into reality.

"Well what do you think of that piece of information Mr Darcy, lawyer/horse trainer extraordinaire?"

"I think I like you even more after hearing that."

"That's good. I was never sure if you liked me at all."

"Can I be honest with you, Sarah?"

"I won't listen to anything other than the truth," she said with a superior look.

"At first I thought you to be a little too sure of yourself, if you know what I mean."

"I do, PJ. And now for more truth: I think I need counselling."

She hung her head and he laughed while leaning back into the hardness of the stylish couch.

"You're certainly not boring, Sarah. I'll say that."

That evening proved to PJ that Sarah was highly intelligent, caring, and as his granddad had said, one of the funniest ladies he'd ever met. He was still a little disappointed that she'd refused to let him in on the joke she'd shared with Tarni, about the nymphomaniac and the kleptomaniac. And Tarni's problems were barely mentioned, as every time he brought up the subject, Sarah steered the conversation away.

By twelve o'clock, PJ excused himself, before kissing Sarah goodnight. A little let down that PJ's passionate kiss hadn't led to an hour or two of bliss, Sarah decided to play it cool. She didn't want to lay pressure on this dreamt about opportunity. After wishing him 'sweet dreams, she closed the door, feeling confident she'd spend more time in his company.

Chapter 7

Days turned into weeks and still no one had come forward to identify the young Aboriginal man found dead on Glenelg beach. And then one evening, Adam phoned his mother to ask if Tarni was home – she was.

At first, he spoke on a bright note. "How are you, Tarni and are you still enjoying your work with the horses?"

"Yes thanks, Adam."

"Well that's good, I'm happy for you." Then he lowered his voice. "Have you heard anything from Blue Boy? I ask, because the last I heard, he was on his way to Adelaide to see you. I'm sorry if he's turned up and has been a problem, Tarni but there was no stopping him. I warned him, that if he caused you any trouble, I would have the law onto him, and they'd send him back straight away. I know I should have rung you sooner but knowing Blue Boy, I thought he was probably all talk about going to Adelaide. I've phoned Mum twice and asked if Blue had turned up there and she said no, she hadn't seen him. Now I've heard there's an un-known Aboriginal man who was found drowned off Glenelg beach. I have to ask you Tarni. Did Blue Boy come and see you at the stables?"

An emphatic, "No," shot back.

Adam couldn't help but feel the dead man was Blue Boy and he was a little put off with Tarni's blunt reply.

"Well Tarni, do you think you could go to the police anyway and tell them what I've just told you? They may ask you to identify the body. It won't be nice, but at least we'll know one way or the other if it's Blue Boy."

Adam waited for an answer; there was none. "I just can't imagine why he wouldn't go and see you, Tarni. He looked up to you. I'm sorry I haven't spoken to you sooner, but as I said, Blue Boy was always threatening to leave. He'd forever say he was going to live in a big city, then he'd just go walk about in the bush and return a few weeks later."

Once again, Adam waited for her reply.

"Tarni, are you listening?"

"Yes, I'm listening. But I don't want to go and look at dead bodies. And it doesn't really matter anyway. Blue Boy had no one who cared for him. He was just a troublemaker."

"Tarni, he's a human being and he loved you. Won't you please go to the police? If you don't, I'll have to fly down and identify the body. It'll probably be a waste of time. Time, I don't really have. I'm still hoping Blue Boy turns up, so I won't have to worry anymore."

"Alright, Adam. I'll go tomorrow morning, after work. I'll phone you from the police station, that's if they let me use the phone," she said sarcastically.

Tarni had no intention of going to the police and thought Adam would be none the wiser when she phoned him later and lied. She'd say, she viewed the body and it was not Blue Boy. What she hadn't counted on was Adam phoning the Adelaide police first thing in the morning and telling them his story. He added that Tarni would be coming to see them by mid-morning, maybe a bit later. The detective in charge said he'd wait until three o'clock and if Tarni hadn't shown up by then, he'd pay her a visit. Come three o'clock Detective Frank drove to PJ's stables.

PJ noticed the police car drive up and went to meet the detective whom he already knew.

"Hello, Paul. What brings you here? After some winning tips are you, mate?" PJ thrust his hand forward. Detective Frank, a tall man with a serious streak shook it.

"I hear you're doing pretty well at this training caper, PJ. I backed you're first winner for our punters club, well done. I suppose it's a silly question, but do you really like training horses more than being a lawyer?"

"Of course I do. Nobody could tempt me to go back to the law. Now, to what do I owe the pleasure?"

"I had a phone call from an Adam Stenning. Do you know him?"

"I know his mother, June Stenning. Why?"

"Well, Adam tells me the young woman who works for you, Tarni, may know something about the Aboriginal bloke who was found dead on the beach at Glenelg."

"She's never mentioned it to me, but I'll go and get her. You can ask her yourself."

Tarni, when being questioned about not showing up at the police station to view the body, looked directly at Detective Frank.

"I didn't go because I had too much work to do. We have ten new horses in the stable. I didn't have the time and I don't think this has anything to do with me. I haven't seen Blue Boy for over two years. I can't imagine how it could be him."

She was convincing. However, Detective Frank thought it best if she went to the morgue with him. He turned to PJ.

"Can you do without Tarni for an hour or so, PJ?"

"Yes of course, Paul."

"This won't take long, Miss. What's your surname?"

"Windsor, my name is Tarni Windsor."

"Well, at least your identification of the body will let us know whether it's your friend or not, Miss Windsor."

The sterile emptiness of the corridor sent a pulse of anxiety through Tarni's stomach. She sensed which door they would open to reveal Blue Boy. She felt his presence, even before she'd identified his bloated corpse. Then the vision of his smiling face appeared, and memories of him following her everywhere at the mission, tugging on her jeans, wanting her attention. She'd shun him. How could she, he just needed a little kindness – a friend. Tarni felt responsible for the way he'd turned out. An avalanche of guilt swallowed her. When finally she stood over Blue Boys dead body her stomach convulsed.

"I feel sick," she said, just before vomiting all over the floor. Detective Frank led her to the nearest bathroom.

"You can freshen up in here, Miss Windsor, and then I need to ask you some more questions."

After Tarni regained her composure, she answered his questions convincingly, especially when becoming emphatic about not seeing Blue Boy since living at the mission. Satisfied with her answers, Detective Frank drove her back to the stables. PJ approached the car.

"Are you all right, Tarni? Did you know him?" PJ asked.

Detective Frank took PJ aside.

"It's been pretty traumatic for Tarni. At this stage there doesn't appear to be any suspicious circumstances. She's free to go."

Tarni hurried past PJ and ran into Volunteers stable. PJ followed and stood watching Tarni cuddle the horse's neck while she sobbed. He felt touched to witness such vulnerability.

"Come here, Tarni, and let's talk about it. I want to help you?"

As tears streamed down Tarni's cheek, she sniffed and shook her head.

"I knew him, PJ, that's all. I'll be alright." Volunteer rubbed his nose on her shirt and snorted, seeming to know his mate had a problem.

"Well at least you have someone other than me to confide in. Volee knows you're upset."

"Of course he does. He knows what I'm thinking." After saying that she smiled a little.

"That's better, Tarni. It must have been a real shock for you."

"If everything's done, can I go home now PJ?

"Of course. I'll drive you."

"No, I need to walk. Thank you anyway."

On Tarni's return home, Mrs. Stenning offered compassion, consoling her with gentle words and held her to her chest before she watched Tarni walk slumped shoulders into her room. Then she phoned Adam.

"I'm afraid Tarni is in shock, Adam. The dead man was Blue Boy. I've given her half a sleeping tablet to hopefully calm her down.

"Please give Tarni my regards, Mum and tell her I hope she gets over this soon."

*

Tarni never failed to keep her weekly appointment with Sarah. Every Monday at eleven am, she would travel by bus to Sarah's office and look forward to finding solace in this woman's humour and wisdom. But ever since Sarah had been keeping close company with PJ, Tarni had closed up and treated Sarah with contempt. In return, Sarah found Tarni's attitude off-putting. She was now concerned that the steps forward they'd taken together would be all for nothing. This Monday's appointment came after the Blue Boy incident, so Sarah approached Tarni gently.

"How are you feeling Tarni? Do you need to talk about your friend who died?"

"I feel fine. I've only come here today to tell you I don't need you anymore. I'm all better." Tarni spoke through a strained smile, her lips pulled tight across her teeth.

Sarah felt her frustration building, especially with being so close to having Tarni confess all about the Robbo business. Sarah was now being told to 'go stick it'. Tarni had changed the rules in one grand sweep. Silence between the pair echoed like a million cicadas – deafening.

"Okay ,Tarni, let's get straight to the point. To the real reason why you've changed your attitude towards me and why you've closed up. I think you've always been in love with PJ and my close relationship with him has caused this rift between us. I think we should work on this or you'll suffer, no matter which way you turn." Sarah softened when she noticed Tarni slump in the chair.

"I must say though; I do know PJ cares deeply for you. He admires you,

Tarni, and he's probably the best friend you've ever had."

Tarni sat up, glaring at Sarah.

"My mother was the best friend I ever had! And those bastards took her away from me and she died because of it! Everything I love is taken away from me!"

Sarah realised then she'd only just skimmed the surface.

"Tell me about it, Tarni. How did you feel the day they dragged you away from your mother?"

Tarni clenched her fist while glaring at Sarah.

"I've told you before!"

"You have, Tarni. But not everything. You have to dig a lot deeper and tell me exactly what it was like. This is where your problem begins. I want you to scream, bash the pillow, do what you have to, but let it all out. I want you to tell me how badly it hurts. Then maybe I can help you heal."

Tarni stood and paced the room, her mind catapulted back to that dreadful day. The day she'd tried so hard to forget. And now it all came flooding back like a tsunami of horror. She yelled.

"I wanted to be bigger, so I could kill them! I still want to kill them! I felt helpless, weak, useless. I couldn't understand why anyone would take me away from my mother. I loved her so much." As her crying became uncontrollable; she spoke between sobs. "I loved her. I loved my mother, so why did they take me away from her? Why? I hate them. I hate them!"

Sarah felt her pain. She held Tarni close, her own tears welling.

"I don't know, Tarni. I don't know why they took you away from your mother, except I know they think it's for the best. They think it's important for the future generations of Aborigines to fit into the white society. But it's not fair, Tarni. I know it's not fair. It's not the right thing to do."

Sarah allowed her tears to flow along with Tarni's and together they sobbed, holding each other tight. When their sobbing subsided, Sarah said with conviction.

"I have my own views on how we should begin helping our indigenous people. And I'm bloody sure, taking them away from their birth mothers is not the way."

After Tarni had calmed, Sarah's made a suggestion.

"You could help me, Tarni. Its young people like you who've suffered from the ridiculous assumption that we white people should take part-Aboriginal children away from their families for their own good. I tell you, it makes me so angry. If I was you, I would have felt the same way. I'd feel like killing someone.

But it's done, it's over. Now you have to heal, so you can help me, help you and the future generations of Aboriginal children to be free and proud of who they are."

Tarni wiped the tears from her eyes.

"What can I do, Sarah?"

"You can join me in my crusade. I'm going to do my very best to have things turned around for the rights of the Aboriginal people in this country. I'll begin as soon as I get all my facts together and gather witnesses who won't be afraid to stand up and tell it like it was and still is."

Sarah held Tarni close again. "What do you say, Tarni. Will you help me put a stop to their un-lawful act?"

"Yes, I will, but what about the horses? Can I still do my horse work?" Tarni asked still snivelling.

Sarah laughed. Of course you can. I'll only need you every so often, not all the time."

Sarah felt maybe she'd gone far enough today, and she should leave their meeting with a final embrace.

"I feel for you, Tarni and I want to help you. If you need to speak with me at any time, please call me." Now would you like to talk about anything else, or do you think we've said enough for today?"

Tarni left Sarah's arms and walked to look out of the window, keeping her back to Sarah.

"I'm sorry for how I've treated you, Sarah. I thought I loved PJ, but now I know he's more like my big brother. And he's over ten years older than me." Tarni shrugged her shoulders. "Maybe when I first met him, I had a crush on him, especially when I knew he liked and respected me. I knew he'd never love me as a man loves a woman. But I lived in hope" Tarni turned and smiled, raising her head high. "He actually saved my life. So, I have to love him for that. I'm happy for you both Sarah, really I am."

"Well, I'm pleased we have one less issue to resolve. Let's make a deal, Tarni. We'll stay friends forever."

Tarni raised another smile. "It's a deal!"

Later, that day, PJ found Tarni in the stables singing along with the radio. She swayed to the music, while brushing a contended Volunteer. PJ stood to watch before he coughed and Tarni turned.

"PJ, that's naughty! How long have you been standing there?" She laughed. "I can't sing or dance I know, but I like to, that's why I do it when nobody's watching."

"You're a better singer than I am, Tarni!"

Tarni's finely arched brows furrowed. "I thought you had a famous aunt, who was an opera star. So you should be able to sing."

"I do, but she is not a blood relation and that's a long story. I don't have time to explain it. But one day I will, or better still, my sister Sally has written our family history. You'll be able to read all about us when it's published."

"I can't wait."

"Good, I'll give you a first edition, signed and delivered. Now tell me, why so happy?"

She went on to tell him all about how Sarah was beginning a massive crusade against the so-called authorities and their right to remove half-caste Aboriginal children from their families. He listened and felt there was no doubt that he'd be dragged into the battle. Maybe not intentionally, but he knew at some stage Sarah would ask for his help with the legalities. And of course, for his experience when in the Northern Territory. There he'd witnessed a half-caste boy being dragged away from his grandmother – screaming. This memory would always un-settle PJ. His compassion doubled for Tarni, on hearing about the pain she'd suffered from having the same experience.

To Tarni, PJ seemed a little reluctant to take up her happiness. He just sat nodding to her enthusiastic spiel on how they'd gather their evidence and then how they'd approach their battle. Without asking, she assumed by PJ's reaction that he didn't want to become too involved. With Tarni still in a state of joy about what she and Sarah were hopefully going to achieve, PJ felt he needed to bring her down to earth a little.

"I'm on your side all the way Tarni, but it will be a long hard fight and I only hope your crusade doesn't take you away from your horse work too often, especially now. It seems we are about to have an equine population explosion!"

"Really, PJ? How come?"

"I suppose it has something to do with the horse you're brushing and of course our strike rate is very healthy. It's ninety percent runners to winners at this stage. I know it's not hard to have a high strike rate, when we have only six horses racing but it's started people talking. I must admit I have to pinch myself sometimes. I think we've been more than lucky, Tarni. I feel we've been blessed. But we shouldn't get too cocky, I'm sure there'll be some tough times ahead. However, our winning streak has brought us some fame and prosperity. And now we have to look for a much bigger complex. We have to expand our stables!"

Tarni's joy was incomparable to anything she'd felt before. This wonderful news, plus the thought of helping Sarah with what Tarni would have loved to have done all by herself, was overwhelming. It was an impossible dream she would never be able to have achieved on her own. And now, realising she'd helped PJ establish himself as the up and coming trainer in South Australia, was the ultimate. Also, PJ referring to 'we' all the time, gave her a solid feeling of self-worth, something she'd never owned before.

"This is amazing, PJ. How many horses will you have to train and where are we going to fit them all? You'll have to employ more strappers and I'm a good judge of character for that job." Tarni smiled and paused a moment before she said cheekily, "After all, I chose you as my friend, didn't I?"

Her laughter turned to hysterics. PJ embraced her to prevent her from falling down laughing. She stopped immediately when she felt his heart against hers. She looked into his eyes.

"I do love you PJ, I told Sarah that today. And we spoke about it. I haven't been very nice to her since you two have been going out together. But don't worry, I've worked it out now. I love you because you've been so kind to me, you're like my big brother. I love you because you are good looking." Her full lips closed into a crooked smile. "I know that sounds silly, but I love a lot of beautiful things, do you know what I mean?"

She left his arms and sat on a bail of straw.

"I love you, PJ, because you've given me the opportunity to do what I have always wanted to do; spend my life with horses. I know you've shown me love, in a brotherly sort of way and that's all it will ever be. I'm growing up now and I can accept you loving Sarah as a woman, especially since I love her to. Sarah and I are going to be friends forever and together we will fight for justice. But I will never leave you, PJ. I'll always be here to help you." Her mood had changed to sombre by the time he answered.

"I've always known you had a crush on me, Tarni and it was hard for me to try and help you, without it seeming like I had the same feelings. God knows you're beautiful, but you're so much younger than me. One day, you'll find a man who will adore you and want to share the rest of his life with you…"

"Actually, PJ, I've met my husband," she said looking up with those big brown eyes in such sincerity. He stood, pinned to the ground – shocked. This made it even funnier to Tarni.

"Yes, it's Volunteer. He and I are going to be married, not that we'll breed of course, but I think he is a fine fellow. I love him, and we'll stay together forever!"

PJ picked up a towel and threw it at her. Tarni ducked while laughing.

"Okay, PJ, tell me where are we going to put all these extra horses?"

"I've been thinking about it and because I like both the country and the beach, I'm going to buy a property near the ocean, say about forty miles south east of Adelaide. There's a place called Seaford Rise and I've driven there many times. I've seen some really nice properties not too far from the ocean."

Tarni's 'whoopee' was so loud, Volunteer pulled away from his tie-up and walked briskly into his stall, standing with his head in the corner.

"You don't think he's trying to tell us something? Do you, Tarni?"

"No, he'll be fine. He's just a creature of habit. If things get out of sequence throughout the day, he sulks a bit. Don't worry. He'll love running free in a paddock and having a daily roll in the sand after he works."

Over the next few weeks, PJ set out to find the perfect property. It had to accommodate fifty or more horses with room to expand. He needed day yards, spelling paddocks and ideally, a railed work track. If there wasn't one already there, he'd build one to meet his requirements.

This vision was almost fulfilled, when PJ found a lovely hundred-acre property near his chosen area, Seaford Rise. This was a mere forty-minute drive from Adelaide. He was also excited to have found the right undulation on the property to create his ideal work-track.

Before he'd found the land, and while searching for it, he'd left Tarni in charge of the Morphettville stables, including the strappers and riders. Tarni was proving she was not only a horse wizard, but she was capable of handling any problem on her own. Not only had she excelled in running their three small lots of stables at Morphettville, but she was also a great help to Sarah in tracking down Aboriginal youths who'd experienced bad, if not horrific times, when living with their white foster families.

Chapter 8

It was now November 1958, one year since PJ had brought Tarni to Adelaide. In that time, the Northern Territory police had not found a trace of Robbo. Granddad Jonathon had turned eighty-seven and still held a sound intellect and a slim physic. He had also remained in touch with the sergeant in charge of Tarni's case. Jonathon remained suspicious about what may have happened to Robbo, but he chose not to worry PJ or Tarni with his assumptions.

Jonathon had enjoyed conversation with Tarni at various race meetings but had not received his wish to see her ride track work. So, as a birthday present from PJ, Jonathon was collected from 'Wildflowers', in a hired chauffeur driven Bentley, (his favourite car) then driven to Patrick's property to watch Tarni ride work on one of uncle Angus's horses. Jonathon also owned a share in that particular horse. Luckily, it was a warm November morning.

"The old bones seem to move a lot better in the warmth, PJ. Did you notice how easily I climbed those steps?"

"Yes, I did, Granddad, and I'm impressed. Are you still taking Doctor Lui's medicine for Arthritis?"

Jonathon almost glared at PJ.

"Of course I am. I wouldn't be able to walk without it."

From the best advantage point in the small grandstand they'd built, Jonathon could watch his two-year-old filly, 'The Bees Knees,' have her final gallop before racing at Victoria Park on the following Saturday. It was no secret that Jonathon admired 'Young Tarni', as he called her, and was duly impressed with her riding ability. She rode 'The Bees Knees' in company with another horse, ridden by a male jockey. By doing so, she made that jockey seem inferior. The boy reefed and pulled on his horse's mouth, while Tarni sat still and calm, seemingly in tune with her mount. The filly pulled up without a blow and Patrick declared her fit and ready to win.

Pleased with what Tarni and PJ reported to him about his filly, Jonathon then enjoyed a guided tour of the property. He sat as comfortably as he could, in the old, well-used motorised buggy he'd gifted to PJ. Jonathon was shown the number one barn, which stabled twenty horses. These horses, Patrick explained, were the ones racing at the moment. A pitched ceiling, high above the stables, enabled a breeze to travel through and expel the hot air in extreme weather. The stalls were roomy and cool, although snug enough for a cold winter's night. Barn number two was built the same way. It held twenty up-and-coming horses that would be ready to race within the next month. The horses that were being pre-trained stayed in day yards with shelters, but sometimes there was an odd horse, already racing, that preferred to be trained from the yards.

"I've seen enough, PJ. It all looks excellent and your horse people all seem very efficient. Now, I would really love a cup of tea and perhaps bacon and eggs. This country air has made me hungry."

PJ always had to laugh at Jonathon's reference to strappers as 'horse people'. He'd even heard him use the phrase in court and he'd argued with him.

"You shouldn't label people, Granddad."

"Not at all, PJ. I'm merely stating a fact. People who work with horses are a special breed. It's like calling a born Aboriginal an Aborigine. A horse person is born a horse person, and therefore will always be a horse person." PJ could never win the argument.

PJ's solid brick home was comfortable, without being palatial. His mother, Addy, had on occasions tried to intervene with her suggestions about re- decorating. However, whenever she mentioned it, PJ would say. 'No thanks, Mum. Sarah is planning to do it.' This statement was beginning to wear thin with Addy, as Sarah's re-decorating had not yet happened, neither had their romance blossomed into a wedding proposal. Addy thought perhaps it may have been Sarah's 'dog with a bone' attitude, with the stolen Aboriginal children cause that seemed to consume all her passion. PJ had found himself on many occasions helping Sarah to bed in an exhausted state. Then, he'd drive the forty miles home to his farm by the sea that he'd named Volunteer.

Every morning at ten, the entire staff at Volunteer, would stop work to enjoy a hearty breakfast. The youngest stable-hand, Jenny, who lived next door to PJ, had asked if there was a job available for her mum, Dawn. PJ happily offered Dawn his job of company cook. She would make breakfast for everyone each day and then clean PJ's home. She'd also prepare an evening meal for PJ if he wasn't staying in Adelaide with Sarah.

At the back of his home, which over-looked the barns, PJ had added a large gauzed-in veranda. It contained a long table and bench seats, which sat around twenty people. A wood-fuelled stove was situated at one end and this is where Dawn would cook. This was also where she'd prepare afternoon tea. Hot scones with homemade blackberry jam and served with freshly clotted cream was everyone's favourite. A newly designed electric refrigerator kept bottles of tank water cool during the hot summer months, to the relief of all.

While enjoying his bacon and eggs, Jonathon was interested in what the young 'horse people' had to say. He found it a welcome change from the intense discussions and demanding work of the law. Before he left, he said to the group:

"I want to thank all of you for the good work you do on my horse and your fine company this morning. Maybe in my next life we shall meet again, as I too would like to have a crack at being a horse person. Perhaps even training a winner or two, maybe three!" He raised his hat in the air and bowed. "I hope to see you again on Saturday, in the winner's circle no doubt!"

PJ helped him into the chauffeur-driven Bentley and kissed him goodbye.

"I'll see you this evening Granddad for your birthday bash. Take a nap so you'll have the energy to dance."

"I am still able to dance without taking a nap beforehand, thank you very much young man." PJ closed the door and Jonathon rolled down the window.

"Try to talk young Tarni into coming this evening, PJ, there's a good lad."

When PJ and Tarni entered the marble foyer of Wildflowers that evening, the first-person PJ spoke with was his sister, Sally. She'd arrived a minute before them.

"Hi Sis. You know Tarni don't you?"

Sally smiled sweetly and held out her hand.

"Of course I do. Hello, Tarni. You look absolutely beautiful this evening and I'm so pleased PJ has finally persuaded you to join a family celebration. Especially this evening, as I know Granddad thinks a great deal of you. I hear you and Sarah are making real headway with your crusade too. I've been out of journalism for many years now, but I still have some powerful contacts. So, when you ladies are ready, let me know and I'll pull some strings!"

Tarni let out a sigh of relief. She had felt inferior to this family, who were all such high achievers and academics. Although the Darcy's never wore their status on their sleeves, so to speak, they were what she would call a high class yet loving and humble family.

"Thank you for making me feel so welcome, Sally. I hope you don't mind me asking but PJ tells me you're writing a book about the Darcy family and it's to be published soon. I just can't wait to read it..."

Sally, although not meaning to, cut Tarni a little short.

"I don't really like to talk about it. Not until I have the book finished and I'm satisfied that all family members are comfortable with what I've written. Then, and only then, will it be published. I hope you understand, Tarni.

"Oh, I am sorry. I knew I shouldn't have said anything. I truly wish I'd not opened my mouth."

Sally took Tarni by the hand.

"Please don't be sorry, Tarni. I can assure you; you will be one of the first to have a signed copy. Now, let's go and join the party, shall we? I'm so happy you're here." Sally squeezed Tarni's hand and led her into the main living room.

Sarah had taken the afternoon off to have her hair done, nails manicured, and her magnificent long legs waxed. She stood out as the most attractive woman in the room and also the tallest – she was six feet tall. Tarni stood beside her and waited until she'd finished her conversation with an elderly gentleman.

"Tarni, what a lovely surprise. I wasn't sure if PJ would be able to talk you into coming." Sarah gave a quick glance around the room and caught PJ's eye, then gave him the thumbs up.

"Tarni Windsor, I'd like you to meet Mr Henry Beer QC. Henry is on our side with the battle and although we perhaps should not be talking shop tonight, I have to tell you, Henry is going to help us. He is completely against what has been allowed to happen. And now I will shut up, because I'm sure I'm beginning to bore everyone with my Jonny-one-note approach to our cause." She threw a charming smile at Henry. Isn't that so?"

"Not at all Sarah, I'd be happy to stand here all evening, admiring your beauty and listening to you preach your sermon over and over. I'd never be bored." He then turned to Tarni. "I am very pleased to meet you, Miss Windsor. I wish you well and I do hope I'm able to help you with your worthy cause. We will of course, converse over many lunches in the future."

"Oh, you are a naughty boy," Sarah said. "I can see you simply want to spend more time with two beautiful young women. But you will have to work hard for the privilege my dear, Henry!" Sarah then excused herself along with Tarni.

"I think we should say hello to the birthday boy now. Come on, Tarni."

Jonathon sat on his beloved tapestry chair in the middle of the room with Margie alongside him. The two looked a picture of serenity.

Sarah almost pushed Tarni through the throng of people to be at his side. His eyes lit up and his hand reached out.

"Oh, Young Tarni. You finally dragged yourself away from those demanding thoroughbreds to come and join an old man at his birthday party. I've been telling everyone about you, and how much talent you have when it comes to horses. I hope you're standing right alongside me when 'The Bees Knees' wins on Saturday. We can cheer her home together!"

Suddenly Tarni felt overwhelmed, expecting someone from her past to come into the room and burst her bubble: to call her a black bitch, or a bloody show-off, or to fondle her, or even try to rape her and then treat her as a nobody. But in the past, she'd never give in. She'd run, she'd fight, and she'd always escape, until they found her and degraded her again. She held back tears, thinking of how she'd battled to survive all the abuse from the so called 'do gooders', whose evil hid behind a charade of honour. But now, yes now, she was accepted into this wonderful family. They all knew her background, they all knew who she was, and they still liked her – genuinely liked her. Tarni had stopped calling herself an Aboriginal and nobody in Adelaide seemed to think otherwise. Was PJ right? Did she look like everyone else who wasn't black?

Her mind drifted into a time warp. She felt confused. What should she believe? Were these lovely people a figment of her imagination? Was this a dream? How could this have happened to the girl, who not long ago was being forced into the path of a crocodile to be eaten? She was the girl who'd almost bitten Robbo's penis off before he attempted to murder her. Her thoughts began spinning like an evil web, turning her head so fast she lost control of her senses. Jonathon's voice seemed to drift far away, and the room began to spin before she passed out.

When she woke, Sarah was sitting beside her, and PJ stood smiling.

"You haven't been eating enough, Tarni, have you? I've told you this will happen if you don't eat." Tarni felt grateful that PJ had found an excuse for her embarrassing display.

"Yes, you're right, PJ. I'm alright now though. I'm so sorry, I feel embarrassed. Have you all finished dinner yet?"

They laughed before Sarah answered.

"No, Tarni. We've been waiting for you to wake up. Granddad Jonathon insisted. He went mad on PJ for not feeding you enough. So, come on; we'd better feed you up now or we'll be in strife."

The dinner was amazing. Tarni had never dreamt food could taste so good. And the conversation was positive, full of hope for all Australians. It seemed she was floating on a cloud. Never could she have imagined being amongst such worldly, refined people.

On their way home, Tarni rested her head on the car door and visualised other evenings spent in the same company. She would never allow her mind to drift back to her past. That is, not until she was asked to do so in a court of law, when she and Sarah would produce the final evidence needed for their human rights case. She drifted off with a smile on her face.

Jonathon's birthday celebrations had been extended to the following Saturday at Victoria Park races, where he watched with Tarni alongside him his filly, 'The Bees Knees,' win with ease. The celebrations began immediately after the race and continued into the evening.

Jonathon stood to make a toast. "I want you all to know my son Angus has finally bred an Oaks filly. Here's to Angus for his good judgement in horse flesh, and to PJ for his fine training effort!"

By the end of the celebrations, 'The Bees Knees' in the owner's minds at least, had not only won the Adelaide Oaks but the Melbourne Oaks as well. This could not happen until the following year, as the filly was only two years old and she needed to be three to win the Oaks.

As usual, Tarni did not join in the festivities. She returned to the farm and tended to the horses. She felt no envy, just happy with her lot. However, the desire to become the first professional female jockey to don a set of silks was now becoming a restless need.

PJ had kept his promise and approached the Chairman of the Board of the SAJC. He'd put forward a thorough and intelligent case. He assured them, many other trainers would be more than willing to give their female track riders the opportunity to ride in races. But as expected, the old, stodgy and most probably chauvinistic Committee men, strongly disagreed with this preposterous suggestion. They whacked PJ's attempt on the head with a sledgehammer.

"At least you tried PJ," a dejected Tarni said as they walked away together from the main office of the SAJC.

Tarni had waited in the hallway with nervous anticipation, even though PJ had told her that in his opinion she would not be permitted to ride in races. However, he was able to lift her spirits by promising her she could ride in picnic and amateur races on an older horse that he'd purchased in a tried horse sale. The seven-year-old, 'Aussie King', had been an old war horse in his day but was sold due to soundness problems. Tarni had nursed him back to health with lots of swimming and long slow work along the beach. He went on from there to win a couple of country cups for PJ, and although not regaining his former glory, he seemed happy enough to keep on racing for Tarni.

This gave her renewed vigour. She took to being an armature jockey with passion, presenting her very serious self in the parade ring, wearing racing silks and carrying her whip with a determined look on her pretty face. It took PJ all his composure not to laugh, but he played along and then watched as Tarni produced her magic in the races. The old horse loved her and Tarni seemed to be one step ahead of the other riders, especially when it came to knowing what pace to travel at, where to have her horse in the running, and then how to get a clear passage in the straight. PJ always praised her.

"Well done, Tarni. Great win! You simply outsmarted the lot of them, and I reckon old Aussie would burst his boiler for you."

This was what Patrick had said on most occasions, until the day-old Aussie collapsed and dropped dead in his paddock, seemingly of a heart attack. Tarni was inconsolable for the next month.

And now, after nearly six months had passed since her first attempt at becoming a professional jockey, she asked PJ if they could try again, since there were many more female track riders and even more becoming amateur riders?

Her wish for this had almost outweighed her eagerness to begin the court hearing on their human rights case, beginning on 20 February 1959.

Soon after, Patrick returned one Sunday afternoon, still slightly hung over from the past evenings celebrations. He went to Tarni's bungalow and knocked on the door.

"Come in, PJ."

She knew it was him because he was the only person who ever knocked on her door. Tarni had remained socially aloof from the young people who worked there. She was amused at PJ's sullen look and the bags under his eyes, not to mention his slumped posture.

"Boy, you must have really drunk a barrel last night, PJ. Here, take a seat."

He rubbed his forehead, pushed his legs forward and hung his arms over the side of the chair.

"Tarni, my dear girl, I promise there will be no more celebrating for me. In future, I'll return straight home after our wins because if these celebrations keep up, I'm either going to turn into an alcoholic, or die of exhaustion. Which brings me to the point. I need a break and so does Sarah. That's why I've come to ask you a favour. We'd like to take a holiday together, so do you think you could cope without me?"

While he spoke, Tarni mixed a glass of ice water with a squeeze of lemon, handed it to PJ and then sat down opposite.

"Sure, I can handle it, don't worry, PJ. We have some really good kids working here now and you know that new boy you hired last month, Craig, well I really like him. He's keen as mustard and I reckon he'd make a good jockey, but he says he can't because his mother would go crazy with worry. His dad died when Craig was five years old. Apparently, he was killed in a horse accident. Craig said it's taken him three years to talk his mum into letting him work with horses. She didn't even know he could ride. He had to sneak off to a friend's place, so he could ride his horse."

She grinned cheekily at PJ, showing the dimples in her cheeks.

"I tell you what, if you do a deal with me I'll let you go on your holiday." PJ raised one brow and waited. "When you come home, PJ, I want you to have another go at the SAJC Committee about allowing women jockeys."

"Oh Tarrrnni", PJ said slowly. "I think you'd have more chance going for a trainer's licence. I've got a better idea. Why don't we wait for the old codgers to retire from the committee and then I think you may just have a chance. I promise I will apply for you then, okay?"

Tarni sat sulking, kicking a sock along the floor as PJ stood.

Tarni finally responded to PJ's suggestion.

"Okay, I suppose you're right. It'd be a waste of time going over it all again with the same old brick wall mentality gang."

He burst out laughing, "Where on earth did you learn that expression?"

"From your fiancé, Mr Darcy."

Patrick stopped laughing. "I haven't asked Sarah to marry me."

"Well you should. You're never going to find a better woman, 'Sir'."

PJ wasn't going to get caught up in that conversation. He quickly moved forward, then paused in the doorway.

"Perhaps you should think about going away on a holiday too, Tarni. When we come back that is, not before. I have a friend who trains racehorses in New Zealand. I reckon you'd love it over there. You could stay with him and his family for a while. Maybe you could bring us back a Melbourne Cup winner?" He didn't wait for her answer but left without banging the door. But Tarni thought about it.

PJ hurried to telephone Sarah.

"It's okay, Sarah. Book the tickets. We have approval from the boss." He then crashed on his bed and slept until four the next morning.

Sarah, although exhausted, started planning their holiday. They'd talked about going to Hawaii, mainly because PJ had distant relatives there and he'd like to visit his grandmother Bernadette's grave. He'd told her.

"It's no good telling you the long and involved story of my mixed heritage Sarah, it's far too complicated. You can read my sisters book when it's published."

Chapter 9

When the first day of December arrived, Sarah could hardly believe she was about to have PJ all to herself for two whole weeks. Four days of this would include flying to and from Hawaii, but she didn't mind.

"What a beautiful feeling," Sarah said as the plane ascended. PJ smiled, admiring her perfect profile. He held her hand up to his lips and kissed it tenderly.

"Now that's an even better feeling, PJ," Sarah said as she snuggled into his shoulder.

"You know you remind me a lot of my Aunty Clare. She's a very funny lady," said PJ.

"I know. I've had many a good laugh with Clare. And your mother has told me stories that would curl your hair and make your beautiful brown eyes go cross-eyed."

PJ sat silently, thinking how he'd now have the time to really get to know Sarah. Their busy lifestyles and the pressures they'd continuously put themselves under, prevented them so often from the love making they enjoyed. He smiled at the humorous memories. Sometimes when he'd hold Sarah tight and was about to kiss her passionately, she'd push him away and ask in all seriousness.

"Are you sure you like my hair straight, PJ, and not frizzy? Because I can let it go frizzy now I've got you where I want you. And I'd really love to wear my bifocals again. I can't see a bloody thing without them."

He'd laugh but be frustrated at the same time. She'd then use force to seduce him. Other times Sarah would be soft and sensuous, not saying a word before she'd cry into his chest. PJ had told her often enough, 'You're certainly not boring Sarah.'

At this moment, glancing sideways at her, he asked himself. Could I be happy spending the rest of my life with Sarah? Would our two worlds combine well enough to make it work? Did she want children?

He knew he did and not too far into the future either. His racehorse business was succeeding, and he was completely content with the choice he'd made. However, another issue may play a major part in their future as husband and wife. And that was, Sarah was consumed with her human rights war. Would she relent, if she lost the case, would she then drive herself mad chasing after something that in her lifetime may never happen? PJ sighed, relaxed in his seat and made a silent pledge. I'll shelve all my worries until the end of our holiday. I will enjoy Sarah's love, her beauty and her humour and I'll give her, my undivided attention and see what happens.

The flight had been smooth, including their descent onto the tarmac in Fiji. This was the first of the stopovers needed for refuelling. While the servicemen worked on the aircraft, the passengers were transported to a small village not too far away, where the indigenous people had prepared a feast.

Flamed torches lit their way, and they breathed in the heady perfume of frangipani. Tiny land crabs crawled as a solid mass across the ground, their shells crunching beneath the feet of the tourists. When closing in on the unmistakable aroma of pineapple and coconuts, the added aroma of roasting pork made their taste buds tingle. It became a night to remember and although the time was two am, PJ and Sarah sat crossed legged on the ground wide awake and welcoming the food with gusto.

Finally, their plane took off again soon after dawn and after their next short-change over, they landed safely in Hawaii. It was an amazing welcome by a group of smiling islanders dancing and singing Hawaiian love songs. Sarah commented as a lei of frangipani was placed around her neck.

"It looks like your entire family has come to welcome us, PJ?"

"Yep, looks like it."

Pleased to be on the ground after a long flight, they sat like rag dolls in the back of the cab as it drove them to their hotel, 'The Royal Hawaiian.' When entering their luxurious joined rooms in the, 'pink building', as Sarah would refer to it for the rest of their stay, they looked at each other through tired eyes.

"A shower and then a nap. What do you say, PJ?"

He agreed.

From the moment they woke, their holiday reflected a honeymoon scenario. They ate like a king, and his Queen, feeding each other sensually until their desire for love overcame their hunger for food. They swam at dusk their bodies entwined and silhouetted by the orange glow of the setting sun, then walked hand in hand like lovers do. This was all done in-between visiting PJ's relatives, who were hard to leave, so welcoming were their embraces and great feasts. Though the most moving and sentimental moment was when PJ stood surrounded by his Hawaiian family and laid flowers on the graves of his grandparents, Bernadette and Barney. Tears flowed and stories untold came about, until it was way past time to wish them farewell.

The second last day of their amazing holiday had arrived and PJ didn't need to think twice about asking Sarah to marry him and of course he wanted to make it special. So, he'd searched out the hidden lagoon on his family's property, which was fed by an ever-flowing water-fall – perfect. It lay unchanged from when Bernadette had swum with Addy and her second husband Barnaby Stuart. PJ remembered what his mother Addy had told him about the day Barney first joined them there. Although Addy was only three at the time, she held a fond memory of Barney's gentleness. Barnaby later adopted Addy and she loved him with all her heart. PJ would now take Sarah to the same waterfall and propose marriage as Barany had.

After a leisurely breakfast on the balcony, on their final morning, PJ sat back in his chair and announced:

"I have a special place that I'd like to take you to, Sarah. I've left it until now for a special reason."

"Really, PJ? It all sounds very special. But what do you mean by special? Special as in you're going to buy a piece of property here, or special because this special place has meant something special to your ancestors?" He took no notice of her attempt at being funny.

"You'll see. I want it to be a special surprise."

Sarah fluttered her thick black eyelashes and flicked her long auburn hair behind her bare shoulder

"Okay. I have nothing else planned, only packing my suitcase ready to leave in the morning," she then faked crying into her napkin.

Confident that Sarah would say yes to his proposal, PJ had organised a private candle-lit dinner on their balcony for later. He'd also contracted a violinist to play for them and enhance the atmosphere.

After taking a leisurely drive, PJ parked the car, took Sarah by the hand and led her into the rain forest.

"You haven't been fooling me have you, PJ? You're not an axe murderer, are you? This place is a bit creepy."

Moments later, the scene took her breath away. A cascading waterfall offered an endless flow of fresh water into the deep blue lagoon. Regal palms spread their canopy over soft, delicate ferns and wild orchids found shelter amongst the moss-covered rocks.

"Oh my God this looks like the garden of Eden." Sarah said in amazement.

PJ looked on it with a dreamy faraway look.

"Yes, it does. I've been here only once before. A long time ago. It was on one of our rare visits, 'back home', as my mum still calls it. She grew up around here, until she was shipped off to Badminton Girls School in the UK when she was fourteen."

"Don't stop, PJ. I want to hear all about your family. I want both sides please, your mum's and your dad's."

"I'll tell you some of it but it's too long to tell you in a short time."

"For now, let's sit on this rock, PJ, and do what you can. I'm all ears."

He went on to unfold some of his family history, in particular how his father and mother had met on the docks of London. It was the day his father had arrived in England to attend Sandhurst Military College and PJ's mother, Addy, stood on the docks with a friend. PJ's eyes softened, as did his voice as he spoke.

"It was love at first sight they say. And I know their love will last a lifetime because they're still crazy about each other. This brings me to a question which I hope you will answer yes to, Sarah."

Sarah's eyes welled with tears; she was unable to contain her happiness.

"YES! Yes, I will marry you, PJ!"

"Ah hah," he said, "I got you. I was only going to ask if you would like to take a swim in the lagoon – naked!"

"You buggar, you were not! Tell me the truth or I'll drown you!"

He began stripping as he laughed.

"Come on then. Drown me and then you won't be able to marry me. Come on just try it!" He dived in with only his underpants on.

Sarah chose to undress slowly, playing the stripper, while PJ watched with anticipation. Floating in the water he admired her perfect body. So flawless were her long shapely legs, that perhaps they should be insured; her full perky breasts that he loved to savour and her long elegant fingers that she used to tease him into submission. When he threw his jocks at her, she stripped completely to his cheers of approval. She dived in and their two naked bodies clung together, their hearts beating in unison, as they slowly dissolved in bliss.

"Do you want children Sarah? That's one question I haven't asked you."

"Anything you want, PJ, I want. But yes, of course I want children. What about you?"

"All I can say is I hope after all my hard work on this holiday, you're pregnant."

"Oh, hard work was it?" Sarah said as she gave him a hard slap.

"Now, now. There'll be no domestic violence in our marriage thank you, Miss Brown, or I'll have you in court!"

"You can have me anywhere you like my darling, I'll even be taken on the kitchen floor!"

"That won't be necessary," and his kiss at that moment was one she was not likely to forget, a perfect ending to their holiday.

*

PJ returned to a problem-free business. As usual, Tarni had held the fort well. She'd even managed to saddle up two winners out of the four starters in the past two weeks. PJ had purposely cut the racing numbers back, which he must remember to do each December, so he and Sarah could take a break.

And now they had a wedding to plan, but Sarah wanted to wait until after the court hearing in February. She felt Tarni needed a short break away, to be refreshed, ready to help her with the witnesses. At first the indigenous people had been shy in coming forth. 'Don't want to make more trouble, Miss,' is how they so aptly put it.

However, Sarah had explained to them:

"This case is based on trouble. It's mixed with deceit and lies, and you were the brunt of it all. You should be compensated, and an apology should be made. And no more children should be taken away from your families."

These were the issues Sarah and her barristers would be fighting for.

Not long after this, a family dinner was arranged by Sarah and Addy, to discuss the wedding. Addy was over the moon about it and felt they should begin to make plans immediately. She'd said to Sarah:

"It's obvious that you'll be far too busy to worry about the finer details of the wedding, so between your mother Mary and me, we will, with your approval of course, do most of the planning and the work. Is that alright with you my dear?"

Sometimes PJ wished his mother had continued being a specialist in plastic surgery. She had so much energy, too much for everybody's good sometimes. However, on this occasion he'd agreed that Sarah and he would be kept far too occupied to organise a wedding, so he appreciated his mother's help.

Sarah then stood and tinkled her glass at the noisy, excited gathering. This included the expansive Darcy family, and her parents, Mary and Wayne Brown.

"I'd like you all to know this. There is only one thing I am absolutely adamant about organising." Sarah paused until they all sat silent on the edge of their chairs. "MY WEDDING DRESS!"

Everyone cheered and raised their glasses.

Sarah then laughed before sculling her champagne.

"Come my darling, PJ, they can fight about the rest.

Let's take a stroll under the moonlight."

Jonathon clapped the loudest before he said to Patrick Snr.

"I'm so pleased I took the liberty of making PJ's first appointment with Sarah. I had a feeling they'd get along."

Chapter 10

Christmas came and went with a rush. The Darcy family had gathered as usual at 'Wildflowers' for lunch and although PJ joined them, by early evening he'd returned to his property. The young strappers and riders who lived and worked on the property were waiting for him to share a Christmas dinner. He was a popular boss.

They also admired Tarni for her horsemanship and her quiet way of explaining what to do and how to do it. If they did something wrong, she'd simply pull them aside and talk to them privately. She amazed even herself with how confident she'd become in dealing with all sorts of people. Maybe the fact that they'd never suspected she was an Aboriginal had something to do with it. This thought gave Tarni last minute doubts about having to expose her heritage in a court room. Having to tell the truth about who she was and what it was like being taken away from her mother. A large part of her wanted the past to be forgotten and for her life to remain as it was now. Tarni's only concern was that there were still many young, half-caste children being dragged away from their families, the same as she'd experienced. And her conscience would not allow her to let those children, and the future generations suffer.

PJ sat down with his staff that evening at the long table in the gauzed-in veranda and was served a Christmas dinner which was almost identical to what he'd eaten for lunch. He would not let this fact be known to his cook and housekeeper Dawn Turner, so upon finishing every morsel he turned to her.

"Thank you, Mrs Turner, the meal was delicious and now, I would like to show my gratitude to you and all the staff, for your loyalty and hard work."

PJ stood and walked over to the Christmas tree where he'd placed twelve identical boxes wrapped in the same red paper, all with green bows on top. He handed every staff member a box, including Mrs Turner. Inside their box sat a bundle of pound notes adding up to fifty pounds. When Tarni wasn't given a box, she was beginning to wonder why, until Patrick grinned cheekily and handed her an envelope. She opened it to find a return air ticket to New Zealand. The departure date was in two days' time, returning twelve days later. She didn't know whether to be pleased, or angry, as PJ had taken for granted that she'd want to go.

"Thank you," was all she said, before offering to help Mrs Turner with the dishes."

Later, when Tarni was getting ready for bed, PJ was kicking the dust on his way to Tarni's bungalow, thinking how maybe he'd made a big mistake, but hoped she'd relent and take up his offer. It would do her the world of good. He knocked tentatively on her door, ready to turn around if she didn't answer.

"Come in, PJ. I thought you'd come." Tarni opened the door with a wry smile on her face.

He stood and sighed, before he spoke.

"I don't like blaming other people, Tarni, but it was Sarah's idea. She thought you really needed a break. And my friends in New Zealand are wonderful people. I knew they'd love to have you stay. They'll make you feel right at home. And I know you never like to be far away from horses, so I was hoping you would be happy about going."

He paused, waiting for her reply. There was none. Tarni sat cross legged looking at him quizzically.

"I'm sorry, Tarni if I've done the wrong thing. I know I should have asked you first. I just left you with the idea the other night. Please forgive me. You don't have to go. I'll be able to cash the ticket in, or perhaps I'll use it myself. Maybe see if I can pick up a good staying type." He smiled and shrugged his shoulders, "Maybe it'll win the Melbourne Cup. Who knows?"

PJ turned to walk out, but Tarni stopped him.

"And where do you think you're going, Mr Darcy? There's a lot that has to be discussed before I go to New Zealand and leave you in charge to run this place."

PJ breathed a sigh of relief, then laughed.

The day arrived and Tarni was airborne. Although she would never admit it, her flight scared her almost to death. She swore she'd swim home, rather than board another plane. The massive turbulence caused by summer storms, rocked the aircraft and caused it to plummet and then suddenly lift. This continued for almost the entire journey.

She disembarked on the isle of the long white cloud, very shaky, but then relaxed when she saw a large sign: 'WELCOME TARNI.' It was held by a blonde-haired, handsome, young man who sported a broad smile. It made her feel she'd come home to the arms of a loving family and it gave her a warm feeling.

Tarni extended her hand to take his. Instead, Harry placed his nose and forehead against hers. She accepted this unusual greeting, but then stepped back a little shocked. He laughed.

"I'm sorry Tarni, I thought PJ would have explained to you. That's our New Zealand greeting, the Maoris call it a hongi. I'm pleased to meet you. My name is Harry Brauer. Come with me and we'll collect your bags."

Tarni walked a step behind this tall, lean, well-built young man and tried to guess his age. She thought him in his mid-twenties and perhaps an athlete of some sort. His physic looked like that of a runner, maybe a long-distance runner. His long well-muscled legs were in knee-length shorts. A white body-hugging tee shirt exposed his broad shoulders and defined biceps. She'd never felt this type of physical attraction to a man before. Well maybe she did, when she had a crush on PJ. But in November she'd turned twenty and she felt something had changed. She decided: Yes, I'm physically attracted to this man Harry Brauer, and then she smiled at her honesty.

Tarni scooped to collected her bags, but Harry beat her to it and smiled. His smile was something Tarni could look at all day. They were on their way in a Mercedes Benz. Harry took her on a sightseeing tour of Auckland and although Tarni had never been a lover of cities, this city did have a certain charm to it. It appeared light and breezy, not overshadowed by too many tall buildings.

"It's a very nice city Harry, especially being close to the sea. I bet there are some lovely views from the hotels here?"

"Yes, there are, and we'll take you to one of our finest hotels on your last night with us. Their restaurant is claimed to be the best in Auckland. We trust you will enjoy our fabulous New Zealand cuisine."

Tarni giggled and Harry loved the sound.

He then drove down to the main wharf in Auckland to where the neck of the Tasman Sea ended its journey. This is where the fishermen would bring in their catch for the day.

"Do you like seafood Tarni?"

"I love seafood. It's my favourite thing to eat. Anything caught from the sea, I simply love."

He smiled across at her.

"Good, then a seafood feast it shall be."

Harry's perfect English with that slight New Zealand twang and his refined looks, reminded Tarni a little of PJ. She asked herself, is this why I'm so attracted to him? It wouldn't worry me if Harry simply drove me around for the entire time I'm here. I just love looking at him and listening to him talk.

They entered a long-sealed driveway leading to the Breuer's home, also his father's training establishment. The stables and buildings were surrounded by flower gardens. Rows of pine trees, manicured into hedges, formed fences to separate the paddocks. An expansive timber barn sat majestically on a concrete slab. Small grassed paddocks encircled it. Tarred paths and narrow roadways shot away in rows, all over the property, from what Tarni could see.

"Why are all the paths and roads tarred, Harry?"

"We have so much rain in New Zealand, we'd be up to our bellies in mud if we didn't seal them."

Tarni looked to the heavens and realised why they called it the land of the long white cloud. Grey stratus clouds had begun to accumulate and some looked ominous.

"I see what you mean. I think we're in for a down pour any minute."

They moved quickly inside where Harry's mother, Valery, welcomed her. Then the sky opened and down it poured. When Tarni entered the cosy living room, she felt at home. The furniture looked expensive but well-worn and comfortable. A newspaper lay strewn on the floor next to an oversized armchair. Its feather-cushion seat had been well and truly sat in. The enormous French windows looked out onto the greenest paddocks she'd ever seen. With horses grazing languidly, it looked like post-card material. Sunlight filtered softly onto the coffee table, which was laden with cakes and biscuits and a tea trolley sat to one side.

Tarni thought Harry resembled Valarie. Tall, about five feet nine, slim and very attractive. She guessed her age was late forties. Her skin was fairer than Harry's, but her hair was just as blonde. Tarni turned when she heard the back-door bang shut and there was Harry's father, Ronny. He came striding towards her with his arms open wide. A ruggedly handsome man, his face creased with deep laughter lines when he smiled. His vivid blue eyes were accentuated against his steel grey hair and tanned skin. Ronny gave Valery no time to introduce him. He shook Tarni's hand with the strength of a bear then gave her a hug in the same fashion.

"Tarni, welcome to our humble abode. I've heard so much about you from PJ. I can't wait to show you around and to see you ride. You've come here with glowing references. I don't know whether we'll be able to allow you to return to SA. We may just have to keep you here," Ronny said with a hearty laugh.

Tarni shrugged off Ronny's flattery, and then sat to enjoy her tea and cake. Their conversation finally slowed and after a time, Tarni asked Ronnie:

"PJ has never really told me how you came to meet. He just said you were very good friends." Tarni accepted a refill of tea into her large china cup and then sat back, listening to more of Ronny's New Zealand twang.

"Well it all began when we sent Harry to boarding school in Adelaide. PJ was in his last year and was the school prefect. Harry was years below PJ and Harry was a shy young lad. He had to put up with quite a bit of bullying but when PJ caught him nursing a black eye, he asked Harry what had happened. Harry told PJ, and PJ asked him who the offenders were. PJ never told the principal, he just knocked their bloody blocks off and told 'em to lay off Harry and if he caught them bullying him or anyone else, he'd give them another hiding. PJ's care of Harry didn't stop there. He showed him how to box and defend himself. They'd go on bike rides together and generally hang out." Ronnie took a gulp of his tea and then continued. "They rode mainly to the racing stables at Morphettville. I was pleased about that because PJ rekindled Harry's interest in horses, also Harry's a very good boxer now and he loves bike riding. Yes, he's very competitive in both sports." Ronny looked at Harry. "Isn't that right, son?"

Harry hung his head a little. "If you say so, Dad."

"Your story sounds just like PJ, Mr Brauer. He actually saved my life you know."

As soon as the words had left Tarni's mouth, she gulped her tea to drown further information and quickly countered.

"I don't like to talk about it though; it brings back too many nightmares." Tarni hung her head while they looked from one to the other, a little concerned.

Ronny changed the subject.

"Harry's now in his last year of studying law. We're very proud of him aren't we Val?"

Valery smiled. "Yes of course we're proud of him Ronny. And we're proud of our twin daughters Emma and Grace too." She looked almost lovingly at Tarni. "They're riding their horses at the moment Tarni. They have a one-day event coming up. Normally they're at boarding school but it's school holidays now." Valery looked at Ronny. "We love having them home with us don't we Ronny?"

"Yes, we sure do, Val."

"They're growing up so fast. They turn sixteen on the 21 of January, the day before they return to school." Valery sipped her tea, still smiling.

"I look forward to meeting them," Tarni said, while still thinking about the Robbo business.

"They should be in soon, so I'll show you to your room now and then you can chat with the girls after you've settled in." Valery rose from her chair.

"There'll be plenty of time for chatting later Val. When you're ready Tarni, I'll show you around."

"I'll go now if you like, Mr Brauer. I can unpack later."

"That's the spirit. Come on then, Tarni. Harry will take your bags to you room." Ronny nodded towards Harry. "You might like to join us son. We'll wait a moment if you want."

Harry gave Tarni an admiring look.

"Okay, Dad." Harry blushed as he turned and lifted her bags.

The tour began and Tarni was astounded with the facilities Ronny had in which to train his horses. The dense turf on the track, she knew, would help ward off the concussion on the horse's joints. And the diverse pastures grown on these volcanic soils were full of nutrients and calcium to build strong bones.

Tarni was falling in love with this property and maybe with Harry too. She felt tingles whenever Harry sidled up close, placing his hand on her shoulder, in a mock shepherding gesture.

Later at dinner, Tarni enjoyed the company of the twins, Emma and Grace. They had a habit of speaking at the same time and giggling at almost everything. She found herself giggling along with them. They were delightful.

"I look forward to watching you compete." Tarni said.

"Well thank you very much, Tarni. We'd love that." They seemed to reply in unison.

Early the next morning, Tarni woke instinctively, dressed in her riding gear and tip toed through the quiet house toward the stables. The lights were on in the barn and Ronny was giving instructions to his staff. She stood in the shadows watching them saddle up. Everything seemed to be done the same as it was at home, so Tarni moved up to the group.

"Good morning, Mr Brauer. Can I help?"

"Good morning, Tarni. I didn't want to wake you because you're on holidays!"

"This isn't work for me. I love every minute of it, even mucking out boxes. I'd like to ride though. Do you have a horse the other riders don't get along with?"

"I wouldn't do that to you Tarni, I'll give you a quiet one first, see how you get on, eh?"

Tarni rode beautifully. Her hands and balance on the horse were admirable. A lesson for Ronny's younger riders, who under Ronny's orders, soon gathered around.

"Take a good look now. Note Tarni's gentle feel on the horse's mouth.

Not like you lot. You all look like you're pushing a bloody pram! See how still and low she sits on the horse, Tarni's part of the horse."

"Good morning, Dad. How's Tarni going?"

"Take a look for yourself, Harry. She's a natural. PJ was right. I've put her on the old mongrel, just to show these kids how to handle him. Look at her, she's having no trouble at all."

"Yes, she's good alright. I've never seen that old boy travel so calmly. I hope you don't work Tarni all day though Dad. I'd like to take her sightseeing."

Harry's eyes squinted against the morning sun as he waited for his father's answer.

"Well, I was going to take her myself, Harry, to have a look at some of our better horse studs. And PJ's asked me to keep an eye out for a horse, with good staying blood lines." He had a chuckle before he said. "I think PJ wants to get in on the Melbourne Cup dream."

"I' can take Tarni, Dad. I'm sure you have more important things to do. Haven't you got a couple of runners at Matta- Matta tomorrow?"

Ronny smiled knowingly. He hadn't missed the admiring glances the two had shared. Ronny clapped his son on the back.

"Yes, come to think of it, Son. I am busy." He nodded towards Tarni, "but just make sure you don't lead that lovely young lady up the garden path. We wouldn't want to upset PJ, now would we?"

Ronny couldn't be happier with the thought of Harry and Tarni mixing it together and it might be a way of getting him even more interested in the horses.

"Tarni will be safe with me, Dad. Don't worry."

Tarni couldn't shower and dress quickly enough for the opportunity to spend an afternoon alone with Harry. Although the plan was almost spoilt when Valery suggested the twins go with them. Harry seemed notably annoyed at his mother's suggestion.

"No, Mum. They talk all the time and giggle at nothing. I can't concentrate when they're in the car!"

"Alright, dear. It was only a suggestion." Valery rolled her eyes and went to check something cooking in the oven. She called out to them as they were leaving.

"Don't eat too much when you're out, Harry. I've made a lovely lamb casserole for dinner."

"Okay, Mum. We won't." Harry winked at Tarni.

Ronny stood at the car window, his hand on the roof.

"You'd better go to Old Hughie's place first Harry; he's got an un-tried three-year old colt for sale. It was passed in at the Karaka sales when it was a yearling. Hughie took him home, gave him time to mature and says he's furnished into a really good type. Take a look at him; see what you both think. He's an old trickster that Hughie, so if you like the horse, don't jump in at his price. I'll go the day after tomorrow and make the deal with him, if a deal is to be made."

Harry gave a wry smile. "So, you do trust my eye with a horse then, Dad?"

"Well, I reckon between the pair of you, you should know what you're looking at," Ronny said as he slapped the roof of the car and with that, they were off.

Tarni was in awe of the scenery. The horse studs were manicured to the last blade of grass and the grand entrances leading into some of the most respected and palatial studs in the world, were simply incredible. The wealth and prosperity of the horse industry in New Zealand seemed to sing its blessings everywhere.

"New Zealand has the most sought-after thoroughbreds in the world. It is the land of plenty with its rich soil and the lush green grass," Harry enthused. "Our horses are simply superior to their rivals."

Tarni was becoming well and truly hooked on this country. She even enjoyed the fact that it was early January and the temperature was attuned to that of a lovely late autumn day in Adelaide. Not like the January temperatures back home.

"What are the winters like here, Harry?"

"To be honest with you, Tarni, they're cold, wet and windy. But you get used to it. We just rug up and wear our woolly underwear."

"What about your rainy season?" Harry laughed.

"It rains whenever it likes here, so it's always rainy season." Harry then slowed up and turned into a dirt driveway.

"Here we are, Tarni. This is old Hughie's place. Now remember if you like the horse don't let on, or he'll put the price up. Just say we have some more horses to look at down the road and we'll get back to him. Okay?"

"Okay, I got it."

Compared to the impressive studs they'd seen so far; this property was a little run down. Tarni would however, be respectful to this obviously battling old trainer. It wasn't in her nature to be cocky, or even get too excited. What she did have though, was a good eye for conformation and the gift to see inside a horse's brain. Tarni could tell within 30 seconds weather the horse would gallop or not. As they drove down the pot-holed driveway and into the stable area, she felt a special vibe – a premonition.

Harry introduced Tarni to old Hughie, who'd limped out of the house to meet them. They exchanged pleasantries before Hughie went to fetch the horse. When Hughie left, Harry placed his arm around Tarni as if it were second nature. She melted, whishing she could stay like this forever. Then Hughie came towards them leading the big chestnut horse with a thin white blaze. Spontaneously, the horse looked straight at Tarni and whinnied with gusto.

Harry whispered, "I really like him, Tarni, but not as much as I like you." Harry's words sent an unfamiliar warmth surging through her body.

She found it hard to concentrate on the horse after that remark. However, she regained her composure and walked around the horse, picked up his feet and felt his tendons. Pleased that they'd passed the test, she stood back for another look. He had a good chest and girth and stood over an enormous amount of ground. All good, but there also seemed to be something special about him. Tarni knew it – she felt it. She'd inspected hundreds of horses with PJ and no horse had ever given her this feeling. This horse had a few surface scars, but nothing to worry about. Tarni placed her hand between his jaw and then around his windpipe. It was huge. She stroked the horse, whispering:

"So, boy. Do you think you could handle the rock-hard tracks and extreme heat in Aussie land, because you'll get plenty of both in SA?"

Tarni then asked Hughie if she could see him move, perhaps in a round yard, or a small paddock where he could stretch out a bit. They watched, as Hughie let him run in a makeshift paddock. The fences were falling down, and wire had been wound in a slap-happy way to hold the rails together. The horse flew around the paddock. His feet barely touched the ground and he seemed to know not to go near the fences, or he'd be in strife.

"I really like him, Harry. He's a beautiful mover. Can we ask Hughie how much he wants?"

"Let me do the talking, okay?" Harry walked over to Hughie.

"How much do you want for him, Hughie? We need to know because there's a few more horses up the road for sale. This is the first one we've looked at, so we'll need a guide. He might be worth a chance, at the right price."

Old Hughie was nobody's fool and he wasn't about to let these two youngsters get the better of him.

"I've put a thousand pounds on him, Harry."

Harry laughed. He knew the horse had decent blood lines, but you'd have to go back to the third dam to find anything worth spruiking about.

"I'd say that's why you haven't sold him, Hughie. You want too much money. He's not worth it!"

Hughie shook his head in disappointment.

"Harry, Harry. You still have a lot to learn about horses, son. This horse is worth more than a thousand pound. I only showed you the horse as a favour to your dad. If the young lady wants to win the Melbourne Cup, well here's her horse. His sire would have won the Melbourne Cup for sure, only he had an accident. And I can tell you this, his mother was the most honest filly I've ever put a bridle on. Anyway, I haven't put him on the market yet. Mark my words though, Harry. When I do, I'll have him sold in a day and for twice the price!"

Tarni knew Hughie was right. The horse would be sold for sure. There was definitely something about him, especially the way he moved with that long easy stride. She needed to get involved now.

"I'll have to phone my boss and tell him all about the horse Hughie. Will you give me until tomorrow morning? I'll give you our answer then."

"Yes, I will young lady. Now there's a real horse woman Harry, she knows a good horse when she sees one. You'd be wise to stick with her!"

Harry couldn't believe Tarni had accepted Hughie's ridiculous price. He threw her a look as if to say, what are you bloody thinking?

They walked to the car in silence. But when the doors closed, Harry couldn't help himself.

"Bloody hell, Tarni. That horse is not even worth half that money." He shook his head in frustration and drove away. Tarni was not fazed at his remark but offended by the way he'd said it.

"You may not think so Harry, but I can see something special in him.," and she fought the tears that were building up. "You may think I'm stupid, but that horse literally begged me to buy him. I feel sorry for old Hughie. The property's so run down. He'll be able to use the money to do it up a bit, at least re-build the fences and make the property safe for his horses." She looked out of the window, thinking she'd ruined her chance with Harry.

Harry burst out laughing, laughing so much he had to pull the car over to the side of the road.

"Tarni, my sweet girl. Old Hughie is one of the richest men in the bloody north island!"

Tarni slapped him on the arm.

"Well why didn't you tell me that before?"

They both laughed so hard, Tarni's laughter turned into tears.

"I can't believe I did that. Now there's no going back. We'll have to pay Hughie the thousand pounds to buy him. Bugger – bum!"

Harry gathered Tarni in his arms and kissed her like she'd never been kissed before. The heat began to rise between them, and all Harry could do was suggest he find a secluded spot off the road. Tarni agreed, then remembered how from the age of twelve she'd fought for her virginity. Now, she was ready to give it up without a moment's consideration the consequences. For God's sake I've only known him twenty-four hours!' But that argument fell short.

It seemed to Tarni that Harry certainly knew his way around the area. Within minutes they were in a remote part, under a weeping willow in a perfectly secluded spot. Tarni murmured through kisses, "I'm a virgin, Harry."

"I can't stop now, Tarni," Harry panted as he pulled her into his chest. "I need you so much," he mumbled. Then he thought about what he'd said and felt guilty. "I'm sorry Tarni, I shouldn't, I mean I…"

"Yes, you should, Harry. I want you too," Tarni whispered as she eased her pants down.

As Harry's fingers travelled down, exquisite vibrations flooded Tarni, sensations that aroused a need she never knew she had.

Harry released the catch on the front seat and the back folded down, so they lay in each other's embrace – skin to skin. Despite the initial stab of pain, Tarni relaxed, wanting to share her soul with Harry the rhythm perfect the sensation unimageable, radiating, building- building. Exploding. Tarni, breathed in the awareness of it all. The air had now changed. The world had changed. Enfolded in Harry's arms Tarni held tight to this incredible feeling. Never- ever did she want it to end.

"I love you, Harry," she whispered over and over again as Harry rocked her and the euphoria slowly subsided.

"I love you too, Tarni. I've never felt this way before. I've wanted to make love to you from the moment I saw you and I want to keep making love to you until I die. So, what are we going to do about it? You'll be leaving soon, and I'll be left all alone."

Harry placed his finger under her chin and gazed into her eyes, searching for an answer.

"Will you stay with me, Tarni?"

"I don't know. What would PJ think and what would he do without me? I owe him so much. I'll have to go home first and talk with him." She paused and gave a cheeky grin. "Anyway, tomorrow you may not feel the same way about me. You know, the morning after syndrome!"

His look had a tinge of playful arrogance.

"Yes, you're right, Tarni. I simply love 'em and leave 'em. That's my motto!"

At dinner that evening, it was almost impossible for them to hide their love for each other. Their only diversion was the discussion about the horses they'd inspected. Tarni was convinced there was only one horse out of the many they had seen during the day, which was worth buying. It was Billy, old Hughie's horse. After dinner, Tarni asked if she may use the telephone to let PJ know about the horse.

When she did, PJ's answer was:

"Yes, if you think he's the one, then buy him Tarni."

Ronny was on Harry's side. He agreed Hughie's asking price of a thousand pound was over the limit, especially for a horse with average breeding, who was already three years old and un-broken into the bargain. However, they hadn't realised the amount of respect PJ held for Tarni's opinion, especially her eye for a horse. If she said the horse had something special about him, then it was good enough for PJ.

"He sounds good, Tarni, but I tell you what. If he's a dud, I'll never let you choose another horse. Is it a deal?"

She laughed, "It's a done deal, PJ!"

The rest of her working holiday became something of a dream. She made love with Harry whenever they found an opportunity. Tarni adored him and couldn't imagine leaving him behind.

Their final evening together was spent as Harry had promised. Ronny had organised a sea view window table at the Auckland Pacific Hotel. Savouring their delicious seafood dinner, a red sunset sank slowly beneath the shimmering silver horizon. It reminded Tarni of twilights spent snuggling up to her mother while sitting on the sands of Victor Harbour. She shook the memory when Roni, it seemed instinctively, asked her a personal question.

Ronny had been aware of Harry and Tarni's love affair and at this point he approved. However, he thought it may be an appropriate time to question Tarni further about her heritage before things became too serious.

"You know Tarni, you've never spoken of your family, or where you came from. All we know is you're a great friend of PJ's and you met on an outback cattle station in the Northern Territory." Ronny looked up from his dinner to see an uncomfortable look on Tarni's face.

He continued carefully, not wishing to push her too much. "Your surname, Windsor. It sounds British, the name suggests royalty?" He smiled broadly with the thought, then he asked. "And where does the name Tarni originate from?"

Tarni coughed before answering.

"Yes, you're right. Windsor is an English name and my mother chose the name Tarni because it means the sound of waves in an Aboriginal language. She loved the sound of waves. And so tell me, is Brauer a German name?"

She intended only to give short answers, or throw one straight back at Ronny, until she was able to excuse herself and go to the bathroom where she would think seriously, if this was the right time to tell the truth. Perhaps not all of the truth, just the fact that she was part Aboriginal. After finishing the last mouthful of her entrée, Tarni excused herself.

"We need to go to the lady's room too, Tarni," the twins said in unison.

The ladies room was lined with marble tiles. White linen hand towels were folded neatly in a white cane basket near the wash basins. An array of freshly cut flowers sat below the makeup mirror. It looked regal and very posh. Tarni remembered she'd said the same thing to PJ, on the first occasion they'd dinned out in an exclusive restaurant. She felt a feeling of inferiority was about to burst her bubble. Now that she thought about it, she realised Ronny only hired Maori youth to do the lowly jobs like mucking out stables, mowing lawns, and taking the garbage to the local tip. Added to this, the Brauers had no dark-skinned friends. Apart from summer tans, they were all white. She washed her hands and waited for the girls, intending to ask them a leading question. She hoped it would give her a sign about whether they had prejudices against Indigenous, or dark-skinned people. The girls exited from the toilets simultaneously and Tarni smiled sweetly as she said:

"I have to thank you, girls, for being so kind to me over my stay. You've taught me so much about your country. I've also enjoyed learning about the Maori culture, especially when we visited Rotorua. I was wondering what your dad would say if perhaps you girls fell in love with a Maori boy and wanted to marry him."

They both looked horrified and for the first time Grace spoke before Emma.

"Oh my goodness, our life wouldn't be worth living. Dad would shun us forever and so would Mum. Why on earth would you ask such a question, Tarni?"

"I don't know. At Rotorua, there were a lot of very good- looking Maori boys admiring you both."

Emma's answer was a little cutting.

"Well I can tell you for sure, Tarni. That's as far as it would go. If those Maori boys even touched us, our father would shoot them."

By the time they returned to the table, Tarni's anger had almost engulfed her. However, she contained it by firing questions at Ronny. She asked him all about the city of Auckland; when it was established; how many people lived in its surrounding suburbs. How did their Government work; was it the same as in Australia? What year did Val and he arrive from Germany; how old were they then? When did he and Valery meet each other? Ronny had no time to return to the questions he would have liked to ask Tarni. She continued asking many more questions about all the places they had taken her to see. Tarni breathed a sigh of relief when the dinner was over, and the family began to bid her farewell.

Ronny had booked a room at the hotel for Tarni. Her plane was to leave early the next morning, so he'd also organised a cab to take her to the airport. He was the first to embrace her.

"It has been such a pleasure having you stay with us Tarni." Ronny held her a little closer and whispered in her ear.

"I'm pleased you and Harry got along so well."

She smiled sweetly as he stood back and before accepting hugs and kisses from the twins and of course Valery, who'd been most gracious towards her. Nothing had been too much trouble. Valery seemed to know exactly what Tarni needed before she had time to ask for it. Last of all, Harry stood waiting his turn.

"Auf Wiedersehen, Tarni."

The family seemed proud of the fact that they were of German descent, although his parents were also proud to have become New Zealand citizens at a very young age and many years before World War Two.

Harry held Tarni so tight she felt her ribs were being crushed. She shed tears like never before, believing this was not, auf Weidersehen but the end of their love affair. Ronny had the good sense to escort the ladies away, so Harry could spend a moment alone with Tarni. Ronny was surprised to see Harry join them so soon, noticeably upset and wanting to leave in a hurry. But Harry kept his last heated conversation with Tarni a secret. How could he tell his father she'd said they were all racists!

Chapter 11

Tarni's tears continued on her flight across the Tasman Sea and while being driven back to the farm. PJ felt helpless in the situation, as he was unable to understand Tarni's tears. It seemed she wouldn't or couldn't explain why she was so upset.

"Just leave me be PJ. I'll get over it; I need a little space. I know you care but there's nothing you can do. So please just let me be sad for a while and then I'll be okay."

Tarni looked across at the man who she would always love. However, she knew now what a passionate love was, the feeling a woman holds for a man when she wants to physically devour him. She'd thought it was impossible to ever feel the way she did about Harry and now the pain of losing him was almost too much to bear.

Tarni was fortunate that her spirits were lifted when Billy, the Kiwi horse, arrived by ship two weeks later, the same day as Sarah's court hearing began. Tarni was upset and a little angry that she couldn't be at the docks to meet Billy, so on the way to the court she gave PJ instructions.

"He won't have a clue what's happening, PJ. He'll be lost. I know you'll be gentle but please be extra gentle with him. It's so bloody hot today. Make sure he goes in the paddock with the big gum tree. Oh, and yes, give him a good hose down. Cool him off as often as you can."

"Yes, Tarni. Don't worry, Tarni. I'll look after him, Tarni. And good luck today in court."

She dismissed his teasing manner with a nervous smile.

"Thanks, PJ. With this ordeal, I'm going to need all the luck I can get."

PJ pulled the car up outside the courthouse, wished her good luck again and drove off towards the docks, thinking Tarni had chosen the right word 'ordeal'. Yes, it would be a very long ordeal. He could only hope and pray that the two women he loved and relied on, would come through without too much pain. And if they didn't eventually win, 'The Sarah Brown case', as it had become known Australia wide, then they would at least make a difference in the social consciousness of the Australian public.

The case had been in the SA headlines for the past month and on this morning, a final consensus had been taken to gauge the likely outcome. 'Will Sarah Brown have laid enough groundwork? Will she produce enough evidence of abuse given by her herd of witnesses, including many young troubled Aboriginal people? Will this be an amazing milestone for Australian history, or will we see Sarah Brown knocked out in the first round?' These were some of the questions asked in the newspapers.

Many journalists it appeared, without putting their necks on the line, were on Sarah's side. The journo's loved this sort of fight, it made for easy news and Sarah was available most times when the press telephoned her. She needed their support and they loved her. She was funny, straight to the point, and the only thing she took seriously was her crusade.

PJ prayed aloud, "Dear God help Sarah and the children. You know what she's fighting for. And it's right and just, so please help them."

By the end of the day, PJ had settled in Billy the horse. He seemed to be enjoying his new home already, despite the blistering heat. And then, as if on cue, a sudden cool change made play with the stubborn heat that South Australia had been experiencing. It was at this time that PJ rang Sarah.

"How did it go in court today, my darling?"

Sarah sounded slightly inebriated.

"Well, it's like this, PJ. We simply have to keep hammering away until we hit home to these stupid bastards. We've produced all the proof they need. We've shown them all the statistics and tomorrow we interview our witnesses. Then our wise judge will make a decision on whether we've established a good enough reason to take our bargaining further. Then, our noble politicians will decide to either stick fast to their idiotic mistakes, or admit they've been dreadfully wrong and then amend the law. Anyway, you should know the procedure, PJ!" Sarah's last sentence sounded angry, but then her voice softened. "So, what do you think our chances are, my darling. Come on, give me the odds."

Patrick would never lay a bet on the outcome. He had too strong a feeling it would all be for nothing, at this stage anyway. However, he'd lay a bet that Sarah had drunk too many wines.

"I'm not going to give you the odds Sarah, I just phoned to say I love you and I'm on your side all the way. And please tell Tarni that Billy has arrived safe and sound. I've left him in the gum tree paddock with the pony. They're getting along really well. I just needed to tell you how proud I am of you both and how much respect I have for you, Sarah. What you are trying to achieve is amazing. But please remember, don't be too let down if it doesn't go our way because we have a wedding to look forward to and I don't want you to be completely worn out."

*

The wedding invitations had been sent out the week before. The marriage ceremony was to be held at Saint John the Baptist church, near Glenelg on Saturday 28 March 1959.

The reception would be held at, 'Wildflowers'.

"Oh shit, I almost forgot about the bloody wedding!" Sarah said, mocking him.

"I'll lay a bet you didn't, my darling!"

She laughed into the phone and then almost whispered.

"My father may have to get the shot-gun out, PJ. I think I'm pregnant."

Patrick whispered back. "Well, you'd better stop drinking. I'm sure alcohol is not good for babies."

Sarah returned the whisper. "Oh dear, then I may have drowned our first child in alcohol, unintentionally of course."

"I love you, Sarah and I hope it's not a false alarm. I can't wait to have our children doing chores and riding their ponies around the farm."

"You're a bloody slave driver, PJ! You just want kids, so they can do all your dirty work!" PJ laughed.

"I hadn't thought of that but come to think of it, it's not a bad idea. How's Tarni handling the questioning?

"She's fine, she cries when she should, and she gets angry when it's expected. So her emotions are in the right place. But I know there's something wrong with her. Something happened in New Zealand and she won't tell me. Have you got any idea?'

"No. And I've only spoken to Ronny twice. All he said was that Tarni was a great rider and a pleasure to have stay in their home. We mainly talked about organising the horse to be sent here by ship. Remember, Sarah, I told you when I picked Tarni up from the airport, how she cried nearly all the way home in the car? She told me to leave her alone and she'd get over it. So I did. It took a while, but she came around."

By the end of the week, all stories and complaints, including the inhumane treatment of Indigenous children had been heard in court. The hard evidence had been produced. Now all Sarah had to do was to wait for the outcome.

Tarni returned to the farm, feeling proud of herself for telling the truth and perhaps helping others to do the same. Her healing in that area had truly

92

begun.

With PJ's help she began to break in Billy, although Tarni preferred to call it, 'tuning in'. As with every horse Tarni handled, Billy was no different. He adapted to her psychological make-up within minutes. It took only five days for her to be on board Billy and cantering him around the yard. Within a few days, she'd progressed from riding in a yard to working him on the track. PJ watched closely and became impressed with Billy's long, easy stride. It seemed from that point on, Tarni was unable to tire Billy. Not that she wanted to, it was just that he seemed to thrive on work.

*

The lull in the court proceedings gave time for Sarah to travel to her parents home and make sure her wedding dress fitted perfectly. After being delighted with the dress they decided to go through the wedding acceptances and the unable- to- attends.

Sarah sat up surprised, when she read the unable to attend letter from the Brauer family.

"The entire family!" she said to her mother. "I can't see why at least Ronny and Val, or even Harry on his own can't attend." Sarah folded the letter and placed it on the table.

"Mmm, this makes Tarni's New Zealand visit a real mystery!" She rose from her chair and apologised to her mother. "I'm sorry, Mum, I can't stay, there's someone I must go and see right away."

Sarah kissed her mother before she left and then drove all the way to the farm.

An hour later she pulled up under a large, sweeping peppercorn tree and walked into the barn. Tarni was talking to Craig about horses, as usual.

"Hi, Tarni," Sarah said after waiting for her to finish chatting. She was a little surprised to see Sarah.

"Hi, Sarah. I didn't expect to see you here today."

"I know. I'm here because I need to talk to you. Have you got time now, or are you too busy?"

"I've got time. I'll ask Craig to finish off." She ran to catch Craig and give instructions and then ran back.

"So, what's up, Sarah? How are the wedding plans going? Everything okay?" Tarni said a little breathlessly.

"Everything's fine with the wedding, Tarni. But I think we should talk about what happened in New Zealand." Sarah looked towards the house and said in a whisper. "I didn't tell PJ I was coming back. So can we slip away, maybe go to the beach and talk?"

Tarni's heart began to race. She'd tried hard to put Harry behind her, even though she'd cried herself to sleep most nights. Tarni said abruptly:

"You should have phoned me, Sarah. I would have told you not to waste your time. There's nothing to tell."

"Don't be like that, Tarni. I know there's something bothering you. And now I'm convinced of it, because I received a letter from the Brauer family to say they were unable to attend the wedding and I think you know why." Sarah paused when she noticed tears welling in Tarni's eyes. "Come on, Tarni. Let's go before PJ sees I'm here. We'll go to the beach where we can have some privacy."

Sarah pulled up on a secluded part of the coast. The lull before the storm she thought, when noticing the wind had dropped and the sea barely moved. Only the shimmer of the fading sun produced the illusion of dancing rays upon the otherwise millpond sea.

"Do you want to sit here and talk, Tarni, or do you want to go for a walk?"

"Let's walk," Tarni said as she opened the car door.

They walked in silence for a while, until Sarah asked. "Could we sit now, Tarni, "I've felt a little worn out since the court hearing. I think it could also be because I'm pregnant."

Sarah plonked herself down on the sand and laughed as she spoke. "Oh God, I feel pregnant. That wasn't very graceful." She laughed a little more before realising Tarni hadn't smiled or said a word. "Well aren't you excited for me? I'm pregnant I'm going to have a baby!"

Tears flowed down Tarni's cheeks, she tried to wipe them dry with her tee shirt.

"What's wrong, Tarni? You know I'm your best friend. Nothing you tell me can shock me."

Tarni looked at Sarah through blood shot eyes. "I think I'm pregnant too."

"OH OKAY—SO, you're not going to let me have all the lime-light. What sort of friend are you, Tarni?"

Sarah's humour always worked its magic on Tarni and she managed a smile before Sarah reached across and held her tight, rocking her in her arms.

"Oh my darling, Tarni. Now tell me what happened in the land of the long white cloud. Did you fall in love or were you forced to..." Tarni butted in.

"I fell in love Sarah. It wasn't rape. I've managed to fight off would-be rapists ever since I was a kid. What makes you think I couldn't do it now?"

Tarni went on to tell Sarah, all there was to know about her time in New Zealand, except there was one twist.

"It was me who'd shunned Harry. I accused him, and his family, of being racially prejudiced. I told him I wanted nothing more to do with him or his family. He asked why I would say such a thing, but my temper was so bad, I'm sure I looked at Harry as if I were about to kill him. Harry wouldn't stop asking me why? That's when I told him I was a part-white Aboriginal. Harry said it didn't matter to him, but then I said, it would matter to your father. He'd shoot me if he knew. He's a prejudiced bastard!

"That was when Harry turned his back and left."

Sarah sighed deeply.

"Oh my dear, Tarni."

They sat in drawn-out silence. Sarah needed to digest the news and Tarni needed to wait for her guidance. Sarah eventually turned to Tarni, who sat still, head lowered. Only her fingers moved, sifting the sand.

"Do you have any regrets Tarni?"

"No not really. I've gone over and over everything and I think if it happened again, I wouldn't change a thing. I love Harry and I couldn't help myself when he was near me, I just melted. But when Grace said their father would shoot the Maori boys if they touched them, that's when I got angry. I can't explain what happens to me when I see other people looking down on others who are different, or when people do something that's inhumane. I just get so angry I can't control myself."

This was another layer within Tarni that Sarah hadn't seen before. It frightened her a little. She'd have to dig a lot deeper into this young woman's psyche, and although Tarni appeared to be an archangel, Sarah thought a temper this intense could land her in trouble.

"I understand, Tarni and I'm feeling your pain. But you know your temper maybe your undoing someday."

Sarah thought it probably would if the authorities ever found out about Robbo's penis being half bitten off.

"We have to work on your rage. Try to relay the patience you have for horses towards humans. I know it's hard but try to feel compassion for those who don't have your insight. Those people need to be shown the way peacefully. Just walk away and think of your horses. Hold your temper, Tarni. I can honestly say that losing control has never done anyone any good." Tarni nodded and turned her big brown eyes towards Sarah.

"You mean, I shouldn't have said those things to Harry and just let him think I approved of his family's bigotry?"

"Not exactly, Tarni. But you only had the sister's word about what their father would do to the Maori boys. I'm certain they overreacted, anyway It wasn't enough evidence to hang the man. And that's what I mean about holding your temper. Learn how to stay calm in situations that you may not agree with. If I were you, I'd write a letter to Harry and explain how you feel about being part-Aboriginal Then finish it with something like:

'If I've been misled about your family's racial prejudices, then I am truly sorry.' That's all you need to say and if Harry replies favourably or unfavourably, then we'll sort it out together." Sarah squeezed Tarni's hand. "What do you say?"

"I suppose your right. But I don't know what to do about the baby. What will I do?"

"Do you know for sure if you're pregnant, Tarni?"

"No, I've just missed a period, that's all."

"Well then, let's go home now. You can wee in a jar and I'll take it to the chemist. He'll do a test and we'll work that one out when we have the results. Okay?"

"Thank you, Sarah. I feel like you and PJ have been sent from heaven. You're my angels. I love you both." Tarni leaned across and hugged Sarah hard.

*

Three days later, Sarah phoned Tarni to tell her she was not pregnant. Another eight days passed before Tarni held Harry Breuer's return letter in her hand. She went straight to her bungalow, poured herself an ice water and sat in her armchair, breathing in and out slowly, trying to relieve the butterflies in her stomach before she opened it.

> *Dear Tarni,*
> *Your comments have certainly caused war*
> *within my family. We had never truly studied our*
> *prejudices, not before you so bluntly exposed*
> *them to us. We have been at logger heads from*
> *the minute you left. However, we have finally*
> *come to the conclusion our family unit is more*
> *important to us, than what each of us thinks*
> *as individuals. It is unfortunate, that some of*
> *my family have harboured prejudice without*
> *realising it. Their attitude may take a long time*

Tarni folded the letter, ran to PJ and asked if she may use the phone.

"Of course, Tarni. Are you okay?"

"Yes, I'm fine, PJ. I just need to talk to Sarah." She looked at him pleadingly. "In private please."

Tarni read the letter to Sarah and Sarah then asked if Tarni could catch the bus into Adelaide and perhaps spend the night with her. They needed to talk further about the letter. Tarni put it to PJ and he agreed.

"No worries, Tarni. We can do without you for a day. But only one day mind you."

Tarni arrived at Sarah's office by late afternoon and was greeted by Ella with the same aloof manner as always.

"Miss Brown will be with you shortly, Miss Windsor. Take a seat please."

Tarni decided not to talk to Ella. She'd tried it before and it didn't work, so she sat and browsed through a fashion magazine. When the door opened, Tarni smiled at who PJ called the butch client. She knew she shouldn't laugh but there was something about women dressing up as men and vice versa that Tarni found funny.

He, or she, greeted Tarni.

"Hi, Tarni. You did a great job in the court room. I reckon you ladies might just pull it off!"

Then Sarah mouthed above the client's head. "That's what she'd love, a dick to pull off."

When the woman left, Tarni burst out laughing. Ella threw Tarni a venomous look before she disappeared into Sarah's office.

"Sarah, you're terrible!" Tarni said after Sarah closed the door.

"I know. Sometimes I wonder who gave me my degree in psychology. They must have been totally mad or madly in love with me? Sit down, Tarni and let's read between the lines shall we?"

After a long discussion about Tarni's thoughts and feelings, Sarah asked.

"What do you think you should do Tarni? I don't want to put words into your mouth."

"I know I love Harry with all my heart. So, I suppose I'll just have to accept his family's prejudices. I think it would take a long time for them to be rid of their ingrained arrogance and it may eventually cause a rift between us. I hope Harry loves me and it's not just lust." Tarni hung her head and Sarah almost flew at her.

"Tarni lift your beautiful head, lift it high and be proud and confident. You have nothing to be ashamed of. The opposite, you are from the most wonderful, spiritual people who are totally misunderstood by the European community. Aborigines are the true Australians. We haven't come this far for me to see you lose what you've gained. Harry wouldn't say or write that he loved you if he didn't. I can see he's had to walk a jagged mile and do some soul searching before he replied honestly to your letter. I think he's laid the cards on the table fair and square. Now it's up to you. If you think you can handle the rest of his family without losing your temper; then do as Harry said. He wrote that he'd like to give the relationship another chance. So please listen to your heart. I'll help you with the rest."

Tarni was about to hang her head once again, but remembered, and so looked Sarah in the eye.

"I was happy when I first read the letter, because all I could see were the words, I still love you, Tarni. Now I have to be honest, I don't want to cause a rift in his family. This may happen, especially if he wants me to live in New Zealand. I would hate to make him choose between me and his family."

Sarah came straight back at her.

"It happens more than you know, Tarni. Harry must stand by his own beliefs. He's a man, not a child. It's time for him to go out into the world and find a wife, have a family and bring his children up under his own guidance. If you think he is truly free from racial prejudice and his family are not, then you have a right to stand by him. You know what's right and what's wrong. As I've said before, follow your heart, see where it leads you. You did it once remember?

And it led you here." Sarah smiled, "and was that so bad?"

Tarni shook her head.

"Could I use the phone to ring New Zealand?

"Yes, please do."

Chapter 12

On the morning of Sarah and PJ's wedding, Harry walked over to Tarni's bungalow and asked if she could straighten his bow tie. She smiled seductively.

"It would have saved you the walk if you'd stayed here last night."

"You know I'd love to, Tarni, but I think we should behave ourselves under the watchful eye of PJ – for a while anyway."

Tarni straightened Harry's tie and then dressed herself in a dusky-pink, satin gown. The colour suited her skin tone and her hair, which she'd recently dyed auburn. The cream shoes and her beaded handbag complimented her dress.

At 11.30 am, Harry, Tarni and PJ, travelled to the church in the same car. The wedding ceremony was to begin at 1.30 pm. As expected, the bride arrived half an hour late. Sarah turned all heads with her grace and beauty as she glided down the aisle, arm in arm with her father, Wayne.

The catholic ceremony continued for almost an hour, before the one hundred guests could leave the church and throw confetti over the happy couple. The weather was almost perfect, while a gentle north east breeze toyed with flimsy fabrics and slightly disturbed the women's hair styles. Tarni held her dress down while trying to brush tears from her eyes.

"This is the first wedding I've ever been to, Harry. It's like a dream. Everyone and everything seems so beautiful and happy."

"I agree. And you look every bit as beautiful as the bride," he said.

Even if Harry was being kind, Tarni loved the way he spoke to her, sincere and with respect.

Tarni noticed a tall, older but still beautiful-looking nun talking with PJ's father, Patrick Snr. She asked Harry if he knew who she was.

"She must be Mother Superior, or Betty, as the family still calls her."

Tarni looked around. She couldn't mistake the very old, Chinese Doctor Liu, whom PJ had told her about.

"I can't wait to meet all the characters Sally's written about in her book." Tarni said to Harry. "I'm so excited to be here. I never dreamt life could be this good."

Harry leant over and kissed her.

"It'll only get better, Tarni. Believe me, I'll make you happy, I promise."

Ella was Sarah's only bridesmaid. She wore a soft crimson dress and carried a bouquet of cream roses. Tarni didn't mean to, but she stared at Ella thinking she looked as good as any plump, full-blooded Aboriginal girl could. Then she scolded herself for being flippant and judgemental. One day I'll invite Ella for a long lunch and then I'll find out exactly what her problem is, she promised herself.

Ella threw a superior look towards Tarni and Tarni smiled sweetly back not wanting unpleasant thoughts to cloud her day.

The crowd stood as one, waiting for Sarah and PJ to let loose the white doves they held in their hands. To the sound of a collected ahh, the doves flew high above their heads and were soon swallowed by the brightness of the sun.

*

The reception was held on Jonathon's property, 'Wildflowers'. Everything had been brought to magnificence. The gardens bloomed in splendour and the French champagne flowed along with the exquisite canapé's. The guests gathered in small groups, catching up with old acquaintances and friends. Tarni stayed close to Harry. He seemed to know most of their friends and all of the family, although he'd never actually met Betty or Mother Superior as was her correct title. Tarni pleaded with Harry to approach her, so they could introduce themselves. This became unnecessary as PJ's sister, Sally, insisted Tarni and Harry meet their beloved Betty.

"Please call her Mother Superior. She only accepts the Darcy clan belittling her superiority by calling her Betty," Sally said. Then she guided Tarni and Harry by the arm.

"Mother Superior, I would like you to meet our dear friends. This is Harry Brauer, a close friend of PJ's and this lovely young lady is Tarni Windsor, who is also an in-valuable working partner with PJ."

While holding out her hand, Betty smiled directly into Tarni's eyes. She then nodded towards Harry.

"I am pleased to meet you both. I've heard so much about the pair of you, especially you, Tarni. I believe you have aspirations of being a jockey. I can only say; may the Lord help you my child. I for one could not imagine galloping those enormous thoroughbreds and being able to control them in a race. It simply astounds me." Betty paused, then leant over, placed her hand on Tarni's shoulder. She lowered her voice almost to a whisper.

"I do enjoy a flutter though and I've been able to bless the poor box

101

lately with the money I've won on PJ's horses." She laughed a little as Tarni stood speechless, mouth agape. As she gazed into Betty's soulful eyes, Betty's hand remained on her shoulder. When Betty had stopped laughing, she said softly, "God has blessed you my child." Her words touched Tarni deeply and lifted her into another realm, one of total peace. She wanted to know more about this amazing woman, but Betty walked away under Sally's guiding hand. Harry noticed the trance-like state Tarni seemed to be in and was slightly amused.

"You seem in awe of Mother Superior. You're not thinking of becoming a nun are you, Tarni?" he chuckled but Tarni felt something different stir inside.

"I don't know. Maybe I will."

Harry simply shook his head laughing as they walked towards Doctor Liu, whom Tarni had also insisted on meeting. He was sitting alongside Granddad Jonathon. The two were in deep conversation before Jonathon noticed Tarni and Harry waiting to speak to him.

"Oh, there you are," Jonathon said. "What a handsome couple you make." He looked toward Dr Liu. "You don't think that was too presumptuous of me, do you Liu. You know, saying they looked like a couple?"

"I think you forgot manners Jon. You should intloduce me."

"Oh, I am sorry Liu. Yes, I am forgetting my manners. You haven't met Tarni as yet, but I'm sure you've met Harry before?"

"No, I only give Haly Chinese medicine. PJ say Haly had bad flu." Liu looked up at Harry as he said this.

"You lemember Haly? It makes you betta vely quick!"

Harry smiled, "Yes I remember, Dr Liu. It did help considerably."

"Yes, I know- vely good vely good. Now you, young lady. I fink you not eat too much. You take Docta Liu tonic for appetite. You need mo' meat on bone. Espesry you get married have babies."

Tarni burst out laughing, blushing at the same time.

"I'm very pleased to meet you too, Doctor Liu. I've heard so much about you. You've been a great friend of the Darcy's for generations it seems."

Liu stood with effort before slowly bowing towards Tarni.

"I thank you, Miss Tarni, but must ask. Pwease not lemind me how vely old I am. Thank you pwease." His contagious laugh rolled from him as he held her hand and shook it.

Harry and Tarni sat with Liu, enjoying conversations about many things, including Sarah's conquest in her human rights case. Tarni felt proud to be able to speak about it freely and intelligently in front of Harry, who seemed extremely interested in becoming involved.

Harry had one year left of his law study before he graduated. As yet, Tarni and he had not touched on the subject of whether Harry would remain in Adelaide to complete his studies or return to New Zealand. But after their talk with Jonathon and Dr Liu, Tarni felt a glimmer of hope that Harry would remain in Australia.

PJ's Uncle Angus approached the microphone, asking everyone to please take their seats inside the enclosure. Dinner would be served as soon as they'd welcomed the bridal party.

The tennis court had been enclosed and lined with white chiffon. From the temporary roof, hung crystal chandeliers; it looked truly amazing. James, PJ's older cousin, escorted Ella down the red carpet. He was introduced as the best man and Ella as the lovely bridesmaid. The applause continued and became deafening, when the bride and groom entered. Their happiness outshone the chandelier's.

Tarni and Harry were seated at a table with PJ's university friends. Tarni felt all eyes were upon her. She was sure her notoriety from the court case had flagged her appearance. However, with clever manipulation, Harry steered any topic that might embarrass Tarni away from discussion. He was her saviour and she would thank him later.

The evening was extremely entertaining, especially when Sarah made her speech. Tarni heard whispers, 'Brides are not supposed to make speeches at their own wedding' but Sarah soon had her critics rolling in the aisles. Her quirky humour and open-minded views on life with all its pitfalls did the trick. There were some speeches that were tear jerker's, especially from Jonathon. He never failed to mention his dearly, departed first wife, Sally. He also mentioned his best friend Jum Watt, who was PJ's deceased maternal grandfather. After the speeches, the guests were highly amused when Sally's inebriated French husband Alain, tried to read aloud the telegrams. Because of his now slurred French accent, he eventually needed help. Angus stepped in, but he'd forgotten his spectacles and as he tried to translate Alain's attempts into recognisable English, the situation became even funnier.

Sarah and PJ left the celebration at 11.00 pm and returned thirty minutes later, dressed and ready for their honeymoon. They'd decided to take a short visit to Queensland to see the Great Barrier Reef.

The single women gathered around, ready for Sarah to throw her wedding bouquet. Tarni was too shy to stand in the front along with most of the girls, so she stood behind. Sarah took one quick look over her shoulder and threw the bouquet towards Tarni, who caught it and smiled at Ella. She who was not impressed.

Harry and Tarni declined the offer to stay overnight at Wildflowers. They made the excuse that Tarni needed to be on the farm first thing. When travelling back home late at night, or early in the morning as it was by the time they left, Tarni usually fell asleep, but not tonight. She was still on a high from her Cinderella night and to have her Prince Harry beside her was the ultimate. Tarni's life seemed fulfilled in this new world, one she wanted to be part of for the rest of her life. She turned to Harry.

"I'm so happy, Harry," and she giggled. Her giggle always delighted him. "That rhymes; Happy Harry. I think it's a good name for a racehorse, Happy Harry. Yes, that's a great name. What do you think?"

"I think if you're going to name a horse after me, it had better be a champion!"

"We haven't named Kiwi Billy yet. We've been arguing about names for the past two months. His name has to be accepted by the SAJC, before we can register him. I'm going to suggest to PJ we call him, 'Happy Harry.' I don't think he'll buck at that because he'll be named after a great bloke."

Harry turned his head to say thank you and as he did a kangaroo jumped in front of the car. He swerved to miss it and lost control. Tarni screamed when she realised they were heading for a giant red gum.

When Tarni woke, she was in an ambulance with the sirens blaring.

"Where's Harry?" The ambulance officer didn't answer. "Where's Harry?" she screamed.

"He's okay love. He's in the other ambulance. Just relax you'll be fine and so will he – hopefully."

Chapter 13

Three months later and Harry was still in rehabilitation. His spine had been severely damaged, and the doctors informed them that he may never walk again. Luckily for Tarni, she was back riding horses within two weeks of the accident, but she stayed with Harry in the hospital whenever she could. Harry's parents had asked for him to be flown back to New Zealand and the cost didn't matter. But Harry wouldn't hear of it.

"I'm staying here with the woman I love until I make a full recovery. And one day I will walk Tarni down the aisle and marry her." He had been adamant.

Harry had proposed to Tarni on the first day he was able to stand unaided, which was exactly three months after the accident.

"I'll walk you down the aisle, Tarni, I promise."

With this statement, Tarni could only pray he hadn't been mentally impaired from the hit on the head he'd received in the accident. But she did know they were lucky to be alive. The ambulance officers and the rescue team said they'd not seen such a horrific accident where anyone had survived.

Under the circumstances, PJ and Sarah had decided they should not go on their honeymoon but Tarni had convinced PJ to go.

"We're lucky to be alive PJ, and you're a lucky man to have such a beautiful wife. So please, go and enjoy your honeymoon. We will be fine and so will the horses. I trust Craig to look after things for five days. He'll do a great job, so please don't worry."

Tarni's words came true. There'd been no problems on the farm at all. And now, three months later, she sat in PJ's office as he opened his mail. Tarni was there to ask if she could stay overnight in Adelaide - again.

"In the morning, the physio therapist is coming to see Harry. If he can walk a few steps, then he should make a full recovery and I want to be there to give him encouragement," Tarni said.

PJ listened while he opened an official letter sent to him from the Darwin Crown Prosecutor. Tarni sat explaining all about Harry's progress while PJ read the letter silently. It explained that the Darwin police had finally found

Robbo's remains. He had been identified from his teeth and the findings were under further investigation by their forensic scientists. The Coroner would soon give his conclusion in a written statement to the police. Patrick Darcy Junior and Miss Tarni Windsor would be informed in due course, when and where the inquiry was to take place. Patrick folded the letter and smiled warmly at Tarni before he said:

"Tarni, I'm so pleased. I truly believe Harry will walk as well as ever. And we all know what a big influence you've been in his recovery. I couldn't be happier for you and I can't wait to see you both walking down the aisle."

PJ paused and then hung his head a little. He was trying to build up the courage to tell Tarni she'd have to go to court for the inquiry. Tarni was about to thank PJ when she noticed the look on his face and also the letterhead.

"Is that letter from the Darwin police? What did it say?" Tarni sounded anxious, so PJ answered quickly.

"Yes, it is. The police found Robbo's remains."

"Well what does that mean? He just died out in the scrub while he was hiding I suppose. He probably ran out of water or something – died of thirst. People die of thirst all the time out in the bush. It hasn't got anything to do with me. They don't want me to go back there, do they?"

"I'm afraid we'll both have to go back, Tarni. The Coroner has called for an inquiry."

PJ noticed sweat beads forming on Tarni's forehead even though it was a cold, windy day.

"Are you alright Tarni? You shouldn't worry. It'll just be a formality."

"I'm not worried, PJ. I have nothing to hide. I didn't kill him."

Tarni stood quickly and hurried out the door. Calling over her shoulder she said:

"I'll just finish up and then Craig will drive me into Adelaide. I'll catch the bus home tomorrow."

PJ didn't have a chance to answer her as she'd disappeared too quickly. However, he phoned Sarah and told her what had happened.

"Maybe you ought to stay in Adelaide tonight Sarah, I think you should talk to Tarni. I'm sure she needs you. She seems worried about going back to Darwin and having to sit through a hearing."

"I will my love. I've already asked the nurse to put a stretcher bed beside Harry. I think Tarni would have slept on the floor if they hadn't agreed. I've offered for her to come and stay at our apartment many times, but she refuses. She won't let Harry out of her sight. I think now, the fact that Tarni will have to leave Harry when she goes to Darwin, may be bothering her more than you realise. But don't worry. I'll have a talk with her.

"That means I won't see you until tomorrow night my darling. I don't know how I'll be able to cope without your love." She pretended to cry, and then said brightly. "The baby's kicking like a bloody footballer, it must be a boy! Good night, PJ. I love you. I love you to bits. And then I'll love you even more! Kiss, kiss."

She slowly hung up the phone, thinking about what Tarni might be putting herself through. Mainly with the fact that she'd almost bitten Robbo's penis off, but after two years, Sarah was certain there would be no evidence of that. It would simply not exist and so Tarni may get away without saying a word about it.   Sarah placed her hand on her stomach and felt her baby kicking. She smiled with the joy, before buzzing Ella to send in her next patient.

*

Later at the hospital, when Sarah opened Harry's door, she stopped for a moment to take in the scene. Tarni sat next to Harry, her head lying on his stomach.

"Oh my God, Harry's not pregnant is he, Tarni?" Sarah screeched.

Harry's eyes opened and Tarni rose guiltily.

"Yes, I think he is Sarah. It's a miracle!"

"You've been mixing with me far too long, Miss Windsor! You're outdoing me with the comedy relief."

The three sat and chatted about Harry's progress and then of course the horses and in particular, how 'Happy Harry' was progressing towards the Melbourne Cup. Tarni was enthusiastic.

"That won't be until next year, of course. Happy's not strong enough for the cup yet. And anyway, he's got a long way to go before he qualifies. I don't think he'll have a problem though. He loves to work and he's very competitive. When I ride him alongside another horse, he relaxes that is until the pace quickens and then he just wants to keep that handsome head of his in front. He won't give in. And that's what will make him a great racehorse."

"You named the horse well then Tarni. Happy Harry is more than a fitting name. Just look at you Harry, the doctors said you may never walk again and tomorrow morning I'm sure you're going to do a lap of the hospital grounds! You really are looking fabulous. Now may I steal your fiancé for a moment?"

Harry, beaming with confidence nodded and Sarah and Tarni left the room. Sarah found a quiet corner in the waiting room and held Tarni's hand. Looking into her eyes, she said softly:

"Tarni, PJ phoned me this afternoon and asked if I would stay in Adelaide, so I could talk to you about the inquest. Now please remember, I know everything there is to know about you and Robbo. So, no holds barred Okay? Just tell me again, every little detail before and after and then we can work it out."

Tarni looked away but her body moved closer to Sarah.

"I keep thinking about what I did to Robbo, you know." Tarni turned her head and leant even closer, 'his thing'. Sarah contained her laughter with difficulty.

"Do you know the structure of a penis Tarni? I know you know the uses of it, but the structure?" Tarni shook her head.

"It is simply a mass of tissue which is highly sensitive to blood flow. There are no bones in a dick. So Robbo's' 'thing', as you put it, will have dissolved. The forensic scientist will not be able to fathom what you did. So don't worry."

"Do you mean I won't have to tell them what I did?"

"Exactly. I'm sure you won't have to. Together we'll write down and then rehearse what you are to say and then you're to stick to it. Don't be bullied into saying anything other than the truth. You won't have to tell them exactly where you bit him, you just say, I bit him. But that's only if they ask you."

"But what if they ask where I bit him?"

"Simple! Just say, 'I can't exactly say where, I was fighting for my life, I was in a frenzied panic'. You just bit him wherever you could. Have you ever spoken to Harry about Robbo or what happened to you?"

"No, I haven't. I can't bring myself to tell him. All he knows is PJ saved my life, but neither of us told him the whole truth. We've just said, I was about to take a swim in the river, when a crocodile attacked me, and it was lucky PJ was there with his 303 rifle."

"I see, Miss Winsor. PJ is your partner in crime, is he not?"

Tarni nodded with a smile,

"Well, I'm not much of a counsellor then am I. I should have spoken with you sooner about telling Harry the truth before it came to this. Now we're forced to tell him. I only hope he'll understand why you haven't told him before, especially with his proposal of marriage. But don't worry Tarni, I blame myself really. I don't think we should say anything to Harry until he is up and walking. And if you like, I will be with you to help you explain the Robbo incident. I think you should tell your entire life story to Harry, right from the beginning. He is sure to understand how you felt and why you fought for your honour. You really are to be congratulated, certainly not put down or even pitied. You have done an amazing job in turning your life and attitude around."

Sarah shook her head, contemplating.

"It's a shame. I think we were born before our time, Tarni. Me with my human rights campaign, and you, with your fight for women to ride as professional jockey's."

*

Two weeks passed, before PJ received another letter from the Darwin Crime Commission. He was told he and Tarni would have to be present at the Darwin Court House on the 14th of August. They were to attend an investigation into the death of a Mr. Robert Timer, in connection with Mr. Timer's alleged attempted murder of Miss Tarni Windsor.

PJ considered this date most inconvenient. Sarah would be nearing her final week of pregnancy, and Harry might be out of rehab by then and needing their help. Tarni feared that if she were not there to care for Harry, he would ask his mother to fly over to Australia. He may even fly back to New Zealand. This was the last thing she wanted.

PJ warned her.

"The inquest may turn into a manslaughter case, if the coroner is not satisfied with the findings."

Tarni had held a dark secret from PJ. After the crocodile attack, Drongo had visited her in the sick room. Gwen was in the next room speaking on the radio to the Flying Doctor Service at the time, so she never saw Drongo enter Tarni's room. Drongo knew there had been serious trouble brewing between Robbo and Tarni. His fears had been justified when he saw PJ pull up and carry her with blood pouring from her leg. Drongo waited until the coast was clear before he snuck into the room to see her. Robbo had made many enemies among the Indigenous community and his attempted murder of one of them, even though Tarni was not a full blood, was a crime against them all. Drongo had assured Tarni on his visit that Robbo would meet with the Aboriginal's most feared death: the pointing of the bone.

*

Two weeks before the Darwin court appearance, Harry was beginning to walk further every day. The time had now come for Tarni and Sarah to front Harry with the truth.

"This is it Tarni." Sarah said. "We made a deal. Now Harry's walking you have to tell him exactly what happened, tell him everything, especially how you felt. And trust me, it will make no difference to him loving you. If I'm

109

any judge of character, Harry will be compassionate, and he'll understand what you've been through." Sarah held Tarni's shoulders and searched her face.

"Is there anything more you want or need to tell me, before we go to Harry?"

"No, Sarah. You know all my secrets."

Tarni crossed her fingers, it's what she did if she told a lie.

"Well that's good. Now I can only hope I'm right about Harry. Allow me to lead the way into the lion's den. We shall face him together – paper tiger that he is." Sarah gave Tarni a reassuring wink.

Harry smiled brightly when both women walked into his room and sat by his bedside.

"Tarni I didn't think you were coming until tomorrow and now Sarah too. What a nice surprise having two great beauties bless me with their company."

"Well, three beauties if you count the baby." Sarah said, before she went headfirst into the reason they'd come to speak with him.

Harry took a deep breath and let it out slowly, "Okay, I'm ready. And I can assure you, I will not judge you Tarni, I—"

Sarah interrupted.

"I'll just go to the nurses' station and tell them we need some privacy for a while."

Tarni sat holding Harry's hand, her head down, not wanting to meet his eyes or speak until Sarah returned. When she did, Tarni stood and paced the room gathering her courage, then stopped by the window her bottom resting in the windowsill, she turned to face Harry. Sarah smiled, giving Tarni a nod of encouragement. She began on cue.

"My father was Irish. He had a beautiful caring soul, but sadly, he was killed in a mining accident at Coober Pedy. After his death, which nearly killed my mother because she was so heart broken. We went to live with Nelly. She was a full-blood Aboriginal who was a great friend of my grandmother. They'd known each other from when they were babies. They grew up like sisters and when they were teenagers they worked on the same property together. It was about forty-five miles south east of Adelaide. Apparently, the owner took a liking to my grandmother and she had his baby. The baby of course was my mother, so she was a half-caste. This meant she had to hide most of her life from the authorities or they would have taken her away. That's if they could have caught her." Tarni paused and smiled, looking out of the window.

"They called my mother Briar Rabbit. She could outrun the wind and outwit anyone. She was never caught and then of course she got past the age when they could legally take her away. When she was eighteen, she left to find work at Coober Pedy in the pubs. That's where she met my father. They fell in love and got married and then I came along. But being a quarter- caste, didn't make any difference to the authorities. They kept an eye on me until I was old enough to be fostered into a white family. My father started educating me when I was four years old. I learnt quickly, and I could read and write by the time I was four and a half. Dad insisted I spoke proper English', as he called it. 'None of that pidgin stuff,' he'd say. My dad protected me from the 'child thieves', not that there were too many out Coober Pedy way. We seemed to get away with it for a while, until Mum and I had to leave there after Dad was killed. She said she could get plenty of work around Victor Harbor with the fishing community and we could live with Nelly in her home for nothing. We did, and Mum supplied the food. We were happy there for over a year, until someone dobbed us in." Tarni sighed deeply, finding the strength to continue.

"The authorities came one day when we didn't expect them. We were sitting on the beach with a fishing line in the water, singing funny songs and laughing. They crept up behind us. There were four men and one woman. One of them grabbed me from behind and took me to a car. I was kicking and screaming, calling out for my mother to help me, but they held her so tight she couldn't get free. She bit and kicked like a mad woman, but two men and one woman were holding her. When Nelly got up from the sand, she started punching and kicking at the men. One of them threw a punch at her and she fell to the ground holding onto her face. My mother screamed. 'My baby, my baby. Don't take my baby. Please don't take my baby!'"

Tears welled and Tarni stopped to wipe them away. Harry used his pyjama sleeve to wipe his own tears and Sarah, her handkerchief. Tarni noticed.

"I'm sorry I can't help but cry when I remember that day. Thank you for crying with me. Do you want me to finish?" She asked hesitantly.

"Of course, Tarni. I need to know everything. I realise now how blessed my life has been compared to yours. Please go on," Harry said.

Tarni's story was quite a saga, including the truth about Robbo and how he'd tried to rape her many times, up until that fateful day when he'd driven her to the river, telling her they were going to deliver lunch to PJ. But he'd tricked her. He sped his ute past PJ, toward the river where the trees and scrub were dense.

"I had to think quick." Tarni looked deep into Harry's eyes and realized he was not judging but listening with his heart. "I'm ashamed to tell you this Harry." She took a deep breath then hung her head. "I told Robbo if he didn't rape me I'd go down on him." She dared not look at Harry again. Instead she kept her head down noticing the white linoleum floor glimmering like diamonds in a shaft of sunlight, it seemed to give her strength to endure the gruesome story. "When Robbo undid his fly I lowered my head slowly then bit his thing so hard I was sure it split in two. I jumped from the car but tripped and fell. He was screaming in agony, but he found the strength to grab his rifle and stagger out of the ute. By the time I got up, Robbo had the rifle pointed at my back. I was going to take my chances and swim across the river, but I could see crocodile eyes watching me I turned around to beg him not to kill me, but he laughed and said, 'turn around again, look what's waiting for ya! Ya think ya can tame anything, well tame that fuckin croc ya black bitch.' Tarni lifted her eyes to see the anger and hurt Harry obviously felt for her predicament, he moved towards her. She shook her head while holding her hand against his chest.

"Let me finish. I heard a crackling sound in the scrub and looked over to see PJ, just before the crock grabbed my leg from behind. I screamed and fell forward, then a shot rang out and then another. I wasn't sure if it was from Robbo's gun, Or PJ's, but I heard him telling Robbo to put the gun down. The next thing I knew, I was freed from the jaws of the dying crock and PJ was then putting a bandage around my wound. I felt faint, but I could make out that Robbo drove off in his ute at a hundred miles an hour." Silence and stillness emanated for a long moment before Harry moved closer to Tarni. Lifting her pretty head he gazed into her deep chestnut eyes.

"I can't believe any human being could do those things Tarni. I don't know how I would've reacted if I were you. All I can tell you is I was not strong like you. I needed to learn how to fight for myself and if it weren't for PJ's help all those years ago, I don't know where I would have ended up. But you have a great inner strength – an un-relenting spirit. I admire you Tarni."

"I call her an archangel." Sarah butted in.

Harry smiled, "That's a good name tag."

After letting go of these emotions, and now having the man she loved understand, even admire her, Tarni felt overcome. She threw her body into Harry's arms and wept.

"It's alright Tarni. I love you even more now you've told me. I'll protect you forever." He thought about what he'd just said and laughed before saying. "Although come to think of it, I think you might be the one protecting me!"

Sarah let out a huge sigh, she loved it when stories turned out the way they should.

"Oh my God, this is like a fairy tale. The princess has finally met her real prince! But now I have some, not so good news for you Harry. The Princess has to go to Darwin and face the web of intrigue regarding Robbo. Thank heavens PJ is going to be with her. He's been Tarni's Guardian if you like. It was the only way the Darwin police would allow her to leave the Northern Territory. So now they have to return together and sit through an inquest into the death of Robert Timer. Can you believe it? Why don't they just say, 'well isn't that a bloody good solution. We've found his bones and saved the taxpayers a lot of money'."

"Unfortunately, it doesn't happen like that, Sarah," Harry said.

Immediately, he thought about the consequences of what had happened between Tarni and Robbo before he disappeared without a trace. He held Tarni's hand.

"Tarni, I certainly don't want to alarm you, but I've studied cases like this. In the Northern Territory, the police seem hell-bent on proving that Aborigine's take the law into their own hands. They may want to use you as an example. I know you couldn't possibly have anyone better on your side than PJ, but I'd still like to be there. I'm going to see if I can be released from hospital earlier than planned. I'm able to use a wheelchair to get around and I can walk unaided for short periods of time, so I don't see how I'd be a burden."

Tarni was lost for words, she looked at Sarah, who answered for her.

"I'll talk to the specialist if you like, Harry. I should be able to explain the situation, not any better than you of course, but I'll explain it with less emotion. If you go pleading through your heart, I'm afraid the doctor's will say no. Doctors think in clinical terms; I know because my grandfather was a doctor."

"I understand what you mean, Sarah. I'll take up your offer. But if you don't have any luck, then I'll simply sign myself out!"

Sarah raised an eyebrow.

"I believe you would Mr Brauer!"

After Sarah's convincing argument, the doctors relented. Sarah's plea had worked, and Harry was released into her care.

Chapter 14

Two days before the hearing date, PJ, Tarni and Harry, waved goodbye to a heavily pregnant Sarah. She only admitted to herself how concerned she was at the length of time the inquest might take. She knew if there were any suspicious circumstances about Robbo's death, then they may have to spend weeks in Darwin. She shunned the thought.

Sarah had also decided to hold onto some heart-breaking news, knowing very well this was not the time to tell Tarni. She had just been informed that their case against the authorities in charge of Aboriginal children had been over-ruled, and she would be unable to take any further action for another twelve months. This was the law.

The morning before PJ's departure, Sally, his sister, was at the publishing company finalising her book deal.

She left the office and returned to her home at Victor Harbour, where her husband, Alain, had many years before, set up a successful lobster trawling business.

Together they sat on their generous veranda, almost mesmerised by the gentle motion of the lapping waves, when Sally confessed to Alain.

"You made the right choice buying this business my darling. I love it here.

But, you know it's times like these, when PJ and Tarni are facing this drama, that I'd love to get back into journalism. I'd like to be there to make sure Tarni's hearing is relayed to the public with honesty and without bias. I have a feeling this may turn into a witch hunt."

Alain hadn't seen the old fight in Sally lately, not since the war days in fact when she was a proverbial Lioness. He just smiled at her suggestion before heartily agreeing that she should go. There was actually no point disagreeing, as Sally would have her own way whenever she thought it appropriate. This is what Alain loved and admired in her.

"Why don't you get in-touch with your old friend and chief of the Adelaide newspaper? I'm sure 'e would be 'appy for you to do an independent story on the 'earring. 'E would buy it for sure!"

"I'm so lucky I found you, Alain. In fact, I think I'm the luckiest woman alive." Sally moved from her chair, placed her arms around his neck, kissed him and sat on his lap.

"You don't mind then if I fly to Darwin tomorrow?" She smiled coyly, "I must admit I've already booked my flight."

Alain simply held her closer and placed a kiss on her neck. She stroked his hair and then rose from his embrace.

"I'll phone my old boss and put in my request. I'll be guided by what he says of course. If it's a 'no go', then I'll just start writing that romantic novel I've been promising you."

Alain laughed.

"Ah, in that case I 'ope 'e says no, because I am looking forward to your sexy story, ma Cherie."

A long passionate kiss followed, before Sally walked inside to make her phone call. The Chief Editor agreed with her proposal.

"It's a story worth telling truthfully, and I know I can count on you to do that, Sally. You know, you're still a darn good looker and television will become the next biggest media outlet. There will be endless opportunities for a woman of your experience and beauty. Please don't say no to the idea. Just think about it on your way to Darwin."

Sally then rang her mother, Addy, they spoke about her plans to go to Darwin. How she'd cover the case as an independent journalist. She then laughed while telling Addy about the TV offer from her boss. She was not so amused.

"I think he's right Sally. You'd look great on television. You're so beautiful, and you look ten years younger than you are. How old are you now?"

Sally laughed. "You must be getting old, Mum, if you can't remember my birthday."

"I remember your birthday. I just can't remember how old you are?"

"I'm forty-four, Mum, and I'm too old to be going back to work full-time, especially in such a demanding job as television. I'd have to live in Adelaide, and I don't want to. I'd better go now; I need to pack my bags. I've made a reservation to fly out in the morning."

"No, don't go, Sally, I mean don't hang up, because your father and I have been talking and we also booked a flight to Darwin. We feel it's important the family support PJ and of course Tarni. Besides, I've never stayed in Darwin. So your father and I are going to turn this trip into a holiday. He says it will be our second honeymoon and you know Sally; I don't think we ever had a first one. He was shipped off to Cairo and I was up to my neck in learning surgical techniques."

"Well, I'm pleased you're going to make it a holiday Mum, because the inquest may be over in a day. It sounds great, so you'd better go pack your bags. I love you. Give my love to Dad. I can hear him in the background laughing, who's there with him?"

"Nobody. He's watching the 'I Love Lucy show'. He never misses it."

Chapter 15

It seemed miraculous, that on the morning of the hearing, most of the Darcy family had gathered for breakfast in the same Darwin hotel. A shocked PJ had not been informed, or even given a clue about his family being there. Tarni was looking a little overwhelmed and Harry found it amusing to see the throng of supporters, especially when two additional family members surprised them at the buffet breakfast. Marjorie and Jonathon literally floated in, looking healthy and cheerful.

"Good morning everyone. What a lovely morning it is," Jonathon said light-heartedly.

Patrick Snr nearly choked on his toast when he saw his father smiling, wearing a red and white Hawaiian shirt, white trousers and shoes.

"Dad, you look so well, I've never seen you dressed like that before. I'd say you look very relaxed and very bright!"

"Yes, well, Patrick, I needed to look a little less like me. I want to fit in with the locals. I've done my investigation work on the case beforehand, so I thought perhaps I should attend the inquiry incognito. That way, I'll be able to adjudicate privately."

Jonathon sat next to PJ and across the table from Patrick Snr. He leant forward and lowered his voice.

"I think what will be in our favour gentlemen, particularly after speaking with Murdoch, is that the Northern Territory police won't want to be written up with any more smears of racism added to their reputation. As it is, there is an ongoing case with an Indigenous man called Max Stuart, which has been put on hold by a British order instructing the Australian Government and the Northern Territory Police Force, to deal with the Stuart case honestly and in an un-bias fashion. If not, a Royal commission would be instigated. Therefore, Tarni's inquest has been blessed with perfect timing."

PJ leant closer to his grandfather's ear.

"I know your right Granddad, but I think there's another conspiracy going on as we speak."

Jonathon seemed alarmed.

"What is it, PJ. What are your suspicions. Please tell me."

PJ could hardly contain his laughter.

"It's called the Darcy Clan Conspiracy. Apparently, the whole family are undercover holiday seekers!"

With that the mood lightened. Soon after, they made their way to the courthouse looking like the new gang in town.

Jonathon lowered his head, looked over his sunglasses and in a whisper to PJ, he said:

"This inquiry will be judged only by the coroner and thank heavens, I know him. I am therefore assuming it will be heard and settled favourably in less than two hours!"

PJ put his arm around the old man's shoulders and gave him an affectionate squeeze.

The first person to take the stand was PJ. After swearing to tell the truth, he was asked by the Coroner to please explain the string of events, which led him to witness the attempted murder of Miss Tarni Windsor. Exactly what did he see and how did he react. With intelligence and an educated understanding of the Law, PJ told his story in fine detail. He was then asked a few more personal but relevant questions and PJ's answers seemed to please the Coroner.

Tarni was then summoned and although nervous, she gathered inner strength and took time to explain the reason why she thought Robert Timer had attempted to murder her. It basically came down to the fact that she'd continuously fought off his sexual advances.

"Yes," she said, "I've fought off Robert Timer's attempted rape many times, but I always escaped. I complained to the station manager, Ian Davies, about Robbo trying to rape me. But Mr Davies would only try to calm me down and then he'd talk me out of reporting Robbo to the police. This happened three times."

Tarni was then asked if she knew of, or if she'd heard of any payback towards Robert Timer on her behalf. For example, did she know if any of her Indigenous friends had conspired to 'point the bone', or in Aboriginal terms, use the Kundela method to take Robert Timers life? Her answer was definite.

"No Sir." She crossed her fingers.

The Coroner then asked Tarni, if she was aware of the fact that Robert Timer was also part Aborigine. Tarni was not fazed by this question. However, PJ was. He was unaware of Robbo's Indigenous blood. Once again, her answer was definite.

"Yes Sir."

PJ had also written in his testimony that Robert Timer had mistaken Tarni's notable horsemanship skills, as being a personal attack on his ability to handle and break in horses. Patrick had witnessed Robbo's physical abuse of Tarni when he'd pushed her away from the horse she was near, or he'd trip her up if she walked too close to him. And then, after PJ had praised Tarni's talent with horses to Robert, Robert rebuked Patrick's praise and threatened to show her a thing or two when the time was right. This was read out in court, while Tarni remained in the witness box.

Tarni was asked, if she found this statement to be correct. She agreed with everything PJ had written and then added.

"It didn't matter what I did or what I said about horses, Robbo would laugh at me. He'd say I was an idiot and I didn't know anything. He said the horses had to be shown who was boss and then he'd be cruel to them. Horses hated him. They only had to smell him coming and they'd run away."

Sally was writing down every word and took note of the body language towards Tarni from the Coroner and the forensic scientist. In her opinion, they seemed to be in awe of this young woman's beauty and probably a little surprised that Tarni called herself Aboriginal. Sally was very rarely wrong about people, particularly about what they were thinking. Her years as a resistance fighter in the Second World War – maybe.

Jonathon felt confident that the Coroner could not possibly attach Robert Timers death to Tarni. And he could only hope that they wouldn't drag this inquiry out with hearsay, based only on suppositions. Jonathon smiled and nodded at Tarni when she stepped down from the witness box, giving his sign of approval.

The Coroner only then, realised who the man in the red and white Hawaiian shirt was. Of course, he's Jonathon Darcy, retired QC and Magistrate. The Coroner lowered his head and smiled to himself before declaring.

"I have one more person I wish to question."

PJ looked around and could see no one of importance to the case. He then noticed the guard leaving the room. Moments later, he returned with Ian Davies, the Merriola station manager.

After being sworn to tell the truth Ian, had to admit to the Coroner that Tarni had been honest in her confession. Yes, Ian had talked her out of reporting Robbo to the police on three occasions. He also agreed that Robbo was a violent man and he'd thought often about firing him from the property.

"The only reason I never fired him, was he was a solid worker. He never complained about what he had to do, or how many hours straight he had to work," Ian said.

Davies seemed humble when he stepped down from the box. He left the court room after nodding with a pained expression towards PJ and Tarni.

The Coroner then announced:

"A lunch break will be taken. The Hearing will resume at 2.00 pm. I will then deliver my findings."

He then asked for the forensic scientist, Gavan Spear, to enter his chambers.

The Coroner, Phillip Keeling, sighed deeply, before he sat behind his desk. He then asked his friend to sit.

Before his behind had touched the leather chair, Gavan Spear asked.

"And so, Phillip, I assume you've decided not to call upon your final witness. I believe he calls himself Drongo, but I think his name is David Smith. He only speaks pidgin. But you know that of course. I find it hard to understand these pidgin speakers." Phillip huffed, smiling as he did.

"Yes, you're right, Gavan. However, I did have a translator at the ready." He sat back in his chair pondering for a moment, before he spoke again.

"I have to tell you, Gavan. I've decided not to call on David, mainly because of the circumstances surrounding our Northern Territory justice system and our reputation at the moment. With all that has been written in the national newspapers, it seems we've been portrayed as being unjust and biased against the blacks. Mind you, it's not that I'm overly concerned about their opinion, but Jonathon Darcy is sitting in the back of the room. I know he's been on this case, right from the start, behind the scenes of course, but he does have a massive pull with Murdoch. One small hint that we may have begun an unsubstantiated claim of attempted murder against this, may I say beautiful young woman and we'll be snowed under! Plus, Jonathon's granddaughter Sally Laurent appears to be writing a piece about the hearing. So whatever Jonathon misses out on, she will report back to Murdoch. I'm telling you, Gavan, they have their guns aimed and their fingers on the trigger."

"Well then, just between you and me, Phillip, do you think as I do that the Aborigines did away with Robert Timer?"

"I'm only assuming they did. Please think about it Gavan. Does he sound like a man who didn't deserve it?"

"Well yes, I suppose he did. But we shouldn't allow these people to take the law into their own hands."

Phillip leaned forward in his chair and put his point across forcefully.

"Of course not, Gavan. However, in this case it may be too difficult to prove and I'm sure it would drag on forever. I've decided to let it go, an eye for an eye. The young woman seems to have the entire Darcy clan supporting her. So she must be a worthwhile project. Also, this Tarni Windsor has been the main witness in a human rights case which Jonathon's grandson's wife, Sarah Brown-Darcy, has begun. She's started an all-out war with the Australian Government to have the laws changed regarding the rights of half-caste children and their families. I tell you Gavan, no matter which way we turn they have us covered."

Phillip leaned back in his chair and studied the expression on Gavan's face. He wasn't sure if he'd convinced his friend that they should simply call Robert Timers death, 'a death by misadventure'. But why did he have to persuade Gavan, when there really wasn't enough evidence. And the main witness, Drongo, would probably be laughed out of court?

No, he'd made his decision and he wasn't going to procrastinate.

Meanwhile, the Darcy clan had gathered in a nearby café. Jonathon tried to put his family's minds at rest. He explained that he still had faith in humane reasoning. And in this case, it should be fair to all. Because Robbo had attempted to murder Tarni due to his contempt for women, he had brought about his own death.   And while there may have been a motive to kill Robbo, the Coroner was unable to offer any findings derived from a forensic investigation, as to why he'd died. He only had the obvious assumption that the Indigenous people had used Kundela, or he'd died of thirst?

By five minutes to two, the Darcy clan had returned to the court room. They waited in silence for the Coroner to enter. When he finally appeared, he gave a short summary.

"I have studied what has been said and written under oath, and I have come to my decision. Robert Timer's death will be recorded as a misadventure. Thank you everyone. You may now leave the court room." He looked toward Jonathon.

"Except you, Sir Jonathon Darcy. Would you kindly give me a moment of your time? In my office if you don't mind."

Phillip opened the door for Jonathon and upon closing it, he laughed.

"I simply need to know where you purchased that shirt Jonathon."

"I'm surprised you haven't bought one, Phillip. They sell them in every clothing shop in Darwin!"

The two shook hands before sitting to discuss the case. Both men agreed it was highly likely that Robbo was a victim of some sort of intervention by the Indigenous people from the mission where Tarni had lived.

"I must thank you, Phillip, for seeing the bigger picture and for not letting this case drag on unnecessarily. However, I feel sure Tarni would have had nothing to do with the death of Robert Timer."

Phillip's manner then changed.

"That is where you're wrong, Jonathon. I held back a witness today. He would have said the opposite, but I chose not to call him to the stand. I'm simply warning you that this young woman may have another side to her personality, which you and your family have not seen yet. The main reason I chose not to call Miss Windsor's Aboriginal friend David Smith, or Drongo as they call him, was his pidgin English is almost unfathomable and our interpreter is unreliable. And, as you said, Jonathon, I was looking at the bigger picture. But actually, it's more like an enormous jigsaw puzzle. I felt it's not the time, nor a case we should try and solve with innuendos. All I will say, is please keep an eye on this young woman."

Jonathon could have argued with Phillip, because right from the beginning, he'd liked Tarni and felt she had a good soul. Yes, she certainly had a fighting spirit and this they'd heard about in court today. Surely this was the only side of Tarni that Phillip was talking about. Jonathon chose to leave it there and thanked Phillip once again for his fair and quick deliberation.

PJ and company were content to stay one more night in Darwin, simply because no flights were available until the next morning. Therefore, PJ, Harry and Tarni had the opportunity to celebrate with PJ's parents and grandparents, who'd decided to remain in Darwin to do the usual tourist thing. After Darwin, they would visit some of the wonders of the Northern Territory, including Uluru. A two-night stay at Alice Springs would end their holiday and then they'd return home just before their third grandchild was due to be born.

Chapter 16

When PJ returned to Adelaide airport, he put Tarni and Harry on a bus headed for home. Then he rang Sarah's mother, Alice, with whom Sarah had been staying. He was informed that Sarah had been taken to hospital. Before Alice had time to say, 'don't worry', PJ slammed the phone down, ran to his car, jumped in and pushed the pedal to the floor.

Sarah was in a private room looking every bit the angel. Her strawberry blonde hair, cascading over the pillow and her white satin night gown flowing over her curves. Although PJ stood enthralled by her beauty, he was also upset.

"You look so beautiful Sarah. But I'm angry. Why didn't you send me a telegram?"

"Thank you for the compliment my darling, but I didn't think it necessary to worry you. They call my condition toxaemia, which means my kidneys, along with other organs aren't functioning properly due to bacteria build-up. I just need to rest and drink plenty of water to flush out the toxins. Please don't worry. I'm fine and the baby is too." Sarah said with a convincing smile.

"Are you sure? Are you telling me the truth? The baby isn't in any danger, is he? And what about you, will this affect you having more children?"

Sarah laughed.

"I am telling you the truth. I think if it was 1859 and not 1959, then I may be in a spot of bother. But medicine has come a long way and I'm being monitored every hour. If there's a problem, then I'll have a caesarean." She furrowed her perfect eyebrows, then continued with her smile in place.

"In a way I'd rather that. I'm not looking forward to pushing this very lively baby out into the world and I'm sure, he, or she, would rather just have the lid lifted. Yes, it would be much easier for both of us." She then gave a fake sigh, placing her hand upon her forehead.

"You're very convincing Sarah. I suppose I'll have to believe you, because I need to get back to the farm." A passionate kiss was shared before PJ left.

Soon after, Mother Superior (Betty), appeared in Sarah's room with what seemed like an ethereal aura surrounding her. The soft golden light remained as she walked to Sarah and placed a gentle kiss on her forehead.

"You simply light up the room with your presence Mother." Sarah's quick wit put an end to having her mouth ajar at the vision. "It's so nice of you to visit, as long as you're not here to give me my last rights!" She giggled, and Betty joined her.

"Heavens no, Sarah. I'd heard you were in hospital and that you would be here until the birth. I've come to inform you that you and your baby have been blessed. All will go well with the birth and thereafter. May I sit down?"

"Of course, Mother and thank you for your blessing. Would you like me to ask the nurse for a cup of tea? How do you like it?"

"No please don't fuss, Sarah. I'd like to talk to you about Tarni. You see I had a visit from Sally."

Sarah cocked her head in puppy dog fashion.

"When was this Mother? Sally shouldn't be home yet, she stayed in Darwin for a couple more days, to be with her parents."

Betty, smiled, taking Sarah's hand in hers. "I mean PJ's grandmother, Sally."

"But she's … "Sarah said, more shocked than surprised.

"I know she's gone from this world. But she is not dead spiritually. Sally comes to me from time to time. She has asked me to tell Tarni that she must go and visit the old lady who cared for her. She has something important to tell her. I know you give counselling to Tarni, Sarah, but you are also a very good friend. I know she loves and respect's you, so you should be the one to tell her. She may not listen to me."

"I hope you don't mind me saying so Mother, but this all sounds a little spooky."

Betty laughed, "I know and sometimes I get a little spooked myself when they appear."

"You mean you see other ghosts too?"

"I don't call them ghosts dear; I call them spirits. We are all spirits wrapped up in skin. When we die we simply shed our skin. Does that explain it a little better?"

"I suppose so, but I probably won't see Tarni until after the birth."

"I think you should ask PJ, if he could bring her with him when next he visits you, because the elderly lady, who Tarni must talk to, is about to leave for heaven." Betty paused, seeming to speak silently with someone – who wasn't there. She then nodded her head in agreement. "Maybe you should phone PJ now, Sarah."

Sarah began to wonder if Mother Superior had lost her marbles.

"Are you able to give me this elderly lady's name Mother? I ask because Tarni knows several elderly ladies who have cared for her along the way."

"I'm sorry, I wasn't told her name, but I felt the urgency of the message. I hope you don't think me a delusional old fool, Sarah. I'm simply God's messenger, or Sally's in this case."

"Not at all, (insincerity smothered), I'm just trying to think who this woman could be. And there's also Mrs Stenning, the lady Tarni lived with in Adelaide before she moved to the farm with PJ."

Betty stood, crossed her chest and gave a silent prayer over Sarah, before excusing herself.

"I have to leave now Sarah. I mustn't be late for Mass. I'll leave you to deliver the message. I'm sure Tarni will know who the woman is that she needs to talk to. The Lord is with you and your baby dear. I shall visit you again when the baby is born, if I may?"

"Of course, Mother, and once again, thank you for your blessings and be assured I will phone PJ straight away."

PJ had driven his sports car to the max, arriving at the farm in record time. He needed to make sure all was well with the horses, and if so, he intended to return to Adelaide to be close to Sarah. Despite what she'd said, he couldn't help but worry.

He found Tarni, along with Harry, standing in the main barn talking with Craig about Happy Harry's progress. Tarni turned with a broad smile.

"Hi, PJ. Craig tells me we have a real star in our stable. Happy beat Joseph Peedy's best horse this morning - hard-held. He clocked him running thirty-four over three furlongs! He's no slouch PJ. If he can stay, and we know he will, then he's on his way to the Cup next year. I think he'll be spot-on for that seven-furlong race at Murray Bridge in two weeks' time and I reckon he'll be hard to beat."

PJ didn't want to burst Tarni's bubble with his worrying news about Sarah, so he went along.

"Sounds great, Tarni." PJ then turned to Craig. "So you have a good feeling about Happy Harry do you, Craig?"

"Yes boss, I reckon he's the best horse I've ridden. Well on the track that is. He still has to prove it in a race though. But I reckon he might just do that at Murray Bridge."

Craig gave Tarni a nudge and who looked a little uncertain before she asked PJ.

"Umm …, PJ, Craig and I have been talking. Would you consider taking Craig on as an apprentice jockey?"

PJ hadn't missed the nudge and he smiled.

"I don't see why not. But are you sure you wouldn't like to have another go at being the first woman jockey to ride in Australia? The SAJC Committee has a few younger, open-minded members now. You haven't given up your dream have you Tarni?"

"No, PJ. I have other more important things to occupy me at the moment." She looked lovingly at Harry. "I think it would be best to have a talk with Harry before I go down that path again."

Harry, still a little shaky on his feet, although well on his way to a full recovery, had only that morning made plans to attend Adelaide University and finish his law degree. It had been agreed beforehand that he would live in PJ's unit at Glenelg while attending uni. Harry held onto Tarni, mainly for balance before he looked down at her.

"You know I'd never stop you from doing anything you really want to do Tarni. In my opinion, if you do nothing, you're a talent going to waste."

"Hang on a minute," PJ said. "Tarni certainly isn't wasting her talent around here. I don't know what I'd do without her. This brings me to the point. I need to go and stay in Adelaide to be close to Sarah. Do you think you and Craig could handle the load here Tarni? I'll drive back on fast work mornings to see how the horses are going, but I feel I should be with Sarah at the moment. I know she's not worried, but I can't help it. This is my first child and I'm as nervous as a pregnant nun!"

They laughed, especially when Harry said:

"You'd be in trouble if Mother Betty heard you say that, PJ."

"And don't I know it!" PJ replied before walking away towards the house. He quickened his pace when he heard the telephone ring. His heart raced, fearing the worst.

"Sarah, what's wrong is everything all right?"

Sarah sighed.

"Please stop worrying about us PJ. Mother Superior, or Betty as you still call her, paid me a visit today and not only to see me, but to ask if I would give a message to Tarni. I figured you would have arrived home by now, seeing you're a speed demon!" Her voice turned to a plea. "I wish you'd leave racing to the horses, PJ and drive a little slower. Will you please drive carefully my love? Remember we'll have precious cargo travelling with us soon."

"I promise I will, Sarah. Now tell me, what's the message I have to give Tarni?"

"Well, it's a bit spooky. Mother Superior said, she was paid a visit by your grandmother Sally."

"What!"

"That's how I reacted. However, she assured me it was normal for her. The spirits as she calls them, not ghosts, come to her all the time. Apparently yesterday, or last night I think she said, grandmother Sally came and told Mother Superior, that Tarni should go and see the old woman who cared for her, as she had an important message to give her. And that's it, she didn't elaborate. She couldn't give me the old woman's name, all she said was, Tarni would know who she meant. So whether I give Tarni the message or you do, I don't see how it would matter. But Mother was adamant that Tarni receive this message as soon as possible, because the old woman will soon be on her way to heaven."

Patrick sat silent for a moment contemplating what he'd heard.

"PJ, are you still there?"

"Yes, Sarah. I was just wondering who the old woman was. It could be Mrs Stenning. I don't think Tarni's spoken to her for a long time. But then I suppose she'd just ring Tarni if she had something to tell her?"

"The only woman who comes to my mind is, old Nelly. You remember, PJ, Tarni's grandmother's friend who took her and her mother in before Tarni was taken away. Nelly cared for Tarni's mum until she passed away. I wonder if Nelly would still be alive. She must be well into her eighties, or even early nineties now."

"I'll go and ask Tarni and see if she knows who it might be. And then I'm coming back to Adelaide to be close to you. I love you Sarah, I'll see you soon."

PJ hung up the receiver before Sarah had a chance to say, 'No please don't come, I'm fine.'

He then went to find Tarni, and as usual she was tending Happy Harry.

"Tarni, I have message from Sarah, via Mother Superior. Come to my office and we can talk." Once Tarni entered and seated herself, PJ filled her in. Immediately she felt the spirit of Nelly surround her, singing to her.

"I feel guilty, PJ. I should've checked to see if Nelly was still alive. I can't remember when I last spoke to her. I assumed she would be dead by now. Maybe I should ring the council at Victor Harbor, they'd know if she were still alive wouldn't they?" The spirit was still in the room. Maybe she'd just passed over?

"Yes, they probably would, but are you sure Nelly is the one?"

"Nelly's spirit is here with me PJ. I'm not sure if she has passed, or she is calling for me to come while she is still here. There were others, but none were as close to me as Nelly. I feel her. She's singing to me."

*

PJ shuddered with the thought. He then phoned Victor Harbor Council, all they could tell him was that Nelly's shack had been demolished and they believed she had been taken to the old people's home. However, that was two years ago, and they weren't sure if she was still alive, because the lady who kept the birth and death records, wasn't' there today. PJ phoned the old people's home. He introduced himself and asked if an elderly Aboriginal lady named Nelly Eagle lived there.

"Yes, Mr Darcy. However, Nelly is not well. She's been delirious for the past few days. She only talks in her native tongue and sings a lot. So we're unable to understand what she's saying. If you wish to see Nelly, I suggest you come quickly because we don't think she'll be with us long."

"Thank you. I'll let my young friend Tarni know. She and her mother spent time living with Nelly and that was many years ago. Tarni would like to see Nelly before she passes."

"Tarni, you say? I'm sure that's the name Nelly keeps repeating."

After PJ had hung up, he turned to Tarni.

"It seems Nelly is definitely the old woman who wants to see you. The carer told me Nelly keeps repeating your name over and over. If you like I can drive you there now. It should only take an hour."

Tarni agreed, "though I think more like half an hour the way you drive PJ." PJ smiled a devilish grin then phoned Sarah to let her know.

Once again, Craig was left in charge of organising the afternoon work, although Harry offered to stay and help fill up the water buckets.

"At least I'm not totally helpless," Harry said to Tarni before he kissed her goodbye.

It was 2.00 pm when they arrived at the Victor Harbor Nursing Home. After entering the building, they were welcomed by the sister in charge, who then showed them to Nelly's room. Nelly seemed at peace while she slept. Tarni walked up and placed a kiss on her forehead. Nelly's eyes opened slightly, trying to focus on the young woman whose face she'd known as a child. Nelly breathed in the familiarity, before speaking in her Nunga tongue.

"Hello Nelly, yes it's been a long time." Tarni said in the same language.

"That really you Tarni? You heard me singing you." Nelly asked her

128

voice husky and trembling. Tarni held her hand and smiled lovingly.

"Yes, Nelly. It's me, I heard you so I came."

The old woman held onto Tarni's hand and while she jabbered in her native tongue, her eyes never left Tarni's. She kept nodding in agreement, replying to Nelly in Nunga. As she spoke, Nelly showed sadness and Tarni would hold Nelly's hand up against her lips and felt their deep spiritual connection. Their talk went on for more than twenty minutes. Just before the old woman's strength had almost left, she reached out to embrace Tarni. Nelly's body then became limp. Tarni lay her down and kissed her. Then she looked up at PJ, tears rolling down her cheeks.

"We best go now. Nelly needs to leave us, and she won't while we're still here." Tarni said, while sniffling back tears. As they headed for the door PJ asked:

"Are you okay Tarni? Would you like a coffee?" He rubbed her back as they stood there.

"Yes, thanks, I'm okay. It's so sad though I feel guilty for not checking in on Nelly before." Tarni wiped her tears away and gave a faint smile. "Coffee would be good. I'll let you in on all she's told me while we're driving home." Tarni cast one last, loving look at Nelly before she closed the door.

In the car and between sobbing and sipping her coffee, Tarni began to relate Nelly's information.

"My grandmother Biny and Nelly were both happy teenagers, best friends if you like. They'd often go on walkabouts together. One day when they were walking along the Darling Riverbank, heading towards Adelaide their home, they came across an old swagman. He looked dead to Nelly, so she crept up close and felt the pulse on his neck. There was a very faint pulse, but Nelly said he was about to die for sure. He was unconscious, and his right hand was clenched around something big. Biny, Tarni's grandmother, unfolded his hand and found an enormous opal. They searched his nap sack and found some smaller ones. Nelly said they didn't want to be blamed for killing him and stealing his stones and then they became scared. But they knew the colourful stones were worth a lot of money in the white man's world, so they ran away with the opals, making sure they covered their tracks well.

"They were going to give the opals to a white man that they knew and trusted. His camp was not too far from their tribe. They thought he could sell them and then give most of the money to their people. Nelly said it was quicker to go home by the roadway and it wasn't long before a strange white man stopped his horse and buggy and asked if they needed a lift. Nelly spoke a little English due to their white friend teaching them a few basic words. The man in the buggy smiled and offered them sweets. He seemed very nice, so they accepted his offer. He kept on driving even when Nelly said. 'Here, you stop here mister.' He smiled saying, 'I live not too far away, I will take you home to my place and give you food for your family, and then I'll drive you back in the morning.' Nelly wasn't too sure about him, but she said my grandmother, Biny, liked the man. She sat very close and giggled when he patted her on the knee. He kept smiling at her all the time. Nelly said my grandmother was very pretty and all the boys liked her." Tarni sighed deeply and looked out the window for a moment before she continued.

"It took two days for them to reach his property. When the man finally pulled the horses up, Nelly noticed Aboriginal half cast children running around. The man's overseer was white, and it appeared he had an Aboriginal wife. She had a half cast baby boy in her arms. She seemed friendly and smiled when she came to meet them. This Aboriginal wife took them to a small cottage and showed them to the bathroom and told them to wash. Later, the woman gave them plenty of good food to eat and then she said the boss would call for them soon. Two hours passed before he ordered my grandmother to come to him in the big house. Nelly said Biny was happy to go because she really liked him. They had sex and Biny loved it, she wanted to stay with him.

"Nelly begged Biny to leave and go home with her. Nelly cried and cried, wanting to go home to her family, but Biny wouldn't go. She told Nelly to take the opals, which they'd hidden. 'Go home you baby,' Biny would say. Nelly was scared to leave by herself. But she did try to leave, many times, though she was soon caught by Birch's Aboriginal tracker. She was trapped for many years with my grandmother, until finally the man died. Apparently, he was gored by a bull and his wound wouldn't heal. It must have turned toxic and he died of blood poisoning. And of course, Grandma Biny had a baby to him, my mother. So that white man was my grandfather."

PJ suddenly pulled the car over to the side of the road. His heart thumped and the blood drained from his face. He turned to Tarni, who sat mystified at PJ's reaction.

"Holy shit, Tarni. Tell me his name again!"

"I said it was Birch."

"I can't believe this! It's either an amazing coincidence, or… You are related to me!"

Tarni looked at PJ as if he'd gone mad.

"What are you talking about, PJ? How on earth could I be related to you?”

“Tell me more and then I’ll let you know if it’s true.”

“Well, I remember Nelly telling me her story and mentioning his name, but she’s never told me the full story before today. She only said that she and my grandmother worked together on the same property. So all of this is a bit new to me. But I remember his name it was definitely Birch.”

“Oh my God, Tarni. He was the man who raped my grandmother Sally and kept her hostage. He’s my father’s, father, my grandfather! And he’s your grandfather! Shit this is amazing!”

PJ sat silently for a moment, wondering how he would tell the rest of the family. Intermittent laughter broke through, especially when thinking about his sister Sally.

“I know my sister Sally will be absolutely livid missing out on this piece of family information. It’s too late now to add it to her book though. The first print run is on the block and set to be delivered to the book shops the day after tomorrow. I just can’t believe this!”

PJ began laughing hysterically and shaking his head. Tarni sat quietly, trying to fathom what had just happened. PJ then turned to her.

“I’d love to find a phone box and let Sarah know, although on second thoughts, I think in her condition she should stay calm, keep her blood pressure down. I’ll have to wait until the baby is born before I tell her, or she’ll crack up.” PJ leant across and kissed Tarni on the forehead. “Welcome to the family cousin!”

He then burst out laughing again while Tarni remained in numbed shock. It took her some time to see the funny side before she smiled and asked calmly.

“Do you want to hear what happened to the opals, PJ?”

“Bugger the opals. This is so amazing; I still can’t believe it!”

“Well I’m going to tell you anyway. Nelly hid them on Birch’s property. Apparently, there’s a hill, not too far from the homestead and there’s an enormous gum tree there and a grave under that tree.”

PJ interrupted. “The person buried there is my great grandmother. I’ll explain it all later. Go on.” Tarni threw him a quizzical look.

“Well anyway, Nelly put the opals in a tin. She dug the hole really deep behind the cross and buried them under a daisy bush. She said no one would suspect anything, even though some of the people who lived on the property went to visit the grave. Anyway, when Birch died, the overseer, Bob, sold all the cattle and gave the workers, or I should say the slaves, some money, including

Biny and Nelly. They used it to build their home, a shack really, near Victor Harbor. There they raised my mum together. They didn't want to return to their tribe with a half cast baby girl. After my grandmother died and when Mum was old enough, she went to Coober Pedy to find work. That's when she met my dad.

Over the years, Nelly sold the opals one at a time, but she kept the big one. She'd told Biny she'd lost it, but she hadn't. She'd buried it, intending one day to take it back to her tribe. Sadly, she never got around to it. Nelly buried it in our special place, and I know where to find it."

"Tarni, please don't tell me anymore. I'm not really interested in the opal. There's so much of our family history I need to tell you. I will explain everything another time. Now we'd better get moving, or they'll be worried about us. And let's not tell Harry or anyone else about this until we have time to digest it."

"I agree, although I'm going back there to dig up Nelly's opal, PJ. Because that was the reason she wanted to see me. I have to sell it and give the money to her tribe. Nelly won't rest in peace until I do, and I owe her that much."

Chapter 17

On 9th September 1959, Sarah gave birth to a perfect baby boy. PJ was present at the birth and held his son close to his heart, his emotions raw. However, he was determined to get something straight with Sarah. He'd decided there were too many family names passed on to the next generations of Darcy's. So he asked Sarah to choose any name, other than, Patrick, Jonathon, James and of course Sarah's father's name, Wayne. Sarah agreed and went on to explain that when she was young, she'd always loved to read The Adventures of Huckleberry Finn and Tom Sawyer. Therefore, the baby was duly named Thomas Darcy. The middle name could be fought over by the grandparents, Sarah didn't care. They now had a beautiful baby boy in their lives and nothing else mattered.

When Patrick Snr and Aunty Clare were informed of the name choice, they thanked Sarah and PJ with all their heart for naming him after Thomas, Patrick's dear friend and Clare's first husband who'd died as a hero on the Titanic. Thomas Norman had saved the lives of hundreds of women and children. As a result, PJ and Sarah decided to keep Sarah's, 'Tom Sawyer' story a secret and duly accept their gratitude.

Another secret, which PJ was bursting to tell Sarah, was of his family connection with Tarni. The two had, with great difficulty, kept it from everyone, because they felt it was not fare on Sarah to be the last to know.

Five days after the birth, Sarah, along with baby Thomas were released from hospital into PJ's care. He'd splurged on a new family station wagon. His sports car had been sold to make way for the growing Darcy family. This is what PJ had told Sarah as he opened the car door. She was impressed, not with the car so much, as the thoughtfulness of her husband.

"I love you so much, PJ. You must be the best husband in the world and I'm sure you will be the best dad in the world."

"Thank you, my dear. Shall we now toddle off slowly back to the farm?"

"Now you sound too bloody old, PJ! Just drive safely, that's all I ask."

PJ decided it was a good time to tell Sarah his secret. It took him nearly all the way home, to relate the tale.

Sarah, after listening intently, turned to PJ with one eyebrow raised.

"I wondered why you seemed to be playing down Mother Superior's visit. You told me it only led to a dead end – fibber!"

"I couldn't risk having you too excited, Sarah. Your blood pressure may have gone through the roof."

"I think you were right. But I'm sure this news has curdled my breast milk!"

PJ laughed as he always did with Sarah's quips.

"Don't you think it's amazing though, meeting Tarni in the outback by chance, then saving her life, only to find out later she's related to me – to us. For as long as I live, it will never cease to amaze me. I haven't even told my sister Sally yet, mainly because I know she's going to be angry. It would have been a real treasure to add to her book."

"Has Tarni read that book yet, PJ?"

"She's reading it as we speak. She couldn't wait."

"Can we talk about it later? Don't get me wrong, I think it's truly amazing. I just need a little more time to take it in. Maybe I should read Sally's book, instead of you trying to explain it to me?"

"Yes, I think that's best. Thank God for Sally. It'll make telling the story to everyone a lot easier. I'm sure as Tarni reads the book she'll explain it to Harry, so he should be up to date."

*

Two weeks later, every close friend and family member had read Sally's book, along with a personal foot note, saying Tarni was their distant relation, this would be added to the next print.

Jonathon and Margie thought it was an appropriate time to hold a celebration at 'Wildflowers'.

"It will be a great opportunity to wet the baby's head and welcome Tarni into the family. We can also congratulate Sally on her book – a three in one," Jonathon said.

A barbeque was arranged for the Sunday after Happy Harry was to have his first race start at Murray Bridge. PJ said to Sarah, before he left for the races.

"Hopefully we'll have another reason to raise our glass tomorrow, my love. I could not have trained Happy to be any fitter. He's literally jumping out of his skin. Fit but fresh that's how I like to race them!"

Sarah sat breast feeding the baby while she admired her husband dressing in his smart, grey suit.

"And what does Billy Paton think of him, PJ? He's ridden Happy in trackwork hasn't he?"

"Yes he has and he's of the same opinion as me. If Harry proves himself to be a stayer, then he'll be a top horse."

A perfect spring day awaited the race goers at Murray Bridge. The track had been blessed with an inch of rain the day before, so perfect conditions were set for Happy to make his racing debut.

After settling near to last, and momentarily being blocked for a run in the straight, Happy Harry forged his way through a narrow opening and went on to win by four lengths. This gave PJ and his staff reason to breathe a sigh of relief. After all the hype that had surrounded Happy for the past nine months, it would have been a massive let down to see him go under, particularly in such a low-grade field.

Billy Paton dismounted in the enclosure and whispered to PJ.

"Keep him under wraps boss. I made it look like I was punishing him, but I didn't hit him. He was only going half pace. I'd start him at Morphettville in two weeks' time. You'll get good odds if you put him up in distance and amongst a stronger field. I tell ya, he'll win no matter what the company."

PJ didn't like the punting side of racing. He was in it for self-satisfaction and to see his hard work and judgement pay off when his horses won. After PJ's first year of training, he'd been placed third on the trainer's premiership, which began on 1 August each year. PJ's number of horses in training had accumulated so he felt confident of claiming first place in the 1960 season.

Life seemed truly blessed for PJ, and on the following day at Wildflowers, he felt it even more so. Everyone who'd meant anything to him was there.

"The only one missing is Happy Harry. I'm sure he'd love to be here and have a beer or two," PJ said as he raised his glass with Sarah.

Baby Thomas became 'pass the parcel', until it was time for him to be breast fed. This Sarah did with decorum. She sat away from the crowd, placing a shawl over the baby and her right breast.

"Do it in private please dear," Sarah's mother, Alice, whispered.

Sarah rolled her eyes as a more open-minded Addy came to her rescue.

"Come Alice, I have someone I'd like you to meet." Addy turned and winked at Sarah, who then mouthed. 'Thank you Addy.'

Harry became a little tired of explaining to everyone, just how lucky he and Tarni were to be alive after the accident. He was asked time and again, to explain about his physio- therapy, which saw him walking again. After much discussion along these lines, he found an excuse to be free from the would-be-doctors and nurses, who'd offered words of advice on what tonics to take and what exercises were best to strengthen leg muscles. Before he left their company, Harry assured them all that he'd found his old passion for bike riding had played the biggest part in returning his strength. On his way through the crowd, looking for Tarni, Harry felt his arm being grabbed.

"Harry, I've been meaning to ask you." PJ smiled and slapped Harry on the back. "But you know, crying babies and all that nappy changing stuff, it can take your thoughts away. Anyway, just between you and me, have you set a date yet to marry Tarni and if so, why don't you announce your engagement today? It's as good a time as any."

"Are you sure, PJ? I don't want to steal your thunder. I'll ask Tarni and see what she thinks but I bet she'll say no. She's a bit shy about public announcements or receiving accolades. Then come to think of it, you probably know her better than me."

"No, not really, she still remains a bit of a mystery." PJ smacked Harry on the back again. "I'll leave it up to you and Tarni then."

Harry smiled and shook PJ's hand. He spotted Tarni sitting on a garden bench talking with Mother Superior and excused himself from the well-wishers.

"Hello ladies, may I pull up a chair?"

Harry said this while dragging a heavy wrought iron chair up close. Tarni seemed a little annoyed that Harry had interrupted their conversation and he noticed.

"I'm sorry if I've interrupted you ladies. I'm sure whatever you were discussing would be most interesting, please go on."

Harry smiled at both women; his charm apparent.

"I was just explaining to Mother Superior, about the opal.

"Have you told Mother Superior the entire story about the opal, Tarni?"

"Of course I have. I can't tell a lie or keep a secret from Mother Superior. God would punish me." Her smile was a little shy. "Which brings me to another topic we've been discussing; I would like to learn more about the Catholic religion. I'm going to have lessons on Catholicism. I'll begin my Bible studies next week. Mother Superior is going to telephone Father Andrew, our local minister this evening. Mother said she was sure he would be more than happy to teach me. I've also spoken on your behalf Harry. I told Mother we will go next Tuesday to Victor Harbour and see if we can dig up the opal, is that alright with you?"

"Of course it is. It'll take me back to my childhood when I loved treasure hunts. Didn't you as a child Tarni?"

Mother Superior interrupted before Tarni had time to answer.

"I know if Tarni finds the opal Harry, she will do as Nelly whished, she will give it to the Nunga tribe. However, I must explain. The opal may be registered to someone. Even back in those days the miners had to make a claim for their significant finds. It was the same for diamonds and gold. So Tarni will have to do a search on this particular opal. The Australian Government's Mining Department should hold the records. If there are no records of it being found, then it belongs to Tarni and she intends to do as Nelly wished. Personally, I think it would be a wonderful gesture."

Mother Superior stood and bent over to kiss Tarni on the forehead.

"I must mingle now. That will allow you two young people to talk about your wedding plans. Bless you both." She then glided away.

Harry looked puzzled.

"Did you tell Mother you wanted to talk to me about the wedding, Tarni?"

She smiled. "No, I didn't mention the wedding. It just seems Mother Superior knows everything. And as Sarah say's, it's a bit spooky."

Harry went on to explain to Tarni what PJ had suggested, about announcing their engagement today.

"No, not today Harry, I'd like it to be private, just the family." Tarni then laughed. "Family, now that sounds funny. It's taken me a long time to register that PJ and I are actually related. It's almost a miracle!"

The rest of the day was full of cheer and good humour. The more inebriated PJ became, the more people he would introduce Tarni to, as his cousin. Every family member, plus extended family were there to congratulate each other on, either being a cousin, an uncle, a grandfather or a grandmother to baby Thomas, and some showed their joy in realising they were also distantly related to Tarni.

A magnificent twilight drifted over the crowd, sealing the end of a special day. The red sunset literally veiled the earth. It set the mood for romance, so Harry took the opportunity to ask Tarni to marry him before he returned to university next February.

"I'd like us to be married next month, Tarni. We don't have to have a big wedding, just the immediate family, as you said."

"I'd like that Harry. We'll set the date tomorrow, but please don't forget your promise about the opal."

Tarni felt a moment of anxiety after Harry said the immediate family. She knew there was no way she could not ask Harry's family to come over for the wedding. This terrible feeling of not wanting to face them ever again, would be something she'd have to discuss with Sarah.

"I haven't forgotten about the opal Tarni. I'll telephone the Mining Department tomorrow." He pondered for a brief moment. "I think the opal would have been mined at Coober Pedy."

"I don't think so Harry. It's a black opal and they're found at Lightening Ridge, in New South Wales."

"Whatever. I'll do the search in both places, okay?"

*

The following morning at 4.00 am, Tarni woke to hear the telephone ringing. She immediately thought it was PJ having a problem with one of the horses. We start at five, not four, Tarni thought as she grabbed the phone.

"Yes, hello, PJ. What's the problem?"

Valery's voice sounded distraught, she asked if Harry was there.

"Yes, he's here Val." She handed him the receiver.

"Mum what's wrong? Please stop crying. I can't understand you. Please just tell me, what's wrong?"

Harry had to wait a moment for Valery to calm down.

"Your father has been diagnosed with cancer. The doctors say it's aggressive and he may only have weeks to live. I need you to come home at once, I've tried to cope and be brave, but I can't. Please come home Harry. I need you and so does your father."

Valery broke down crying again and Harry tried to console her as best he could. It was only when he promised to catch the next flight home to New Zealand that she pulled herself together.

The look Harry gave Tarni after he'd hung up said it all.

"I know you have to go home Harry, I heard enough of the conversation." That was all Tarni had to say. She was unable to offer any sympathy. She quickly dressed and left to begin her work a little earlier than usual.

Harry remained sitting on the bed, shocked at the news and what Tarni had said, or not said. A knot began to form in his stomach. How could she leave me here, without even saying, I'm sorry Harry, I hope your father beats the odds and lives, please give your family my blessings. I'll pray for him every day. Or she could have said, I love you with all my heart Harry and I feel for you. I understand you must go home. I'll be waiting for you, unless you need me to come to New Zealand with you.

Tarni hadn't said those things; instead she'd left in a rush. He reluctantly packed his bags and went to make arrangements with PJ to drive him to the

Airport. PJ was devastated by the news. Despite the friction between Tarni and the rest of Harry's family, PJ really liked Ronny and Val, as well as the twins. PJ explained to Sarah what had just happened and that he would drive Harry to the airport immediately. "I've just phoned the airlines and they had a cancellation on the only flight to NZ today."

Harry approached Tarni just before she was about to mount a horse. He hoped he'd hear words of love and support after he embraced her to say goodbye. Instead she said bluntly.

"Have a safe trip Harry." She then flung her body effortlessly on top of the horse.

Craig was holding the horse with one hand and shook Harry's hand with the other.

"Gees that's terrible news, Harry, I'll pray your dad gets better. I'm so sorry mate, we'll miss you." Harry nodded as Craig threw Tarni a quizzical look.

"Thanks, Craig. Take care of Happy Harry for me."

"I will, and you take care of yourself." Craig's smile disappeared as he said in a sombre tone: "I really hope the doctors are wrong about your father, Harry."

*

The next day, Tarni had somehow found the strength of heart to catch the bus to Victor Harbour. PJ had offered to drive her and help find the opal.

"If it still exists," he'd said.

"I need time alone, PJ. But thanks anyway."

He knew better than to argue with her, especially with that look of determination he'd seen so many times, so he drove her to the bus stop and wished her luck.

"If it's as big as you say, Tarni, it could be worth a fortune. So ring me and I'll come and pick you up. You won't want to be responsible for carrying it around on your own. And don't worry I'll phone the Mining Departments of South Australia and New South Wales as soon as I get home."

"Okay. Thanks again, PJ."

Tarni sat on the bus resting her head against the window, her breath fogging up the glass. This gave her a misty view of the giant gums and the pasture, which, due to recent rain had turned a pale shade of green. A lone kangaroo stood in the distance with a look of surprise, or was it danger registering? It was ready to flee, the same as Tarni had so many times before.

With Harry's departure, her love and her main purpose in life had gone, been taken away like everything else she loved and cared for. She knew Harry would be held duty bound by his family in New Zealand. His heart would always be pulled toward the needy and the weak. She knew Harry well. Sooner or later, he would ask her to come to New Zealand and live with him and she would have to say no.

She pushed her thoughts of Harry away and concentrated on comforting news. Tomorrow night, she was to begin bible studies with the Reverend Andrew Baker. He was the preacher at the nearby Seaford Rise Catholic church. This thought gave her joy and a certain peace of mind. Even her heart felt healed whenever she trusted in God.

The bus pulled up in front of the Victor Harbour Post Office. Tarni stepped down and took in the unmistakable smell of seaweed. She smiled when listening to 'the sound of waves', (meaning her name), as she walked to the familiar milk bar to buy a drink. She would need one, as it would take her at least thirty minutes to reach the spot where Nelly told her to look. Her riding boots had been replaced with sand shoes and her jodhpurs with shorts.

Standing in the shop, Tarni reminisced. It all looked the same. Only years ago, they had huge lolly jars sitting on the counter. Not so today. Most of the lollies were in packets, displayed at the back of the counter. Tarni bought a Coke-a-cola and her favourite Choo- Choo Bar, wrapped the same as it was when she was a little girl. She put it in her pocket and quickened her pace towards Nelly's shack.

After twenty minutes of brisk walking, she reached the spot where Nelly's home used to be. She stood for a moment amazed that a large wooden house frame had been erected on the site. Huge window spaces allowed full views of the ocean, obviously someone had grand plans. While studying this, she hadn't noticed a young man sitting under the shade of a tree eating his lunch.

"Hello," he called. "Are you looking for someone?"

Tarni was a little startled.

"Um, ar, no. I'm just admiring your work. It looks like it's going to be a lovely home when it's finished."

"It may never be finished. The owner's running out of money. I'm the only builder on the job. He can't afford to pay anyone else."

Tarni smiled and moved closer to talk to the young man who seemed familiar.

"I used to live here on this spot with my mum and my Aunty Nelly. It was years ago, thirteen to be exact."

He literally dropped his sandwich and stood up.

"Tarni, is that you?"

"Yes, my name's Tarni, but I don't remember you. I'm sorry?"

"I'm Johnny! Remember? We used to build sandcastles together and dig for pipis along the beach. We built our hideaway in the tee-trees."

"Oh my goodness. Yes, I do remember you! Little Johnny. So you're still here and you're a builder."

They stood studying each other for a moment before they laughed. After sitting down on a pile of timber and sharing many happy memories, Tarni said she had to take a walk.

"Could I join you, Tarni?"

"No, I'd like to be alone." She saw the disappointment in his eyes. "It's just that Nelly and I had a special place where we used to sit, and she'd tell me stories; dream time stories. Nelly passed away only two weeks ago. I need to be alone and remember my time with her."

"I understand, but will you come back and see me before you go home? I'm really happy you've had a good life Tarni. You know I remember how you used to tell me every day; 'one day my mother is going to buy me a pony'. I used to think, I hope she doesn't because then the pony would take you away from me." His smile was shy, the same as it was when he was a small boy. "I'm sure you were born to love and care for horses, Tarni,. I'm still scared of them. I'd rather ride a motor bike." He gave a nervous laugh and combed his fingers through his hair.

Tarni smiled back at him as she walked away.

"Okay, I'll drop back and say goodbye. I shouldn't be too long. See ya."

She'd kept her in-between-years a secret from Johnny. Tarni had merely told him she was adopted out to a white family and then she'd met the Darcy family who now, it turns out, are related to her through a paternal grandfather.

Johnny had also kept a secret from Tarni. His mother, Maude, had been the person who'd told the authorities about Tarni. Maude had become jealous of her only child, Johnny, loving a little half-caste Aboriginal girl more than he loved her. Johnny's mother, a few years after that episode, was placed in a mental institution and then later, his father became an alcoholic. Johnny had had a sad life.

The sun was beginning its decline, and a cool sea breeze stirred the sea grasses, but Tarni's perspiration still trickled down her brow as she dug deeper, using the miner's shovel that she'd carried folded in her backpack. She began to think Nelly had given her a bum steer, when she struck something solid. The large tin, mostly rusted, fell apart the moment Tarni tried to pull it from the earth. Once she freed the contents, she studied the uncut opal. It was almost as big as her fist with a depth measuring three inches. She sat in awe of the precious stone and considered its value for a moment. Looking into the hole again, Tarni noticed a piece of paper, she reached for it and shook away the dirt, then unfolded it. The words had been written in ink and were smudged by age. The Victor Harbour Council on this day, the twelfth of December 1902, sold to Nelly Eagle, a one-acre block of land situated on the far north cliff of Victor Harbour for the sum of ten shillings, etc, etc.

Meantime, PJ, back at his farm, had phoned the Australian Mining Department. He'd asked for any information held on major opal finds, dating back to the mid-to-late nineteen hundred period. He was informed that he would have to put his inquiry in writing. All opal finds recorded in that period would then be sent to him via the mail, which may take up to three weeks. Or subsequently, if he needed the information sooner, he could go personally to Canberra and search the mining archives.

That evening, a chilly August night, had shrouded the farm in an early darkness. PJ began to worry about Tarni. He assumed she would be home by now. Sarah noticed his disquiet.

"PJ, if you're that worried, take a drive, maybe the bus broke down or something? I'm sure she would have caught the last bus home. Tarni knew what time it left didn't she? But if you're that worried why don't you phone the police to see if there's been an accident."

"Yes, you're right Sarah. I'll phone the police."

Just as PJ was about to dial the number, car lights appeared up the driveway. He hung up the phone and hurried outside. Sarah could hear him say.

"Tarni, we were worried about you."

"PJ, really, you should know better than to worry about me. I can look after myself."

She introduced PJ to Johnny and went on to explain how they'd met. PJ was pleasantly surprised.

"Come inside Johnny, I'll introduce you to my wife Sarah." PJ said as he guided Johnny in doors by the shoulder.

After the introductions, Johnny and Tarni both told how they'd been discussing happy childhood memories.

"I think I may have even proposed marriage to Tarni back then!" Johnny laughed it off, but Sarah could see the love in his eyes and how Tarni shifted in her seat, uncomfortable with the thought. Sarah changed the subject.

"Would you like something to eat Johnny, there's plenty of casserole left over from dinner?"

Johnny stood up.

"No, no thank you. I have a long drive home and we had something to eat before we left. I apologise. We should have phoned you earlier. I'll say goodnight and it was a pleasure to meet you both. I hope we meet again." He looked at Tarni before saying, "soon I hope."

Tarni escorted Johnny outside and gave him a kiss on the cheek. She returned, and her eyes lit up as she unravelled the opal, placing it on the dining table.

"Oh my goodness, Tarni! That's the biggest opal I've ever

Seen," Sarah said. "It's so beautiful, just look at the colours. The light makes them dance, it looks so alive. Just imagine when it's polished! I don't know how they measure opals, but I reckon it would make at least four hundred carrots."

PJ stood, eyes downcast – mesmerized by the opal. He'd never seen anything like it, not even in the mining journals where the biggest finds had been photographed.

Tarni surprised them again when she unfolded the deeds to the property. It seemed it was PJ's turn to be confounded.

"Why didn't Nelly tell you about this when she was dying? You thought she was just a squatter on the land, didn't you?"

"I don't know. Maybe she forgot, or just ran out of energy before she had the chance to tell me. I think perhaps we should've waited for her to wake up," Tarni said guiltily.

PJ said in his own defence. "Well I had to get back to Sarah. And you said, we should leave Nelly alone, let her go to heaven and you were right. Remember, they said she died only minutes after we left. It doesn't matter anyway, because if Nelly didn't leave a legal will, then the land will automatically go back to the Government, unless she has relatives. And that may be hard to prove." PJ gave Tarni a shrewd look and said:

"I think you'd better say you simply found the opal."

"I would have said that anyway PJ, we think alike. And I'm not worried about the land. I don't want to open that can of fish. I'm just concerned about the opal and what I should do with it. I know I promised Nelly I'd give it to the Nunga tribe, but they'd probably be ripped off by some crooked dealer." Tarni gave PJ that determined look of hers. "I think you're going to have to help me with this one PJ."

"Of course I will, but I think you mean a can of worms," and they all laughed.

Chapter 18

After that evening of opal revelation, and each morning after PJ had finished working his horses, he would then travel to Adelaide and search the state records for all major opal finds at Coober Pedy and Lightening Ridge. After a week of looking in every archive, he came to the conclusion that the black opal now belonged to Tarni. She needn't feel guilty because it seemed the old man whom Nelly had found dying all those years ago, had died as an unknown person. PJ knew this for a fact, as he'd searched the death register. He then spoke to Tarni about him meeting with the elders of Nelly's tribe. Tarni was happy for him to go alone.

It was only the second week of September but already the midday sun was a searing ball in the sky. PJ drove slowly along the parched, cracked earth up to the mission. He parked, then walked to where a group of Aboriginal men sat cross legged on a fallen-down veranda. Their deeply lined black faces squinting into the blinding light. They each held their hand out for PJ to shake. After introducing himself, PJ asked to see their elders. One spoke up, who actually looked the youngest, PJ was a little perplexed.

"We are elders. I'm oldest. My name Joe."

"Well, I'm pleased to meet you Joe. I've come to talk to you about a story I've been told. It's about two young Aboriginal girls that went missing from here around the year 1893."

They listened intently while PJ told the story slowly and clearly. He was then informed that Nelly and Biny were not the only girls who had been stolen or disappeared. Their story had been handed down from generation to generation.

"Warra Wirrin man; he come to sacred ground. He take young girls and women. Them disappear."

"Didn't your elders follow their tracks? Surely they would have seen the girl's footprints or maybe the ditches left by a horse drawn carriage?" PJ found it all a little hard to believe.

Then, the Elder who appeared to be the youngest, smiled with a twinkle of mischief in his eyes.

"You white man. You can't change our story now. How we know for sure what elders do back then? Me just tell you their story but today when full-blood goes missing, we call police." His raspy laugh sounded almost evil. "But that do no good, hey, they don't care. And you white man take em away them half-castes. Yeh. Police don't care about us black fellas. Hey, you got any smokes or grog?"

PJ shook his head and sat silently, unconsciously doing an impression of his grandfather Jonathon when he'd take time to deliver an answer.

He spent a moment looking at the government-built houses, which had been constructed for the tribe. The sight saddened him. Half the homes had gaping holes in their walls, probably the structure ripped out to use for firewood. Torn curtains blew about through broken windows. Skeletal dogs roamed the surrounds sniffing for anything edible. Children laughed while playing cricket with a long piece of wood and a large round stone. Most were dressed in rags.

PJ chose then not to tell the elders about the opal. He'd only waste his time talking to men who seemed to have lost interest in everything, including the truth. They lived in their own world, neither black nor white, but in what he thought of as 'no-man's-land'. It was heartbreaking, and he would have to explain to Tarni that in his opinion, selling the opal and simply giving the money to these people would do no good. Maybe there was another way to help them, a more constructive way. Perhaps by giving the children a proper education, they would then find a way of escape, a reason to live and prosper. Yes, give them a scholarship of some sort?

Tired after his long drive home, PJ was met by the aroma of roast lamb as he entered his home. He smiled when he heard Sarah playing with baby Thomas; she was making him chuckle.

"Hello, my darling. So, tell me what's been happening since I've been gone?" PJ kissed Sarah on the head as he removed his shoes. She was on the floor, blurting on the baby's stomach. He was giggling, and Sarah looked up at PJ.

"Oh, not much, although we did have a scare with Happy Harry this morning after you left. Apparently, he had a mild case of colic, but he seems fine now. The vet has just left. He's checked Happy twice today and I think Tarni is going to sleep with him tonight. The horse I mean, not the vet." Sarah was always able to put a smile on PJ's face with her quips.

"I'd better have a talk with her then. I'll fill you in on all my details when I come back." He paused in the doorway. "When will dinner be ready?"

"In half an hour, don't be late!"

PJ found Tarni talking to Happy Harry in his stable.

"Hi, Tarni. Sarah told me that Harry had a slight bout of colic. He looks okay now?"

"He's fine."

Tarni appeared to be in one of her solemn moods, so PJ decided to cut the conversation short.

"I'm a little tired after all that driving. What say I tell you about what happened out at the mission in the morning?"

Tarni didn't answer, or look his way, she simply shrugged her shoulders.

"Okay Tarni what's wrong."

"Not tonight, PJ. I'm tired too. Let's talk in the morning."

PJ lost no sleep worrying about whatever it was upsetting Tarni. He was exhausted, but relieved that he'd kept his promise of helping her with the opal dilemma. Now it would be up to her and her conscience, as to what to do with 'the dam thing', as PJ had come to refer to it.

*

Morning light came too soon for PJ. He dressed slowly, made a cup of tea and took his time walking to the number one barn. However, getting back to his normal duties did put a smile on his face. He entered, with his mug of tea in hand and realised just how fortunate he was to have such honest and reliable staff. This reminded him; he should concentrate this week on applying to the SAJC for young Craig's apprenticeship.

It was also time to have a talk to Tarni, about her travelling back to New Zealand and supporting Harry for a while. Maybe this was what she was worried about last night. He took the last gulp of his tea and smiled at his strappers. All were busy, either saddling up horses or mucking out boxes. Patrick breathed in the heady smell of horse urine mixed with straw, the smell he'd loved, from as long as he could remember. Above the noise and chatter he called.

"Good morning all."

A chorus came back.

"Good morning boss."

It amused him that no one looked his way, they just kept working. PJ took another moment to realise what Tarni had helped create, this well-oiled machine – the team. She's a gem, he thought. PJ then walked to the grandstand carrying his two-way radio.

Each morning, before dawn, Tarni would exercise the horses that had just returned to training. So that later, when the sun rose, PJ was able to see clearly, his racing team doing their fast work. At first light, Happy Harry trotted onto the track, seeming very full of himself. PJ was a little surprised that Tarni had kept to the initial plan of galloping him three furlongs. Perhaps we should have waited another day after his bout of colic PJ' thought, but he put these doubts aside after watching Happy's impressive work. Placing his binoculars on the bench, PJ scurried down the steps and over to Tarni, who was still on board Happy.

"How did he feel Tarni?"

"He feels really good PJ. And he ate up last night. I wouldn't have galloped him if he hadn't. He's tough. He'll be fine. Anyway, we needed to see how he feels for Saturday."

"So, what do you reckon? Is he ready for the mile?"

"I think so, but you'd better get back up in the stand. Remember you wrote on the work board for Craig to gallop Volunteer. It's his first gallop after his spell. I think he's twice the horse now but see what you think."

PJ felt relieved, not only because his horses had worked well this morning, but Tarni seemed to be over the doldrums.

After having breakfast with his staff, PJ suggested that Tarni stay back and have a talk with him. She nodded and waited until everyone had left.

PJ began by explaining, what he thought about the Nunga elders and then his opinion on what should be done with the opal. Tarni listened, however, she seemed to be on another plain, not interested in what she should or shouldn't do with the opal. Sarah joined them for a coffee and noticed Tarni's mood.

"Is there something wrong Tarni, you seem a bit despondent?"

Tarni threw Sarah a venomous look before she demanded.

"I'm not despondent Sarah, I'm angry. How well do you know your stepdaughter?"

Sarah sat back hard on the chair.

"I'm sure I know Ella very well. Why?" Tarni, sighed deeply, remembering the tools Sarah had given her, to control her anger.

"I'm sorry Sarah. I didn't mean to fly at you like that. It's just that I received a very upsetting letter from Harry. He told me his mother Val, received a telephone call from a young woman who said she was very close to you Sarah. She said there were some important things Harry and his family should know about me. Val told her they already knew I was part Aboriginal and then the woman asked Val, 'but did you know she was an accomplice to two murders.'"

"How do you know it was Ella, Tarni?" Sarah asked humbly, but shocked.

"Because, Harry said he grabbed the phone off his mother when he saw the horrified look on her face. He asked who it was. The person on the other end didn't answer, but he heard in the background another woman saying. 'Hang up Ella'. Harry said he'd swear on the Bible the woman said, hang up Ella."

The colour left Sarah's face. She needed to recover and think for a moment about what Tarni had implied. Patrick on the other hand donned the lawyer's hat.

"What did she mean by you being an accomplice to two murders Tarni?"

Tarni's anger rose again and she let it rip this time.

"How do I know PJ. Why don't you ask Ella?" She hung her head and took a deep breath – in control again. "Anyway, I have to go. I'll be late for Bible studies and I don't want to lose my temper. It wouldn't be Christian of me." Tarni rose from her chair and left in a hurry.

PJ and Sarah sat gob-smacked until PJ said:

"I don't often say this, but, Holy Shit!"

"You can say that again if you like, PJ. I find it hard to believe Ella would do or say such a thing. I'm going to phone her now," and with that, Sarah rose immediately.

PJ was unable to move, he sat in a trance while Sarah spoke to Ella on the phone. Ella denied everything, until under pressure she began to lose it. Sarah then received a clear picture when Ella yelled at her.

"Why don't you bail that bitch up and interrogate her like you're interrogating me!" Ella hung up and Sarah turned to PJ.

"It was definitely Ella, PJ. I'll go and see her tomorrow. I'll take Tom and leave him with Mum for a couple of hours. It's about time I went to the office anyway. I need to catch up and have a talk with my new fill-in psychologist."

Sarah walked over to PJ and kissed him tenderly.

"Try not to worry. There's always been something between those two. I'm sure it's just a jealousy thing. I'll sort it out, but I won't let Ella off lightly. It was a terrible thing to do, especially with Val being so heartbroken and stressed about Ronny."

"It's not Ella I'm worried about, Sarah." PJ looked her in the eye. "I haven't told you, but Granddad said he had a meeting with the Coroner, Phillip Spear, after his findings at the Darwin inquiry. Phillip said. 'Just keep an eye on that young woman Jonathon. I think she may have more sides to her than you and PJ have seen.' When Granddad told me what Phillip Spear had said I just scoffed. He then told me, Phillip had decided not to call on his final witness, a man called Drongo. He's a full-blooded Aboriginal who only speaks pidgin. He was Tarni's only friend on Merriola Station, apart from me. It appears Drongo snuck in to see Tarni when she was in the sick bay after the croc attack. Granddad thinks they collaborated on a payback for Robbo. Now I'm wondering how Ella knew about this and why she said two murders. What was the other murder?"

Sarah shrugged. "I don't know, PJ but I'll see if I can find out."

*

Tarni sat listening to Father Andrew. His words gave her peace and she felt grateful for that.

"The Lord is your saviour, Tarni. Only the Lord is able to forgive your sins. If you truly believe in Him, He will welcome you into his kingdom. And if you give your life to the Lord, He will love and cherish you for eternity."

Tarni needed desperately to repent, to confess her sins. This sounded like the best offer she'd ever had. She began to sob rocking her body back and forth. Father Andrew placed his hand gently on her head.

"I shall ask God for His blessing." He then looked to the heavens and prayed. "Dear God, I pray you will bless this child. Please free her from her guilt and forgive her, her sins."

Father Andrew held Tarni at arm's length and waited until she looked up at him.

"Now, Tarni. Please offer your sins to the Lord, ask for His forgiveness and He will hold you in His arms forever. His love will conquer all and you will be totally forgiven."

The following morning, Father Andrew telephoned Mother Superior, who picked up the receiver on the first ring.

"I've been waiting for your call, Andrew." Mother Superior then listened to his explanation. It was what she'd suspected. "It's alright, Andrew. I'll handle it from now on. Tarni has made her peace with the Lord and now the Good Lord will guide me. We'll speak again, thank you for letting me know, goodbye."

Mother Superior sat upright, closed her eyes and breathed in the presence of the Lord, crossed her chest and thanked Him.

*

PJ rose from bed feeling sleep deprived. He'd had a restless night worrying about Tarni and the two murders. He'd never wanted to believe she could be capable of such a thing. However, over time there'd been signs, verbally and in her manner, which made PJ think that maybe Tarni was capable of at least being an accomplice to murder.

After dressing for work, PJ clicked in the numbers on his safe and

150

removed the black opal. He held it up to the light, exposing its dancing colours and smiled at the magic. He then remembered the classic novel written by Walter Scott, about Anne of Geierstein. Apparently, Anne had worn a talisman of opal around her neck, until the day she spilt a drop of Holy water on it. The opal immediately turned to a colourless rock. Anne then cried herself to sleep. Tragically, during that night, she was turned into a pile of ashes. PJ felt his mind heavy once again with the decision of what he, or Tarni, should do with this gem.

Tarni was tending to the horses in the barn and organising the staff when PJ appeared.

"Good morning everyone," and as usual he heard the chorus.

'Good morning boss.'

PJ then took the time to speak alone with each of his workers. He inquired if they were happy in their work, or if they had any personal problems, which perhaps they needed to take some time off to attend to. His unusual display of concern attracted Tarni's attention.

"What's up PJ, are you thinking of going on another holiday?"

"No just wanting to know if everyone was happy, that's all, Tarni."

"Well that's nice PJ, but you haven't asked me."

"I suppose that's because you're different. We always talk privately, so if you're not happy then we'll talk about it later."

Tarni smiled before she mounted Happy Harry.

"Yes, we'll talk about it later, PJ, after breakfast."

Sarah had left early to go and see Ella and so after the usual chatty breakfast with the staff, PJ and Tarni sat in the living room to discuss a multitude of concerns and decisions.

"I feel a lot happier this morning, PJ. Something wonderful happened to me last night." She paused to witness his face light up. "I've found the Lord."

PJ's expression then changed to shock, but it didn't faze Tarni.

"The Lord has forgiven me all my sins. I feel free and completely loved. I'm a different person now, I truly believe I've found my calling. I'm going to speak with Mother Superior about becoming a nun."

If Tarni had puzzled or shocked PJ before, this proclamation was beyond anything she'd ever done or said prior. He cleared his throat and sat bolt upright in his chair, stiff with shock.

"I think you've been under a lot of strain lately, Tarni. Why don't you take some time off? I could book you a flight to Queensland. I'm sure Suzie would love to go with you, she's due for her holidays. You two get on so well and I'll pay your airfares. Have some fun like other young people do. You've had a hard time with Harry having to leave."

PJ felt guilty that he hadn't found the courage to tell Tarni he'd received a letter from Harry only yesterday. Harry had made his decision to remain in New Zealand to complete his law degree. His father Ronnie was putting up a brave fight against cancer and it appeared he was winning the battle but for how long the doctors couldn't guess.

Val was forever grateful that Harry had come home to help her cope with the situation. In other words, Harry felt duty bound to stay. He knew this would appear to Tarni as if he'd placed his family above her, especially knowing how she felt about them. So Harry had asked PJ, if he would try and explain his predicament. Harry had written, 'I can only hope and pray that Tarni will come and join me in New Zealand, or she will at least wait another year for us to be married.'

PJ was aware of the telephone calls between Tarni and Harry, however each time he'd inquire about how Harry was handling things over there, or how Ronnie was, she'd give him a blunt answer: 'They're fine.'

And now, there was the mystery of why Ella would accuse Tarni of being an accomplice to two murders. He would have to wait for Sarah to return home with the answer. Hopefully he could then phone Harry and let him know that the accusation was all absolute nonsense.

Tarni and PJ sat opposite, in silence, with Tarni thinking. My horses will be the hardest thing to give up. And then Harry's love, I still ache for him. But I've found the Lord and I will prove my love is for Him and only Him ... PJ disturbed her thoughts.

"I'm not taking it lightly what you've just told me Tarni. I just want you to consider everything you'll have to give up. That is if you do take this road. It's a long journey into a totally selfless world…"

Before PJ was able to continue, Tarni quoted a passage from the Bible.

"I gave up everything I loved that I might gain your Love. Romans.8:31-32."

"I hadn't realised the extent of your Bible studies. I'm surprised. Although I should remind you, you do have some earthly problems here to deal with first before you go running into the arms of the Lord."

PJ stood and paced the room, his anger rising. I'll be left without my right hand, she's made my training a breeze, I never have to worry about a thing. The whole place is so organised. All I have to do is write out the training program, then watch my horses work. Of course I have to deal with clients, but that's usually over a long lunch or at the races. I don't know if I can handle things without her.

PJ turned abruptly.

"You can't really be serious about becoming a nun Tarni?"

Tarni gave such an innocent smile, PJ felt like calling her a fraud.

"I am, PJ. I've never felt the way I did when l confessed all of my sins to Father Andrew. I felt as if my body and soul had been lifted and placed in the arms of the Lord. Sublime peace and happiness overcame me. I find it hard to explain, except I've been blessed. I cannot refuse the Lords love."

PJ gave a frustrated sigh, feeling at that moment, there was nothing he could say or do to change her mind. This will not be the end of it though; I'll phone Mother Superior the moment Tarni leaves. I'll ask Tarni to leave now. I have book work to do, but the opal, what about the dam opal.

"What about the opal Tarni, what are you going to do with it?"

"I don't know, PJ. I'll speak with Mother Superior when she comes to see me at Father Andrew's church tomorrow. I must go now; I know you like to do your book work in peace."

'Oh Christ', PJ said under his breath. Now she's beginning to sound like Mother Superior. She even knows what I'm thinking.

"Yes, you're right, Tarni. I'd better get on with it. We'll talk later when Sarah comes home."

Tarni stood and kissed PJ on the cheek. This was another surprise, as Tarni rarely showed him any affection. She left PJ wondering if he'd been dreaming. But never in his wildest dreams would he think of Tarni as a nun, and he really couldn't believe it now.

It was late afternoon, by the time Sarah arrived home. Baby Tom was due to be fed and when taking him from his car bassinet, he squawked, demanding his feed. It was the first time PJ had not consoled the baby with, 'there, there little man, don't cry. Mummies going to feed you'. Instead, PJ was annoyed that he'd have to wait for the news about Ella. He poured himself a stiff whisky and sat in his armchair waiting for Sarah to finish the feeding.

PJ had decided not to phone Sarah and tell her about Tarni's news of becoming a nun, simply because he was unable to accept it, so he'd sat brooding. He poured another whisky, almost downing it just as Sarah appeared. She bent over and kissed him on the head.

"What a day I've had, PJ! I almost phoned you to come to Adelaide and cross examine Ella. She had me so bloody mad, but finally I forced her to confess." Sarah noticed the faraway look in PJ's eyes but chose to continue. "You know the young Aboriginal man who was found drowned on Glenelg beach and was a friend of Tarni's? Well, it was only by chance that Ella and her flat mate Trish, asked their white friend to go into the pub and by them some wine. While they waited, they were approached by an Aboriginal man who called himself Blue Boy. He asked if their friend would buy him some grog too, because he was going to meet his girlfriend on the beach later. They obliged him and when they saw how much money he had, they asked where he got it. He said his girlfriend's name was Tarni and she had a good job working with horses at Morphettville. She'd given him the money because she loved him, and she wanted to have a drink with him and make love to him on the beach. Ella, being Ella, wanted to know more, so they took him home and they had a drink together. That's when Blue Boy told them the whole story about Robbo and how Tarni had given Drongo the word to use the Kundela on Robbo."

Patrick stood and poured himself another whisky.

"But why didn't Ella tell us this as soon as she knew?"

"Because she'd always thought there was something evil about Tarni and she was frightened Tarni would turn on her. They all believe in the Kundela; you must know that, PJ."

"Yes, I do, but do you really believe there's something evil about Tarni?"

"No, of course not, but we all have good and bad in us. I definitely don't think Tarni's evil and I told Ella that. I told her, her dislike for Tarni, came from jealousy. I may be wrong, but I think she's jealous of Tarni's beauty and her closeness to me and also the full-bloods look down at quarter-castes. I told Ella that Tarni's had to fight for everything in life and she only reacted the way she did with Robbo, because he'd pushed her to the limit. Blue Boy had probably come to Adelaide to bribe, or blackmail Tarni. And I don't believe she intentionally killed Blue Boy. She probably didn't even show up at the beach, so he drank himself into oblivion and drowned. However, I'm going to ask Tarni to explain that story later."

"I'm pleased you're going to because I'm not in the mood to talk to her. I've had enough of her theatrics. Plus, this news about Blue Boy could reopen the case. It would take months, if not years to clear Tarni of any wrongdoing. I hope you told Ella not to repeat this to anyone. I'll pour you a drink Sarah. You're going to need one when I tell you what Tarni intends to do with the rest of her life."

Sarah accepted the drink.

"Yes of course I did, Ella is sworn to secrecy. Now tell me PJ, what is it?"

"She wants to be a bloody nun!"

"PJ, please don't use that language when you're speaking about nuns."

At that moment, PJ held enough alcohol and anger in his veins to dam the Lord as well.

"I don't give a fuck Sarah, it's ridiculous. She's running away, like she always does, whenever she's in trouble. It's the bloody Abo in her. Now she wants to go walk about and hide behind a nun's habit!"

PJ's outburst was totally out of character. Sarah honestly didn't think him capable of such crass language.

"Maybe you should take a long walk darling. Try and calm down, it's not the end of the earth if Tarni has leanings towards being a nun. I'll go and have a talk with her right now. Please just calm down. I'll sort it out."

Sarah walked sideways as she left the room. Her eyes remained on PJ pouring yet another whisky.

She knocked on Tarni's bungalow door and could hear her singing a Hymn.

"Oh my God she's hooked," Sarah said, then let herself in. "Tarni, its Sarah. I've come to have a talk with you."

"Okay, I won't be long. I'm just getting out of the shower."

Tarni appeared with a towel wrapped around her head, turban-like and wearing a tee shirt, baggy track suit pants and fluffy slippers. She sat cross-legged on her armchair.

"Sarah, it's nice of you to pay me a visit."

Tarni was what Sarah would describe as over-joyed. She even suspected Tarni may have smoked a little dope, she seemed so happy. Sarah went straight to the point.

"Did PJ tell you that I paid Ella a visit today?"

"No, but I knew you would. So what did Ella have to say?"

Sarah went on to explain the whole story. Tarni sat unemotional until Sarah stopped. She then said light-heartedly.

"Well, now you know everything Sarah and so does the Good Lord. He's forgiven me you know." The smile left her face. "Now I'll tell you the truth, Sarah. I can't remember what I said to Drongo that day at Merriola, I was in so much pain, I was delirious. I may have agreed to teach Robbo a lesson, but honestly, I can't remember saying anything like pointing the bone." Tarni's brown eyes lit up once again.

"I've made a decision to become a nun Sarah, did PJ tell you?"

Sarah couldn't help herself, she laughed. Tarni smiled.

"I'm pleased you're happy for me Sarah. I knew you would be."

Sarah knew then to contain her amusement. In her opinion, Tarni seemed to be having a nervous breakdown, or was it some sort of joke. However, she soon realised it was no joke, not to Tarni.

"Yes, you're right Tarni, I am happy for you. But I must tell you, I've spoken at length with Ella today, about what she knows, well, what she has been told. She has assured me it is all in the past. She will never speak of it again. But please answer honestly. Did you meet with Blue Boy down at the beach on the night he drowned? Did you have anything to do with his death?"

"I wished him dead, but I didn't kill him, he killed himself."

"You didn't entirely answer my question. Did you meet with him that night?"

"I went to, but I got as far as the footpath. I could see him drinking and then I watched and listened, he was talking to himself. He spoke in our native tongue. I couldn't hear everything he said. But I heard him say, he was going to catch a big fish and then he'd light a fire and cook it for Tarni. I watched him go into the water, but I didn't wait around, I just walked away."

"Did you know if he could swim Tarni?"

"Yes, Blue could swim alright, but he was really drunk. He was not a good person, Sarah. He'd always cause trouble and he'd steal from everyone at the mission."

"That's no reason to wish him dead, Tarni. Did he bribe you? Did he say he'd tell the police that he knew you'd conspired with Drongo to do away with Robbo?"

"Not exactly, I knew he would though. Blue Boy would have drained me of my money and then he'd keep on wanting more. Or he'd end up telling lies about me to the police. I had to do something."

"Oh my God Tarni, you said you didn't kill him!"

"No, I didn't. I didn't kill him. I just wished him dead. Honestly Sarah, I never laid a hand on him. I just wished him dead and that's as bad. Don't you see I confessed all of this last night? Father Andrew was with me; he knows I'm telling the truth. I was taken into the Lords embrace I felt like an Angel; He forgave me. Can you understand how I feel Sarah? I'm free of guilt, I belong to God now. He's washed away my sins and I will be forever grateful. I have repented. I will be the Lords bride one day."

The look on Tarni's face when she spoke, gave Sarah shivers down her spine. It was as if Tarni had become an Angel already. Her expression had changed into pure radiance, like the Biblical paintings Sarah had seen in the church. Sarah's eyes welled with emotion: Tarni had bared her soul.

"Tarni, I'm truly happy for you, although I'm a bit concerned with PJ's attitude at the moment. He'll miss you terribly. We all will."

The ethereal look on Tarni's face disappeared and she saddened.

"I'm sorry Sarah, I will never forget PJ, or you, or anyone here for that matter. The Lord has sent you to me, to be my friend, everyone has been so wonderful. Granddad Jonathon, PJ,'s family." Tarni giggled a little, "Well my family really if you look at it that way. I'll miss you all. And Harry, poor Harry I should have been kinder to him with his father dying of cancer. But I am a changed person now. I'll telephone him tomorrow and try to explain about my spiritual calling." Tarni hung her head. "I can only pray he understands."

While Sarah and Tarni were talking, an inebriated PJ telephoned Harry.

"Harry, I'm just phoning you, to let you know that your fiancée is going to be a nun and you'd better come back here quickly! You have to talk her out of it!"

Harry laughed.

"You'd better ring me back in the morning, PJ. I think you've been on a bender mate. You're not making any sense."

"I'm fuckin serious Harry! She's gone crazy, ever since that bloody Ella said those things about her murdering that fuckin Robbo and that other whatever his name is. You know Harry, the one that drowned in the beach. Oh shit, I'm gonna be sick."

PJ hung up the receiver just in time to reach the toilet and vomit.

By the time Sarah returned, PJ had found his way to bed and although it was only seven o'clock, he was sound asleep – snoring.

The phone rang at six am and Sarah answered it just before she was about to feed the baby.

"Oh, hello, Harry. I was going to ring you later. No, PJ's not here. He's managed to go to work with a massive headache. He'd be up in the grandstand by now, watching his horses work."

Harry went on to tell Sarah about PJ's drunken phone call. He laughed when he relayed what PJ had said about Tarni becoming a nun. There was a long silence before Sarah gave Harry the sobering news.

"I'm so sorry, Harry. It's true. You must understand that Tarni has had a lot to deal with in her short life. It seems ever since she began her Bible studies some months ago, she feels closer to God. It amazes me how she's able to remember all the scriptures and commandments. It appears after Tarni received your letter Harry, explaining about what Ella had said to your mother, she went to her usual Bible study class and found something miraculous happened after Father Andrew coaxed her to seek God's forgiveness. Tarni said it was like an awakening. She felt like she was one of God's angels and I believe her, because I've never seen her so happy. It's more like an inner glow of happiness that's almost indescribable. Mind you, I still find it hard to believe how somebody, so in love with horses and you of course, could leave it all behind and enter into a completely selfless world. Plus, I'm unable to fathom how Tarni could make this life-changing decision overnight. It just doesn't seem possible."

Sarah waited for Harry to speak and when he didn't, she could only imagine he was in shock. "Oh Harry, I am truly sorry, but please don't give up hope. Mother Superior is coming here today, after she and Tarni have visited Father Andrew. I phoned her last night and she promised me she would come and talk to us before she returned to Adelaide."

"I'm sorry too, Sarah. It seems like one thing after the other. I've been praying and hoping Tarni would come to New Zealand, if only for a short while, to make peace with my father before he dies." Sarah's eyes welled up, sniffling back her tears made it hard for her to speak.

"I know, Harry. We've always known Tarni can… well she can be complicated, even an enigma. But if you had seen her last night when I spoke with her about becoming a nun, she seemed a different person. She simply radiated happiness. I have to apologise before I say this, Harry, but I only hope it lasts. Then maybe we'll both be happy that Tarni has left us and found what the Good Lord intended. If you truly love someone Harry, they say you have to let them go."

"Thank you for explaining things to me, Sarah. I've heard that saying before. Could you please ask Tarni to phone me later?" His reply was short and abrupt.

"Of course I will. I'll ask her when she comes over for breakfast. Goodbye, please give my love and best wishes to your family and…"

Harry had hung up.

*

In the days that followed, there was no persuading Tarni against joining the sisterhood. She said her calling had grown stronger every day.

"God is guiding me towards being a spiritual teacher within the Indigenous community of Australia." She preached this to as many people as she met.

Mother Superior and Father Andrew both truly believed that Tarni had received a genuine message from above. So it was, that on the morning of 31

October 1960, Tarni packed her bags and said farewell to her beloved horses and friends.

PJ and Sarah stood watching as Tarni stroked each horse and blessed them. Not one tear was shed by Tarni. However, Sarah's tears trickled down her cheeks and PJ found it hard to hold back his emotions. When the goodbyes were done, Tarni joined Father Andrew in his car and waved her friends goodbye. He would drive Tarni to Adelaide where she'd be left in the care of Mother Superior and that would be that as far as PJ was concerned. Tarni had made her choice and he would get on with the job at hand, which was to become next year's leading trainer in South Australia. This would be decided on the 1 August 1961.

Chapter 19

That same afternoon, PJ walked into the number one barn and faced his sombre staff. Attempting to lift their spirits he offered.

"Cheer up you lot, I'll shout you all a night out on the town if Happy Harry wins next Saturday."

"Thanks, Boss," was their un-excited reply.

"I know it's a bit of a cover up for how we feel about Tarni leaving, but it's the best I can do." PJ shrugged his shoulders, before taking Craig aside.

"I need to ask you, Craig, whether you'd like to be my foreman now, or if you still hold a passion to ride in races?"

"I've thought about it; Boss and I think if I don't give it a go now I'll miss the boat. I turn twenty next month and most jockeys start when they're fourteen or fifteen. I'll still do most of the riding in the morning though. It's when I have to go and ride in races that it'll be a bit of a problem for you. Maybe you should find another worker, someone with experience, a good foreman?"

"Okay, Craig. I'll put an ad in the paper." He shook Craig's hand turning to walk back home, when Craig said:

"If you don't mind, Boss, without Tarni and now with Suzie on holidays, we could do with a bit of a hand. Would you mind, although I understand if you have book work to do."

"No of course, I'll lend a hand. Sorry I didn't think to offer."

*

In the weeks since Tarni had left, PJ found solace with his horses. He surprised himself with the degree of satisfaction he found from being in total control once again. Sometimes, he felt guilty that most of the time, Tarni had to run the show without him. Her overseeing had allowed PJ to act as the 'Lord of the Manor' for far too long.

Saturday morning arrived and the race meeting at Victoria Park was in doubt due to torrential rain over night. At 7.30 am, PJ sat by the phone, waiting for the stewards to call their decision about the races going ahead or not. He sat sipping a cup of tea when Sarah walked in. She brushed a strand of wet hair off his forehead and kissed him.

"I know you'd really like Happy to race today PJ, but I think it would be a perfect day to cuddle up on the lounge with a good book. You know, just take it easy. You've been working almost nonstop since Tarni left."

"I have to work, Sarah. We're understaffed, and it will only get worse when Craig starts riding in races. I'll be run off my feet unless I can find an experienced foreman. Anyway, I need to see if Happy handles the wet. I've got a couple of races planned for him in Melbourne. I reckon he's good enough to take on the 'big guns' this spring, and it's always bloody wet in Melbourne this time of year."

The telephone rang, and PJ grabbed the receiver.

"Hello, yes, that's good. Thank you, Sir." He turned to Sarah. "The races are on!"

The sky was a mass of threatening clouds, looking about to burst before the first race. Thankfully the rain held off, at least until the horses paraded and while the race was run. Then it bucketed down. The jockeys rode back into the enclosure, race colourers' clinging wet to their skin.

PJ hated to race his horses in these conditions. It posed far greater risk to horse and rider, especially after six more races, when the track would be turned into a ploughed paddock. Still he needed to know if Happy Harry could handle the going. There would be too much prize money at stake in Melbourne for him not to know. The expense to travel Happy Harry there, rent stables, plus the strapper's accommodation and cost, would all be pointless, unless PJ was confident that Happy could handle the wet.

Every owner, including PJ's family, arrived at the races

dressed to the 'nines' and full of hope. One by one they approached PJ to ask his opinion on whether Happy Harry would handle the mud. PJ spoke honestly.

"I'm not sure. I think you should hold all bets until he's proven himself in the wet."

PJ hadn't felt this nervous since Volunteer had his first start at Murray Bridge. He confided this fear to Patrick Snr when having a drink in the trainers' bar.

"I don't know why, Dad, but I'm really nervous. I hate racing in these conditions, especially in the last race. The track will be a bloody quagmire. I've been thinking about Tarni. She'd always stay positive and keep me calm. I still can't believe why she chose to be a nun. I think she's just running away, even though she has nothing to run away from. I just can't fathom her Dad."

"I know what you mean, Son. I loved Mother Betty with all my heart when I was young, and I could never understand why she chose the Lord above me!" Patrick Snr laughed, as if it were only a joke then stopped abruptly when he saw the pain behind PJ's smile.

"As you've always said, Dad, maybe it was meant to be, and I know I'll just have to accept it. But I feel like my right arm's been chopped off and I'm still angry. We were such a good team. I needed her; I still do."

Patrick placed his hand on PJ's shoulder and looked him straight in the eye.

"You're more than capable of training winners, PJ. You don't need Tarni. Let her go Son and concentrate on your own family and your own business. You have a beautiful wife and a healthy son and plenty of good horses. You too have been blessed."

"You're right, Dad. Let's have another whisky and drink to it!"

By the time the second last race was about to be run, PJ and Patrick almost staggered out of the bar towards the jockey's room.

The seventh race was run and won by a fair-dinkum mud lark, called Big Joe. He'd literally bolted in by ten lengths, leaving his rivals floundering like fish out of water.

PJ watched that race, drinking three glasses of water to dilute the whisky in his gut. He then felt a little steadier on his feet when he left the Jockeys room with the saddle, although he was disappointed that his jockey Billy Paton had taken ill after his ride in the previous race. PJ then had to choose another jockey. He was forced to ask a rider he'd never liked as a person, but who rode well. 'That's if he's on your side-and trying', PJ had heard comment. There were too many rumours about Sammy Brown pulling up horses, not to believe that some of them were true.

A stunning Addy, in her latest horte' couture, lingered at the horse stalls talking good sense to Happy Harry.

"I'm here to assure you, Happy, that you will definitely handle the mud. After all you are a New Zealander. I hear the country is up to its belly in mud all the time."

Harry snorted, and Addy gave him a pat before she turned to see her two Patrick's walking a little unsteadily towards her. Patrick Snr planted a kiss on her cheek.

"Patrick, you smell like a brewery!"

"I've just been partaking of a little Dutch Courage with our son, my dear."

"A little! I'd say a lot."

Patrick laughed, his amazing blue eyes could still draw Addy in "Well, maybe we needed a lot. Now don't be angry Addy, this is a Happy Harry occasion."

She smiled and kissed him back.

"God, I could get drunk on the smell of you!"

Happy was saddled up, and led to the mounting enclosure by Craig, who was excited because he'd just been given permission to ride in trials. However, his excitement was dampened a little with his worry that Happy may not handle the mud. Craig was the only one who'd ridden Happy since Tarni left. And each time he rode him after the rain had turned their home track into slosh, Happy would shorten his stride, keeping himself safe.

When Craig informed PJ of his concerns, he simply waved them off.

"It'll be a lot different in the race, Craig. Happy's adrenaline will see him through, plus he's far above this lot in ability. He'll only have to stay upright to win."

The starter pulled the leaver and the barriers flung open. Happy faltered when jumping, but soon regained his balance to sit fourth on the fence. The three horses in front were running along at a decent pace and seemed to be handling the mud. Sam chose to keep Happy on the fence, even though there was plenty of room to move out and onto better going.

PJ's heart thumped in anger. He could see the back markers making their move around Happy and he'd be blocked for a run if Sam didn't get off the fence.

"Get off the bloody fence Sam!" PJ yelled.

Sam stayed where he was. The pattern of the race continued in the same order until they entered the straight. Sam then went to make a move out into the open, but another runner came from behind, preventing him. The horse in front of Happy began to tire over the final two furlongs and dropped back into Happy's chest. Another two horses had crept up on the outside, they were only just battling in the going and so kept Happy locked in a pocket. Sam got desperate and pushed him through an opening that wasn't quite there. The sudden fling onto the off foreleg saw Happy dip dramatically. Amazingly, he recovered in time to put in two amazing strides and win by a nose.

Happy's heroic win, had the owners excited and heading straight to the winners' bar, all except PJ. While Craig walked Happy back to his stall, PJ noted a slight lameness in Happy's off-side fore-leg. After hosing down the horse, taking him for a ten-minute walk and then tying him up in his stall to rest,

Happy's tendon began to swell. For it to come up so quickly, PJ knew it must be the worst possible scenario. The race vet was called and Happy was bandaged extensively. The vet then gave PJ instructions on how to care for Harry's bowed tendon and then more bad news. In his opinion, 'for Happy Harry to have any chance of returning to the races, he will need to rest in the paddock for at least twelve months.'

This news, along with returning home to find his main string of horses off their food and running temperatures, literally fell on PJ like an avalanche. Later, in the lounge room, Sarah tried with all her charm and good sense to talk him around. But PJ was in his own world – devastated.

"I can't believe this Sarah; everything has gone from bad to worse. I feel like giving up. It's no bloody good kidding myself. I'm not cut out for this game. I haven't got the heart. I'd be better off going back to law; at least I'd earn a steady living." PJ sat forward in his armchair, head in his hands. "Fuck this! Get me another whisky, will you Sarah?"

"Yes, I'll pour you another whisky, then I want you to pull yourself together. We all get tested in life, PJ. I never dreamt you would give up this easily. And I know you think you need Tarni because she's some sort of horse wizard, but honestly, you have as much talent as her with horses and this is the time to prove it. If you don't try now, then you'll just be giving into your insecurities. You'll be falling back to where it's safe and comfortable, to where your family will help by providing you with clients and easy wins in court. Is that what you want, PJ? Or do you want to finally grow up and prove to yourself that you have talent?"

Not another word came from PJ. Sarah handed him the Scotch and left the room. She didn't look back.

"What's the time," PJ said aloud to himself while scratching his head. "Is New Zealand behind us, or in front? Ahh, it doesn't matter, Harry'll be home."

PJ picked up the receiver and dialled Harry's number. He was just about to hang up when Harry finally answered.

"Hello, who is it?" Harry said, sounding half asleep.

"It's me, PJ. I just need to talk Harry, are you awake?"

"I am now. What's the problem?"

PJ went on to fill Harry in on all the bad news, plus his thoughts on giving up training horses.

"I can only say, PJ that I'm very sorry things aren't going as well as they did when you started. How long ago was it, over a year, nearly two? But

Christ, please get things in perspective. Don't get me wrong, I know all things are relevant, but my father's dying of cancer, my mum's a mess and the woman I love has left me to join the church. I can't believe one or two setbacks with horses could knock you off your perch. I've always looked up to you, believed you could handle anything. I know how much hope you had in Happy, but he's not finished yet, he'll come back, better and stronger. It'll just take time. Something my father hasn't got much of. So, chin up old mate and keep on keeping on. Now there's a couple of good old clichés to carry on with. Good night PJ. Keep me posted on how things progress with Happy." He hung up abruptly.

"Well now. I've just been told – twice – in the same evening! I guess I'd better get a grip on life," PJ exclaimed to no one.

Chapter 20

Christmas 1960 came and went and as usual, the family gathered at Wildflowers, where Jonathon it seemed, had found what appeared to be a hidden supply of strength and vitality. This delighted everyone, especially Margie who'd thought him well enough to take a cruise around the Pacific Islands. They left on the 2 January 1961.

It had taken three months of intense care and recuperation before PJ's horses could start racing again after their viral set back. Reluctantly at first, he'd given every waking moment to his horses' wellbeing. They duly progressed to the fitness level needed to race. He took pride and satisfaction in knowing that he'd done it almost on his own. It had given him the confidence he needed.

However, the only winner they'd cheered home during this spate of time was Craig. Craig had completed his desired number of barrier trials with success and booted home his first winner in his race debut. He continued to ride winners and place getters from then on and was fast becoming the most sought-after apprentice in Adelaide. Although PJ was proud and happy for Craig, it did leave him a lot of the time, without a trustworthy foreman. He'd tried out a few young men, but they hadn't come up to PJ's standard. So Suzie was given the opportunity to be in charge when PJ wasn't there, this was after she'd begged PJ for the chance to do so.

After Volunteer had taken many weeks to recover from the virus, he proved he was back firing on all four legs by winning his first start back. It was the relief PJ had been praying for. It seemed his hard work and perseverance had seen him through the doldrums. Now he looked forward to his string of promising gallopers performing at their best and put him, as he'd said, 'back on the map'.

Sarah had stayed home that day and greeted PJ on his return from the races. He was literally beaming. This was something Sarah had missed seeing over the past six months. He picked her up a swirled her in the air like a rag doll.

"Congratulations, PJ. You really deserved that win," Sarah said when PJ landed her on the floor.

"I couldn't be happier, Sarah. Thank you for the kick in the bum. I know I needed it."

Sarah leaned into his chest, not wanting to see his happiness disappear. Her words vibrated against his chest as she said:

"Harry phoned while you were at the races. Ronny passed away today."

PJ held her tight, rocking her back and forth, like his mother would whenever he was sad.

"I suppose I should say, it's a blessing. But then maybe I should say, life's a bastard sometimes …"

Sarah stayed in his arms. Her perfume hadn't changed since the day they met. PJ would remember it forever, the same as he'd remember Ronny's piercing blue eyes, his welcoming smile and his bone breaking handshake.

"Did they tell you when the funeral is? We should go Sarah, or I'll go alone if you'd rather."

"No, I'd like to go with you, PJ. I'm going to phone Tarni and see if she'd like to join us. That's if she's able." PJ's grip was firm, as he held Sarah away from his chest.

"No, Sarah. I mean, I don't think the church would allow it and I don't think she'd want to go. It would make things uncomfortable for Valerie and the girls." He walked to the window, looking out to the horse-filled paddocks.

"Please, PJ, that's all buried and forgotten now. You know Valerie's a devout Catholic; she'd be proud of Tarni becoming a nun. I believe after six months, if Tarni's proven her commitment to God she's allowed to take her first vows. I've written to her many times and it appears that will be the case. But until then, she's free to come and go."

As PJ turned to face her, Sarah studied his expression. It was still mixed with anger and disappointment.

"When are you ever going to get over this, PJ? Don't you want Tarni to be happy?"

"Of course I do. But as long as I live, I'll never be able to believe that Tarni wants to be a nun. I think she's locked herself away from life. She's living in a make-believe world."

"Well, you think what you like. But I believe she has a calling and I'm pleased for her." Sarah paused, thinking perhaps this was not the right time to mention the opal but what the heck. "I've been talking with Mother Superior about the opal. I've asked her what we should do with it and she said, just keep it in the safe until Tarni receives word from the Lord what should be done with it."

"You know that's a pretty big ask, Sarah. Why don't they just take it and put it in their own safe. I'm sick of worrying about it being here."

"I didn't realise you'd been worrying about it, PJ?" Sarah said with a little sarcasm.

"I don't want to talk about it anymore." A huge sigh escaped PJ and his shoulders lowered, always a sign to Sarah that he'd given in. "Do as you wish with the opal and ask Tarni if she wants to go with us to NZ if you like." His look softened into what Sarah new well. "Now let's wind back the clock to when I picked you up off the floor."

Sarah moved in like a lioness, slinking towards her mate until her chest rubbed PJ's.

"Can we compromise? I've always felt more comfortable in bed, naked of course."

All problems dissolved as the two gave everything to each other. Still wrapped in one another's arms, PJ drifted off to sleep leaving Sarah to contemplate her thoughts.

Love is the strangest messenger of all. It virtually orders us to give all we have to another. I adore my husband. I accept every fault he has. Some come from the fact that he's been catered to all his life, it plays out like a pantomime sometimes. Does this change my love for him? No and it never will. I'm paid to study people's thoughts, their feelings and the reason why they are who they are. I've come to the conclusion that most problems stem from self-esteem, our ability to believe in ourselves. Why does PJ lack this? Some may say he does not. But I know the truth; he has great difficulty believing in himself.

Sarah slowly untangled her long limbs from PJ's grasp, kissed him on the cheek and heard him moan before he reached for her once again.

"I'm tired my darling, go back to sleep PJ."

*

Two days later, PJ parked the car outside the convent. Tarni stood waiting dressed in a dull grey skirt and what PJ would have described as a moth-eaten jumper. Her hair was cut into a short bob and she was clutching a worn suitcase. She looked every bit the lonely orphan. Sarah rose elegantly from the front seat of the car and opened the rear door. Tarni placed her bag next to theirs then held Sarah close for a long time. Sarah kissed Tarni on both cheeks, before indicating the back seat of the station wagon. Baby Thomas held his chubby hand out and Tarni pulled it to her mouth blurting on it, he chuckled.

"More," he said.

"Oh, he's grown so much, and he's talking. I can't believe it." Tarni said, all smiles.

"He's two now and yes, sometimes we can't shut him up," PJ replied.

"How are you, PJ?" Tarni asked brightly.

"I'm fine, Tarni. How are you?"

"I'm very well thank you."

Their trip to the airport was interrupted, when they stopped to deliver Thomas into the care of Sarah's parents, Alice and Wayne. Only polite conversation was shared from then on, until they boarded the plane. Sarah then suggested she sit next to Tarni. PJ didn't mind, as he'd found an old lawyer friend on the flight that he could sit next to.

"So, Tarni," Sarah began. "Now we have the time to talk, without anyone else butting in, if you know what I mean?" She glanced towards PJ. "Let's start by being honest with each other. I hope you don't mind me asking you the obvious question. Do you think you still have what it takes to be a nun?" Sarah could have kicked herself. Usually she wouldn't jump in so fast, even though she thought the question fare. However, she was close enough to Tarni to be forthright.

"I knew you'd ask that Sarah." Tarni said, amused at Sarah's serious expression. "And no, I'm not becoming more like Mother Superior. I'm not a mind reader and I don't see spirits. I simply guessed it would be your first question. And my honest answer is, I think so. Sometimes I have doubts, I dream a lot, but mainly about the horses." Tarni turned to look out of the window, as the plane climbed through the clouds. "It's funny, I was so scared on my first flight to New Zealand, but now I'm not afraid. It's almost as if I'm expecting to see God waving to me from a cloud. That sounds silly, I know. It's just that I feel God is with me all the time. I feel safe, and so close to him."

"When you said, you think so, Tarni, does that mean you're hesitant about taking your final vows?"

"There's not a specific time in which we have to take them. And my final vows won't be given until after I've taken my first vows. At this stage, I'm convinced I am exactly where God wants me to be."

Sarah knew immediately that she'd made the right decision by encouraging Tarni to join her and PJ. She had an overwhelming feeling of being correct in her assumption about what may happen, or at least be encouraged to happen. This satisfied her to the point where she would let her next question lie. The answer she knew would be shown to her when they met with Harry. In the meantime, Sarah fired leading questions, in a nice way, to judge for herself if Tarni would indeed 'stick it out', as PJ had put it.

Nearing the Auckland airport, wild winds caused the plane to shudder. It rattled as if it were a toy being shaken by an excited child. Sarah grabbed the arm rests tight, while Tarni appeared relaxed, reading her Bible.

"I hope you're praying Tarni?" Sarah said nervously.

"Of course I am. However, the Good Lord holds our life in his hands, Sarah. So, what will be, will be." Tarni sent Sarah a quick smile then held onto her hand.

"I must be honest with you Tarni, what you have just said is of no comfort to me. I'd like to see my son grow up!" Her voice vibrating with the plane.

"You will Sarah, I have no doubts."

"Now you do sound like Mother Superior!"

*

"Oh Dear ,Lord. Help me. Give me strength," Tarni whispered, as Harry walked towards her. He'd matured into a magnificent specimen of manhood. The intense exercise regime he'd taken on, purposely to get himself walking unaided and then running in marathons, had sculptured his body to perfection. His blond hair, now even lighter, accentuated his tan. Tarni's heart fluttered before it almost stopped when Harry engulfed her in his arms. PJ stood alongside Sarah, watching helplessly while Harry wept silently onto Tarni's shoulder. Slowly Tarni's dangling arms reached up and slid around Harry's body. Her tears welled and spilled onto his chest.

Sarah took PJ's arm, a sign for them to walk on. Out of ear shot.

Sarah said. "If that doesn't shake her out of it, nothing will."

"I can't believe you said that! You told me she had a calling and now you're telling me she's going to leave the Lord for Harry? As I've said before, Sarah. You're never boring!" PJ shook his head laughing.

"Shut up, PJ. I'm a woman and we women have more intuition than men, that's all."

Sarah had booked the three of them into a hotel for the two-night stop over. The funeral would be held the next day and then the day after that, they'd fly home again. However, Harry begged them to stay at his family's home and reluctantly, they accepted.

"Are you sure it's not too much trouble for your mother Harry?" Sarah asked.

"No not at all. Mother was the one who suggested it. She'd love you all to stay with us. So please don't disappoint her."

Val looked a lot better than Tarni had expected. But then Tarni thought, Val did have time to accept Ronnie's ending before it actually came.

"Hello, Mrs Brauer." Tarni said extending her hand, "I'm so sorry for your loss."

"I know you are Tarni and I thank you. Ronnie thought a lot of you. He admired your talent with horses and always sang your praises. He was pleased to hear you were studying to be a nun." Val leaned towards Tarni and spoke softly. "But secretly, he wished you would have come back here to marry Harry."

"Mother! Harry said shocked at her forthrightness. Tarni didn't know which way to look until Harry guided her away by the arm.

"I'll show you to your room, Tarni." He turned and said: "You may as well come too, Sarah. Your room is next to Tarni's."

The evening that followed became a pleasant, memory- filled journey back through Ronnie's life. Tarni listened to the stories told by the family, with love and humour. She knew by feeling this way that she'd totally forgiven Ronnie and the girls. The sisters, in return, who now knew who Tarni really was, showered her with love. It came freely without any mention of the past. However, every now and then, Tarni would notice Grace studying her. Tarni was never sure about Valerie's true thoughts as Valery lived in a simple world caring for her family and nothing else seemed more important to Val than that.

Then a surprise.

When Tarni was about to retire to her bedroom, Grace approached and asked if they could talk.

"Of course, Grace. Come in. Sit down." Grace sat on the only chair in the room, while Tarni sat in her usual position, cross-legged on the bed.

"Firstly, I must apologise for what I said all that time ago Tarni …"

"Please don't Grace. It's in the past. All is forgiven."

"I know Tarni. I can see it in your eyes. Do I call you Sister now?"

Tarni laughed. "No I'm still a pre-novitiate. I haven't taken my first vows. I intend to do so when I return home."

"I wish you wouldn't," Grace said with a rush. "I know that's not the right thing to say, but we really like you and I know Harry still loves you with all his heart." Grace hung her head. "I have to tell you something, something that you may find surprising, but it's true. I've fallen in love with a half- Maori boy, Noah." She then looked up smiling, showing her perfect white teeth which Tarni had only seen hidden behind braces on her last visit. "He's studying to be a doctor at the same Uni as me. I didn't know whether to tell Dad, or not. Not when he was so sick. But Harry said I should. I was really scared Dad would disown me, or worse still, he'd die with worry. Instead, when I told him, Dad held me close and asked me to forgive him. He said he'd been brought up with this biased attitude, but when he really studied his own feelings, he felt he was not prejudiced. He gave us his blessing and wished Noah all the best with his studies. We have to thank you for that Tarni. You woke us up. We never really went out purposely to dislike or put down Maoris, or Aborigines. It was a subconscious thing I suppose. We had to face ourselves, our own true feelings and be honest. I have to say, it wasn't until I met Noah, that I knew my prejudices had been unfounded. I suppose it has been a big part of my growing up." Grace stood then bent to kiss Tarni on the cheek. "That's all I wanted to say Tarni, but I will say once again that I am truly sorry for what I said about Dad. And I'm sorry you've chosen the Lord above Harry. I don't think he will ever get over the love he has for you." She then turned quietly and left the room.

Tarni spent half the night awake, asking God if he'd sent her there to test her strength. Yes, she would be strong and resist the desires of the flesh. Or would she? Could she, knowing how much she still longed for Harry's touch. His embrace today was overwhelming, every sense in her being cried out to be loved, just one more time. Yes, just one more time, before she took her final vows. Surely the Lord would forgive her that.

Once again Tarni was surprised, that she, along with PJ, was asked to give readings at Ronnie's funeral. The church was packed with mourners. They also converged onto the footpaths outside. A loudspeaker sent prayers and readings out to all who had gathered. The ladies of the Church Committee had been up since dawn preparing the lavish morning tea that was offered to the family members and friends after the lengthy service.

Harry was overwhelmed by well-wishers and Tarni felt relieved. This would keep him away from her. However, it didn't prevent him from giving her 'that look' every chance he had. The one he hoped would stoke her fire. Tarni slowly slipped away and re-entered the Church, she knelt directly in front of the crucifix and prayed until Harry tapped her on the shoulder.

"Tarni, we're leaving now. We're going home. Are you alright?"

"Yes, I'm fine. I was just making peace with Ronnie." She stood and wiped away tears. "I'm so sorry Harry, I've treated you terribly. I know the Lord has forgiven me, but I need your forgiveness, so I can move on."

"Move on to where Tarni? You know you still love me, and I adore you. I always have, and I always will. Please don't leave me again. I'll come back to Australia; I'll do whatever you want." With that Tarni turned and hurried outside to find Sarah, Tarni almost bumped into her, then asked almost breathlessly:

"Can we go and stay at the hotel now, Sarah. I don't want to go back to the house."

Sarah nodded, took Tarni by the hand and found PJ.

"PJ, I think it best if Tarni and I stay at the hotel tonight. You stay with Harry. Help him out will you please. I'll call you later."

Their flight home was taken in silence. At the Adelaide airport, Tarni informed them she would take the bus back to the convent.

"I'll be fine. I just need time alone. I hope you understand. Thank you for asking me to go with you." Tarni smiled, kissed them both. "I'll see you around I suppose. Will you come to my first vows?"

"I wouldn't miss it, Tarni." Sarah said, while PJ simply nodded.

Chapter 21

The moment PJ arrived home; he went straight to the safe and took out the opal. Sarah looked at him quizzically.

"What are you doing?"

"I'm just taking another look. Tomorrow I'm going to have it polished and valued. And then I'm going to drop it off at the convent." PJ held Sarah to him with one arm and held the opal up with the other. "You know I think this opal could be the biggest Black Opal, ever found. I've been reading all the journals that I could get my hands on. It may be worth a small fortune, and I don't think we should be the ones held responsible for it. Tarni should."

"I agree, let her work it out with help from God and Mother Superior."

PJ clasped Sarah in his arms and kissed her.

"I love you, Sarah. You're the best thing that has ever happened to me."

"I'm pleased to hear it. I've always had my doubts. I thought perhaps Tarni was, or Happy Harry, or Volunteer, or..."

"You're not jealous, are you?" He asked before kissing her passionately. She accepted his lips before retaliating.

"Jealousy is one fault I do not possess, PJ. You know that," then Sarah released herself from his arms. "I'll just go and put Tom down for a nap. Then we can continue this conversation in bed if you like?"

"No. Sorry, Sarah. I have to check on the horses."

"Now I am jealous, you bugger!"

The following morning, straight after his horses had worked, PJ travelled to the Adelaide registrar of minerals, where he'd made an appointment with the man responsible for polishing and valuing the opal. He took time to walk around the city, have a bite to eat before he returned to listen to the expert's opinion.

"This is a solid, flawless Black Opal; it's worth well over a million pounds."

PJ felt weak at the knees. He also felt guilty that later on when driving to the convent that he drove even more carefully with this precious gem on board, than he did with his own son. He pulled up outside, took a deep breath, held the opal in his hands, and spoke to it as if it could understand.

"You, my friend, will be the deciding factor on whether Tarni becomes a nun, or she returns to Harry. Work your magic and stay clear of the holy water Big Boy!"

"PJ, how nice to see you," Mother superior said surprised when he presented himself in her office unannounced.

"I'm sorry Mother, I didn't phone. I just assumed you'd be here."

He unravelled the enormous opal, placing it gently on her desk. The deepness of colour was captivating. The ray of light that seemingly shone upon Mother Superior, hit the opal like radar sending its glorious rainbow colours to dance on the walls.

"Oh, my goodness. I never realised the opal was this huge. Do you know how much it's worth, PJ?"

"Yes I do, Mother. They say it's worth well over one million pounds."

"Oh, my goodness was the right phrase then. The question of what to do with it will need serious deliberation." She looked PJ in the eye with a look that he hadn't seen before. Was it shock, or determination, or even envy? He couldn't tell, but her angelic look had momentarily disappeared.

"Yes it will, Mother and I don't want any part of the decision making. I've brought the opal here because I felt it unfair that I should be the one held responsible. That is until Tarni has made up her mind. Perhaps when she's told its worth, it will lead her into making a decision. As a matter of fact, I think we should call Tarni here now? I think it would be best, if the news came from me."

"Yes, perhaps you're right." Mother Superior softened, and her well known Mona Lisa smile appeared on her flawless skin. "I've been thinking about calling you here, PJ. You've saved me a phone call turning up as you have. I do feel something has changed within Tarni since her return from New Zealand. She is not herself. Well, not the Tarni I knew when she first entered these walls. I've asked if there's anything she wishes to speak with me about, but she says, 'No Mother, I'm simply concentrating on taking my first vows'. However, I feel there is something more, something she is not telling me. Would you have any idea what that could be, PJ? Is she still in love with Harry? Maybe she can't get him off her mind? Or more to the point, is she unable to free him from her heart?"

"You're spot on Mother, if you'll excuse the slang." He managed a slight smile. "Both Sarah and I knew it would be a real test for Tarni to see Harry again. I knew, well, probably Sarah knew before me, that their meeting would tell the tale. When Tarni first saw Harry at the airport, they immediately held each other tight without saying a word for what seemed like an hour. Harry then talked us into staying with his family and all went well with Tarni and the girls. It was a wonderful evening full of fond memories, mostly about Ronnie. Tarni even joined in, telling funny moments she'd shared with Ronnie when staying there. Then, the next day, after the funeral, Tarni insisted on staying at a hotel. She wouldn't say why, and on our way home, she hardly spoke a word. That maybe an exaggeration, but I know Tarni was having a fight within herself about her feelings for Harry. Sarah agreed. I think she knows more than me. But you know all about the therapist-patient code."

PJ leaned forward in his seat, hung his head and ran his fingers through his hair, sighed then looked up.

"You probably know how I feel, Mother, but I have to voice it anyway. I think this whole thing about Tarni becoming a nun is preposterous. I think she is the least likely person." Mother went to interrupt. "No please, Mother, hear me out and then you can have your say. I know Tarni has been a runner. What I mean is, she runs away from whatever it is she can't physically fight. She's good at that. But being demure and giving the rest of her life totally to the Lord? Well, I just can't buy it. And that's all I have to say."

Mother Superior sat silently, studying the look of frustration on his face. PJ then began to think she'd mixed it too long with his grandfather Jonathon. Her deliberation finally came after a two-minute interval.

"I know what you mean, PJ. You must understand, Tarni needed the Lords help and He gave it to her. Now she has to decide for herself, if the sublime peace she felt in that moment, was indeed a calling, or just pure relief in knowing that the Good Lord loves her unconditionally. This is what we all need, to be loved unconditionally. It doesn't mean we should go on committing sins, it means we have repented, and we will do our very best not to sin again. I know Tarni has promised this over and over to the Lord. I also know Harry will be her cross to bear, that's if she chooses God above him. I must tell you though, PJ, most nuns have the same cross to bear. I myself carried a man in my heart for many, many years."

"Really, Mother! And who may I ask was the lucky man?"

"No, you may not ask! That is between God and me," she said sternly.

"I am sorry, Mother."

"Please don't apologise, PJ. I should not have snapped at you like that. Mother turned to the window, to hide the tears welling. "Oh dear, it seems I still bear the cross. I shall go and find Tarni, shall I?" She rose from her chair and glided, head lowered, across the room and out the door.

PJ sat contemplating, wondering if the fun jibes he'd heard between his mother and father about his father's love for Betty, Mother Superior, actually held some truth. He knew Betty was the little girl who'd found his father at two months of age on the doorstep of the convent. Surely it would be just sisterly love? His thoughts were disturbed when Tarni appeared.

"Hello, PJ." Tarni's eyes turned like a magnet to the opal. "You've had it polished. It looks much bigger now."

"Yes, it does. Did Mother tell you I had it valued?"

"No."

"Well I have, and its worth over a million pounds!"

"Shit! Oh, I mean… I am sorry Mother." Tarni said, a flush spreading over her cheeks.

"What should I do, PJ?" She turned from one to the other expectantly.

"It's up to you, Tarni. The opal belongs to you and no one else at this stage," Mother said firmly.

"I'll need to think some more, I never thought it would be worth that much. So much good could be done with such an amazing amount of money."

"But please remember, Child. When you take your vows next week, you'll have to give up all your worldly goods, including this opal. So you must think clearly about your decision." Mother Superior took Tarni's hands in hers and smiled warmly. "You know, and I know, Tarni, that only the Good Lord has the answer. Go to the chapel and pray. Listen to Him. His answer will be written on your heart." She turned to PJ, "And you, young man, you are free from the opal burden. Go home now and give my blessings to your beautiful wife and tell her my prayers are with you both in this, your second pregnancy."

PJ opened his mouth intending to make a comment but chose not to. He would hold onto this unforeseen knowledge until he returned home to Sarah.

*

PJ handed Sarah a perfect yellow rose on his return home.

"For you my love, I believe we are pregnant again?"

Sarah's jaw literally dropped.

"How do you know, PJ? I only found out today when I took my own test. Ah yes!" Sarah said with the conviction of detective. "I know the answer, it's simple: Mother Betty the clairvoyant! God she amazes me. How does she know these things?"

"Never mind, I think it's wonderful." PJ held her close and breathed in her familiar scent. "Let's celebrate, I'll take you out to dinner, I'll check with Dawn and see if she can look after Tom."

"We can't, not tonight. Your father phoned and he's coming over. He wants to talk to you."

"What about?"

"I don't know. He just said he'd be here about 7.30 and asked if he could stay the night. It's probably because he knows how much whisky you two will consume!"

The reason Patrick Snr had come to talk, was because Mother Superior had phoned him about Tarni. On his arrival at PJ's home, Patrick gave PJ the latest news.

"Apparently, after you left, PJ, Tarni asked Mother Betty if she could keep the opal with her. She thought if she held it in her hands it would send a powerful message to God and then he would tell her what to do. So Mother Superior gave Tarni the opal and escorted her to the chapel where she left her to pray. A long time passed before Mother realised Tarni hadn't returned to her office. She then became anxious and went to find Tarni, but she'd disappeared. Mother Superior knows Tarni is not stupid, PJ, and that she's quite capable of looking after herself. But she's still worried, because not long afterwards, Tarni phoned to say she had to go alone to the mission. She needed to talk to the Elders about the opal." He paused when he saw the shocked look on PJ's face. "I don't know if we should go there, PJ. But you did say after you visited them, you didn't hold much faith in just giving them money, or the opal. You said it wouldn't help and in your opinion, they would simply squander it. Your home is closer to the mission, so I thought, if you agreed, it would best if I came here first and we can go together. What do you think?"

"You're right, Dad. Let's go but I wish you'd phoned me first with this news."

"That's exactly why I didn't. I knew you'd be off like a greasy pig!"

Although anxious to get to the mission, PJ was still dwelling on the question he'd asked himself about Mother Superior and his father.

"Dad, were you in-love with Mother Betty when you were young? I know you said you loved her, but I assumed it was a sisterly love."

Patrick Snr laughed, "What brought that on?"

"Oh, just something she said today, about nuns carrying crosses for the men they loved. When I asked her who she carried a cross for, she snapped and said it was none of my business, or something like that."

"It was a long time ago now and I still love her, but not in the way I did back then. And I'm going to tell you the truth PJ. If I hadn't met your mother in England when I did, I would have come home and fought the Lord for Betty's love. But it was not meant to be. Everything is as it's meant to be I reckon." He glanced sideways at PJ and saw Addy's profile. "You're so like your mother, PJ, in looks that is. Maybe not like her in temperament but I agree with Jonathon, you're more like Sally your grandmother. Just look at us now: off to save the victim!"

"Tarni's no victim, Dad. She's part of the family remember?"

"Yes, I know. How could I forget something like that? It's so profound, almost unbelievable."

After a further two hours driving they saw flames blazing from a cast iron drum. The glare added light to the night sky and a pink glow to the dark faces. A group of Aboriginals sat cross-legged on the ground, squinting at the headlights shining towards them. PJ parked the car to the side and with his father beside him, walked over to the group. The Elder, Joe, remembered PJ.

"Hello, PJ. Come join us." With a beckoning hand, he then tapped the ground beside him, "Our women caught giant goanna taday. You eat with us." He peered at Patrick Snr. "Who you got there, your Dad?"

"Yes, Joe. This is my father, Patrick Senior." They shook hands and the women shuffled their heavy frames aside for them to sit on the ground.

"So, you come lookin' for Tarni hey? There she is!" He pointed his bony finger towards Tarni, who was shielded behind a lubra. Tarni was not surprised at seeing PJ but astonished to see Patrick Snr. "Tarni tells us opal, pretty bloody big hey?" They all laughed including the two Patricks.

"Yeh, it's pretty bloody big alright! What do you reckon Joe? What should Tarni do with it?" PJ asked.

"I tell her. She sells that bloody big opal and helps our kids. Lots of kids want to learn, have better life. Not like us here. We too old – set in our way. We no need money, we live off land. But young people mixed up with our way and white fella way. I reckon day will come and not enough food for us on land. The young ones have to work in white fella job. Need educatin'. We talk plenty good sense Tarni and me."

PJ breathed a sigh of relief and turned to Tarni. "So you've worked it all out have you Tarni?"

"Yes, I just needed to come and make peace with the elders and ask them if I'd made the right decision. I'm going to buy a home, a halfway house if you like, where teenagers and young adult Aboriginal's can be safe. Give them a roof over their head until they've sorted out a job, and an education. I will provide counselling, food, lodgings and a general helping hand to those in need."

"And are you going to do this from behind a nuns' habit Tarni?"

"No, PJ. I prayed today, and I listened. The Lord said I would do better working outside the convent. This work, this need, is urgent. Help is needed now. I'm sure I'll be able to get this up and running within a couple of months. If I take my vows and stay amongst the cloistered, my time would be mostly taken up with prayers and learning. It would take too long for the church hierarchy to even discuss the opal, let alone decide what they should do with it. This is my journey; PJ and I intend to follow the Lords wishes." She smiled broadly. "And I can tell by that look on your face, you're going to ask will Harry be included in my journey. All I can say is, I hope so. I'm tired of running. I want to stand and fight for what is right and just."

Joe tapped a stick on the ground.

"Okay, no more talk. We eat now. Then we smoke peace pipe, ha, ha, ha. You got smokes, PJ?" Joe said with a twinkle in his eye.

"Yes Joe, I bought them especially for you."

"You good bloke you know."

Chapter 22

Tarni had been right; it was three months later when she'd finally paid for and moved into the house that Johnny had been building at Port Lincoln. Apparently, Johnny's predictions were correct. The owner had run out of money and therefore he'd sold it cheap to Tarni. Johnny had been re- employed by Tarni, along with another two of his mates, to finish the house. Tarni had another five bedrooms added, making it a total of nine, giving comfortable living to twenty or more youths. Free bus rides to and from Adelaide every day had been set up by Tarni for the young people who needed to attend Uni and work.

Sarah offered counselling to the youth at 'Opal Farm,' as it was named, and a new office was added to the home. Travelling was difficult now that she was pregnant with her second child.

The entire Darcy family rallied, helping Tarni in any way they could. This included cousin James, who set up a trust for the aptly named, 'New Life Foundation.'

Suzie, who was now PJ's foreman, had become a regular visitor to the home, while remaining a key member in PJ's racing staff. However, she'd offered in her spare time to teach the young Aboriginals horsemanship skills. Working and learning alongside horses was a valuable tool when learning to respect others. Suzie also taught them how to ride, and from there, some showed interest in becoming track riders, even jockeys. During this time, Suzie and Johnny became close. He'd even dared have his first riding lesson from Suzie, despite his fear and her amusement. He handled the lessons well.

When Happy Harry's twelve months' spell was up, Tarni returned each morning to the farm and rode track work. She'd then take her time walking Happy along the beach for half an hour or so.

"I think we should take him slow PJ, just walk him through the water every day for about a month and then trot him for another four weeks before we slow canter him."

"I agree, Tarni. But he's all yours now, so you do what you think is best."

"Really? Well if I get this right and Happy Harry returns a winner, then

I might just go for my trainer's licence."

"Good luck, but I think you'll have more chance going for your jockey's licence!"

"Ha-ha-ha. I remember when you said the opposite."

Harry Brauer had now graduated with a law degree and was on his way back to Australia. Tarni and he were to be married in two weeks' time in the gardens at 'Wildflowers.' Only the immediate family were invited.

Ella had surprised Tarni with a sincere apology, plus her pledge to help tutor the Aboriginal youths in secretarial skills on weekends. Now that things were running smoothly at the New Life Foundation, Tarni confided to PJ.

"My only worry is that we may unintentionally be giving safe harbour to nymphomaniacs with kleptomaniac tendencies."

"Now you'll have to let me in on that joke you've shared with Sarah for so long," PJ said, his frustration showing.

"Oh, for heaven's sake, PJ. I thought you would have worked it out by now. Think about it! A nymphomaniac, who's a kleptomaniac is a fucking thief!